Napoleonic War Stories

Napoleonic War Stories

Tales of Soldiers, Spies, Battles & Sieges from the Peninsula & Waterloo Campaigns

Sir Arthur Quiller-Couch

LEONAUR

Napoleonic War Stories: Tales of Soldiers, Spies, Battles & Sieges from the Peninsula & Waterloo Campaigns
by Sir Arthur Quiller-Couch

FIRST EDITION

Published by Leonaur Ltd

This selection copyright © 2005 Leonaur Ltd

ISBN (10 digit): 1-84677-014-9 (hardcover)
ISBN (13 digit): 978-1-84677-014-2 (hardcover)

ISBN (10 digit): 1-84677-003-3 (softcover)
ISBN (13 digit): 978-1-84677-003-6 (softcover)

http://www.leonaur.com

Publisher's Notes

In the interests of authenticity, the spellings, grammar and place names used by the author have been retained.

The views expressed in this book are not necessarily those of the publisher.

Contents

Corporal Sam Vicary • 9
Three Men of Badajos • 39
The Two Scouts • 62
The Lamp and the Guitar • 123
The Cellars of Rueda • 152
Rain of Dollars • 182
The Laird's Luck • 212

Corporal Sam Vicary
1st (Royal) Regt. of Foot

1

Sergeant David Wilkes, of the First (Royal) Regiment of Foot -- third battalion, B Company -- came trudging with a small fatigue party down the sandy slopes of Mount Olia, on the summit of which they had been toiling all day, helping the artillerymen to drag an extra 24-pounder into battery. They had brought it into position just half an hour ago, and already it had opened fire along with another 24-pounder and two howitzers mounted on the same rocky platform. The men as they descended heard the projectiles fly over their heads, and paused, distinguishing the scream of the shells from the dull hum of the round-shot, to watch the effect of the marksmanship, which was excellent.

Northwards, to their right, stretched the blue line of the Bay, where a single ship-of-war tacked lazily and kept a two-miles' offing. The smoke of the guns, drifting down on the land-breeze from the summit of Mount Olia, now hid her white sails, now lifted and revealed them in the late afternoon sunshine. But although blue held the upper heavens -- cloudless blue of July -- the sunshine that reached the ship was murky, almost copper-coloured; for it pierced through a cloud of denser smoke that rolled continuously along the western horizon from the burning houses of San Sebastian.

Sergeant Wilkes and his men, halting on the lower slope of the mountain where it fell away in sand-dunes to the estuary of the Urumea, had the whole flank of the fortress in view. Just now, at half-tide, it rose straight out of the water on the farther bank -- a low, narrow-necked isthmus that at its seaward end climbed to a cone-shaped rock four hundred feet high, crowned by a small castle. This was the citadel. The town, through which alone it could be taken by force, lay under it, across the neck of the isthmus; and this again was protected on the landward side by a high rampart or curtain, strengthened by a tall bastion in its centre and covered by a regular hornwork pushed out from its front. So much for the extremities, seaward and landward. That flank of the place which it presented to the sandhills across the Urumea was clearly more vulnerable, and yet not easily vulnerable. Deep water and natural rock protected Mount Orgullo, the citadel hill. The sea-wall, for almost half its length, formed but a fausse braye for the hornwork towering formidably behind it. Only where it covered the town, in the space between citadel and hornwork, this wall became a simple rampart; stout indeed and solid and twenty-seven feet high, with two flanking towers for enfilading fire, besides a demi-bastion at the Mount Orgullo end, yet offering the weak spot in the defences.

The British batteries had found and were hammering at it; not the guns upon Mount Olia, which had been hauled thither to dominate those of the citadel, but a dozen 24-pounders disposed, with a line of mortars behind them, on the lower slope above the estuary, where an out-cropping ridge of rock gave firm ground among the sand-dunes. The undulating line of these dunes hid this, the true breaching battery, from view of Sergeant Wilkes and his men, though they had halted within a hundred yards of it, and for at least an hour the guns had been given a rest. Only, at long intervals, one or other of the mortars threw a bomb to clear the breach -- already close upon a hundred feet wide -- driven between the two flanking towers. It was behind this breach that the town blazed. The smoke, carried down the estuary by the land-breeze, rolled heavily across the middle slopes of Mount Orgullo. But above it the small castle stood up clearly, silhouetted against the western light, and from time to time one of its guns answered

Corporal Sam Vicary

the fire from Mount Olia. Save for this and the sound of falling timbers in the town, San Sebastian kept silence.

"Wonder what it feels like?"

Sergeant Wilkes, not catching the meaning of this, turned about slowly. The speaker was a tall young corporal, Sam Vicary by name and by birth a Somerset lad -- a curly haired, broad-shouldered fellow with a simple engaging smile. He had come out with one of the later drafts, and nobody knew the cause of his enlisting, but it was supposed to be some poaching trouble at home. At all events, the recruiting sergeant had picked up a bargain in him, for, let alone his stature -- and the Royals as a regiment prided themselves on their inches -- he was easily the best marksman in B Company. Sergeant Wilkes, on whose recommendation he had been given his corporal's stripe, the day after Vittoria, looked on him as the hopefullest of his youngsters.

"Feels like?" echoed the sergeant, following the young man's gaze and observing that it rested on the great breach. "Oh! 'tis the assault you mean? Well, it feels pretty much like any other part of the business, only your blood's up, and you don't have to keep yourself warm, waiting for the guns to tire. When we stormed the San Vincenty, now, at Badajoz -- "

Someone interrupted, with a serio-comic groan.

"You've started him now, Sam Vicary! Johnny-raws of the Third Battalion, your kind attention, pray, for Daddy Wilkes and the good old days when pipeclay was pipeclay. Don't be afraid, for though he took that first class fortress single-handed, you may sit upon his knee, and he'll tell you all about it."

"It's children you are, anyway," said the sergeant, with a tolerant smile. "But I'll forgive ye, when the time comes, if ye'll do the Royals credit -- and, what's more, I'll never cast up that 'twas but a third battalion against a third-class place. Nor will I need to," he added, after a pause, "if the general makes a throw for yon breach before clearing the hornwork."

"I wasn't thinkin' of the assault," explained the young corporal, simply, "but of the women and children. It must be hell for them, this waitin'."

The same voice that had mocked the sergeant put up a ribald guffaw.

"Didn't the general give warning," it asked, "when he summoned the garrison? I've got Sam Vicary here along with me," he said, "and so I give you notice, for Sam's a terror when he starts to work."

"If you fellows could quit foolin' a moment -- " began Corporal Sam, with an ingenuous blush. But here on a sudden the slope below them opened with a roar as the breaching battery -- gun after gun -- renewed its fire on the sea-wall. Amid the din, and while the earth shook underfoot, the sergeant was the first to recover himself.

"Another breach!" he shouted between the explosions, putting up both hands like a pair of spectacles and peering through the smoke. "See there -- to the left; and that accounts for their quiet this last hour." He watched the impact of the shot for a minute or so, and shook his head. "They'd do better to clear the horn work. At Badajoz, now -- "

But here he checked himself in time, and fortunately no one had heard him. The men moved on and struck into the rutted track leading from the batteries to camp. He turned and followed them in a brown study. Ever since Badajoz, siege operations had been Sergeant Wilkes's foible. His youngsters played upon it, drawing him into discussions over the camp-fire, and winking one to another as he expounded and illustrated, using bits of stick to represent parallels, traverses, rampart and glacis, scarp and counterscarp. But he had mastered something of the theory, after his lights, and our batteries' neglect of the hornwork struck him as unscientific.

As he pursued the path, a few dozen yards in rear of his comrades, at a turn where it doubled a sharp corner he saw their hands go up to the salute, and with this slight warning came upon two of his own officers -- Major Frazer and Captain Archimbeau -- perched on a knoll to the left, and attentively studying the artillery practice through their glasses. The captain (who, by the way, commanded B Company) signed to him to halt, and climbed down to him while the fatigue party trudged on. Major Frazer followed, closing his field telescope as he descended.

"What do you say to it?" asked Captain Archimbeau, with a jerk of his hand towards the great breach.

"It can be done, sir," Sergeant Wilkes answered. "Leastways, it ought to be done. But with submission, sir, "twill be at wicked waste, unless they first clear the hornwork."

"They can keep it pretty well swept while we assault. The fact is," said Major Frazer, a tall Scotsman, speaking in his slow Scots way, "we assault it early to-morrow, and the general has asked me to find volunteers."

"For the forlorn hope, sir?" The sergeant flushed a little, over the compliment paid to the Royals.

Major Frazer nodded. "There's no need to make it common knowledge just yet. I am allowed to pick my men, but I have no wish to spend the night in choosing between volunteers. You understand?"

"Yes, sir. You will get a plenty without travelling outside the regiment."

"Captain Archimbeau goes with us; and we thought, Wilkes, of asking you to join the party."

"You are very good, sir." There was hesitation, though, in the sergeant's manner, and Major Frazer perceived it.

"You understand," he said coldly, "that there is no obligation. I wouldn't press a man for this kind of service, even if I could."

The sergeant flushed. "I was thinkin'" of the regiment, sir," he answered, and turned to his captain. "We shall have our men supportin'? -- if I may make bold to ask."

"The Royals are to show the way at the great breach, with the 9th in support. The 38th tackle the smaller breach. To make surer (as he says), the general has a mind to strengthen us up in the centre with a picked detachment of the whole division."

Sergeant Wilkes shook his head. "I am sorry for that, sir. 'Tisn't for me to teach the general; but I misdoubt all mixin' up of regiments. What the Royals can do they can best do by themselves."

"Hurts your pride a bit, eh, sergeant?" asked the major, with a short laugh. "And yet, my friend, it was only yesterday I overheard you telling your company they weren't fit to carry the slops of the Fifth division."

"It does 'em good, sir. A man, if he wants to do good, must say a trifle more than he means, at times."

"You can trust 'em, then?"

"And that again, sir -- savin' your presence -- would be sayin' more than I mean. For the lads, sir, are young lads, though willing enough; and young lads need to be nursed, however willing. As between you and me, sir" -- here he appealed to Captain Archimbeau -- "B Company is the steadiest in the battalion. But if the major takes away its captain, and upon top of him its senior sergeant -- well, beggin' your pardon, a compliment's a compliment, but it may be bought too dear."

"Wilkes is right," said the major, after a pause. "To take the both of you would be risky; and unless I'm mistaken, Archimbeau, he thinks you will be the easier spared."

"I haven't a doubt he does," agreed Captain Archimbeau, laughing.

"But I do not, sir." The sergeant seemed on the point to say more, but checked himself.

"Well?"

"It's not for me to give an opinion, sir, unless asked for it."

"I ask for it, then -- your plain opinion, as a soldier."

"An officer's an officer -- that's my opinion. There's good and bad, to be sure; but an officer like the captain here, that the men can trust, is harder spared than any sergeant: let alone that you can easily spread officers too thick -- even good ones, and even in a forlorn hope."

"He wants my place," said Captain Archimbeau; "and he salves my feelings with a testimonial."

"As for that, sir" -- the sergeant conceded a grin -- "I reckon you won't be far behind us when the trouble begins. And if the major wants a good man from B Company, you'll agree with me, sir, that yonder he goes." And Sergeant Wilkes jerked a thumb after the tall young corporal, a moment before the sandhills hid his retreating figure.

2

The assault had been a muddle from the start.

To begin with, after being ordered for one day (July 23rd) it had been deferred to the next; on reasonable grounds, indeed, for the town immediately behind the great breach was burning like a furnace; but it gave the troops an uneasy feeling that their leaders were distracted in counsel. Nor, divided by the river, did the artillery and the stormers work upon a mutual understanding. The heavy cannon, after a short experiment to the left of the great breach, had shifted their fire to the right of it, and had succeeded in knocking a practicable hole in it before dusk. But either this change of plan had not been reported to the trenches, or the officer directing the assault inexplicably failed to adapt his dispositions to it. The troops for the great breach were filed out ahead of the 38th, which had farther to go.

Worst of all, they were set in motion an hour before dawn, although Wellington had left orders that fair daylight should be waited for, and the artillery-men across the Urumea were still plying their guns on the sea-wall, to dissuade the besieged from repairing it in the darkness. To be sure a signal for the assault -- the firing of a mine against the hornwork -- had been concerted, and was duly given; but in the din and the darkness it was either not heard or not understood.

Thus it happened that the forlorn hope and the supporting companies of the Royals had no sooner cleared the trenches than their ranks shook under a fire of grape, and from our own guns. There was no cure but to dash through it and take the chances, and Major Frazer, waving his sword, called on his men to follow him at the double. Ahead of them, along the foot of the sea-wall, the receding tide had left a strip of strand, foul with rock and rock pools and patches of seaweed, dark and slippery. Now and again a shell burst and illuminated these patches, or the still-dripping ooze twinkled under flashes of musketry from the wall above; for the defenders had hurried to the parapet and flanking towers, and their fire already crackled the whole length of the strand.

Sergeant Wilkes, running a pace or two behind the major, slipping and staggering at every second yard, was aware -- though he could not see him -- of young Corporal Sam close at his shoulder. The lad talked to himself as he ran: but his talk was no more than a babble of quiet unmeaning curses, and the sergeant, who understood how the lust of fighting works in different men, did not trouble to answer until, himself floundering up to his knees in a saltwater pool, he flung out a hand for support and felt it gripped.

"Damn them!" The corporal, dragging him to solid foothold, cast a look up as a shell burst high overhead, and his face showed white with passion in the glare of it. "Can't any one tell them there's no sense in it!"

"Take it easy, lad," panted the sergeant, cheerfully. "They're bound to understand in a minute, hearin' all this musketry. Accidents will happen -- and anyway they can't help seein' us at the breach. Look at the light of it beyond the tower there!"

They floundered on together. The tower, not fifty yards away, jetted fire from every loophole; but its marksmen were aiming into the darkness, having been caught in a hurry and before they could throw down flares. As the sergeant rushed to get close under the wall of it, a bullet sent his shako whizzing; but still he ran on, and came bareheaded to the foot of the breach.

It ran down to the foreshore, a broadening scree of rubble, ruined masonry, broken beams of timber -- some of them smouldering; and over the top of it shone the blaze of the town. But the actual gap appeared to be undefended, and, better still, the rubbish on the near side had so piled itself that for half the way up the stormers could climb under cover, protected from the enfilading fire. Already the major had dropped on hands and knees and was leading the way up, scrambling from heap to heap of rubbish. Close after him went an officer in the uniform of the Engineers, with Corporal Sam at his heels. The sergeant ducked his head and followed, dodging from block to block of masonry on the other side of which the bullets spattered.

"Forward! Forward the Royals!"

The leaders were shouting it, and he passed on the shout. As yet, not a man had fallen on the slope of the breach. Two, more agile than he because by some years younger, overtook and passed him; but he was the sixth to reach the summit, and might reckon this very good work for a man of his weight. Then, as he turned to shout again, three more of the forlorn hope came blundering up, and the nine stood unscathed on the summit of the gap and apparently with none to oppose them.

But beyond it -- between them and the town, and a sheer twenty feet below them, lay a pool of blazing tar, the flames of which roared up against their faces.

"Forward the Royals! Ladders -- ladders! Oh, for your life, forward with the ladders!"

The major started the cry. Corporal Sam, taking it up, screamed it again and again. In the darkness, behind and below, the sergeant heard Captain Archimbeau calling to his men to hurry. One ladder-bearer came clattering up; but the ladders were in six-foot lengths, and a single length was useless. Nevertheless, in his rage of haste, Corporal Sam seized it from the man, and was bending to clamp it over the pit, when from the parapet to the right a sudden cross-fire swept the head of the breach. A bullet struck him in the hand. He looked up, with the pain of it, in time to see Major Frazer spin about, topple past the sergeant's hand thrust out to steady him, and pitch headlong down the slope. The ladder-bearer and another tall Royal dropped at the same moment.

"Hi, sergeant!" spoke up the young Engineer officer very sharply and clearly, at the same time stepping a couple of paces down from the ridge over which a frontal fire of bullets now flew whistling from the loopholed houses in the town. "For God's sake, shout and hurry up your men, or our chance this night is gone."

"I know it, sir -- I know it," groaned Wilkes.

"Then shout, man! Fifty men might do it yet, but every moment is odds against. See the swarm on the rampart there, to the right!"

They shouted together, but in vain. Four or five ladder-bearers mounted the slope, but only to be shot down almost at their feet. The Engineer officer, reaching forward to seize one of the ladder-lengths and drag it behind a pile of masonry under which he had taken cover, and thus for an instant exposing himself, dropped suddenly upon his face. And now but Sergeant Wilkes and Corporal Sam were left clinging, waiting for the help that still tarried.

What had happened was this. The supporting columns, disordered by the scramble along the foreshore, arrived at the foot of the breach in straggling twos and threes; and here, while their officers tried to form them up, the young soldiers behind, left for the moment without commanders and exasperated by the fire from the flanking tower, halted to exchange useless shots with its defenders and with the enemy on the rampart. Such fighting was worse than idle: it delayed them full in the path of the 38th, which now overtook them on its way to the lesser breach, and in five minutes the two columns were inextricably mixed, blocking the narrow space between wall and river, and exposed in all this dark confusion to a murderous fire.

At length, and though less than a third of his men followed him, Captain Archimbeau led the supporters up the breach; but by this time the enemy had packed the ramparts on either side. No soldiery could stand the hail of musketry, grape, and hand-grenades that rained upon the head of the column. It hesitated, pushed forward again, and broke some fifteen feet from the summit, like a spent wave. Then, as the Royals came pouring back, Lieutenant Campbell of the 9th, with all that could be collected of his picked detachment, forced his way up through the sheer weight of them, won clear, and made a fling for the crest. In vain! His first rush carried him abreast of the masonry under which Sergeant Wilkes and the corporal clung for cover. They rushed out to join him; but they had scarcely gained his side before the whole detachment began to give ground. It was not that the men fell back; rather, the apex of the column withered down as man after man dropped beside its leader. He himself had taken a wound. Yet he waved his sword and carried them forward on a second charge, only to reach where he had reached before, and be laid there by a second bullet.

Meanwhile the Royals, driven to the foot of the slope, were flung as a fresh obstacle in the path of the 38th still striving to press on for the lesser breach. From his perch half-way up the ruins, Sergeant Wilkes descried Captain Archimbeau endeav-

Corporal Sam Vicary

ouring to rally them, and climbed down to help him. The corporal followed, nursing his wounded hand. As they reached him a bugle sounded the recall.

The assault had failed. At the foot of the breach a soldier of the 4th Regiment, mad with rage, foamed out a curse upon the Royals. Corporal Sam lifted his bleeding fist and struck him across the mouth. The sergeant dragged the two apart, slipped an arm under his comrade's, and led him away as one leads a child. A moment later the surge of the retreating crowd had almost carried them off their feet. But the sergeant kept a tight hold, and steered his friend back every yard of the way along the bullet-swept foreshore. They were less than half-way across when the dawn broke; and looking in his face he saw that the lad was crying silently -- the powder-grime on his cheeks streaked and channelled with tears.

3

"I don't understand ye, lad," said Sergeant Wilkes.

"Fast enough you'd understand, if you'd but look me in the face," answered Corporal Sam, digging his heel into the sand.

The two men lay supine on a cushion of coarse grass; the sergeant smoking and staring up at the sky, the corporal, with his sound hand clasping his wounded one behind his head, his gaze fixed gloomily between his knees and across the dunes, on the still unrepaired breach in San Sebastian.

A whole fortnight had dragged by since the assault: a fortnight of idleness for the troops, embittered almost intolerably by a sense that the Fifth Division had disgraced itself. One regiment blamed another, and all conspired to curse the artillery -- whose practice, by the way, had been brilliant throughout the siege. Nor did the gunners fail to retort; but they were in luckier case, being kept busy all the while, first in shifting their batteries and removing their worst guns to the ships, next in hauling and placing the new train that arrived piecemeal from England; and not only busy, but alert, on the watch against sorties. Also, and although the error of cannonading the columns of assault had never been cleared up, the brunt of Wellington's displeasure had fallen on the stormers. The Marquis ever laid stress on his infantry, whether to use them or blame them; and when he found occasion to blame, he had words -- and methods -- that scarified equally the general of division and the private soldier.

"Fast enough you understand," repeated Corporal Sam savagely.

"I do, then, and I don't," admitted Sergeant Wilkes, after a pause. The lad puzzled him; gave him few confidences, asked for none at all, and certainly was no cheerful companion; and yet during these days of humiliation the two had become friends, almost inseparable. "I've read it," the sergeant pursued, "in Scripture or somewhere, that a man what keeps a hold on himself does better than if he took a city. I don't say as I understand that altogether; but it sounds right."

"Plucky lot of cities we take, in the Royals," growled Corporal Sam. He nodded, as well as his posture allowed, towards San Sebastian. "And you call that a third-class fortress!"

"Accidents will happen." Sergeant Wilkes, puffing at his pipe, fell back philosophically on his old catchword. "It takes you hard, because you're young; and it takes you harder because you had fed yourself up on dreams o' glory, and such-like."

"Well?"

"Well, and you have to get over it, that's all. A man can't properly call himself a soldier till he's learnt to get over it."

"If that's all, the battalion is qualifyin' fast!" Corporal Sam retorted bitterly, and sat up, blinking in the strong sunlight. Then, as Sergeant Wilkes made no reply, or perhaps because he guessed something in Sergeant Wilkes's averted face, a sudden compunction seized him. "You feel it too?"

"I got to, after all my trouble," answered Sergeant Wilkes brusquely.

"I'm sorry. Look here -- I wish you'd turn your face about -- it's worse for you and yet you get over it, as you say. How the devil do you manage?"

Still for a while Sergeant Wilkes leaned back without making reply. But of a sudden he, too, sat upright, drew down the peak of his shako to shade his eyes, and drawing his pipe from his mouth, jerked the stem of it to indicate a figure slowly crossing a rise of the sandhills between them and the estuary.

"You see that man?"

"To be sure I do. An officer, and in the R.H.A. -- curse them! -- though I can't call to mind the cut of his jib."

"You wouldn't. His name's Ramsay, and he's just out of arrest."

"What has he done?"

"A many things, first and last. At Fuentes d'Onoro the whole French cavalry cut him off -- him and his battery -- and he charged back clean through them; ay, lad, through 'em like a swathe, with his horses belly-down and the guns behind 'em bounding like skipjacks; not a gun taken, and scarce a gunner hurt. That's the sort of man."

"Why has he been under arrest?"

"Because the Marquis gave him an order and forgot it. And because coming up later, expecting to find him where he wasn't and had no right to be, the Marquis lost his temper. And likewise, because, when a great man loses his temper, right or wrong don't matter much. So there goes Captain Ramsay broken; a gentleman and a born fighter; and a captain he'll die. That's how the mills grind in this here all-conquering army. And the likes of us sit here and complain."

"If a man did that wrong to me -- " Corporal Sam jumped to his feet and stared after the slight figure moving alone across the sandhills.

Had his curiosity led him but a few paces farther, he had seen a strange sight indeed.

Captain Norman Ramsay, wandering alone and with a burning heart, halted suddenly on the edge of a sand-pit. Below him four men stood, gathered in a knot -- two of them artillery officers, the others officers of the line. His first impulse was to turn and escape, for he shunned all companionship just now. But a second glance told him what was happening; and, prompt on the understanding, he plunged straight down the sandy bank, walked up to a young artillery officer and took the pistol out of his hand. That was all, and it all happened in less than three minutes. The would-be duellist -- and challenges had been common since the late assault -- knew the man and his story. For that matter, every one in the army knew his story.

As a ghost he awed them. For a moment he stood looking from one to the other, and so, drawing the charge, tossed the pistol back at its owner's feet and resumed his way.

Corporal Sam, who had merely seen the slight figure pass beyond the edge of the dunes, went back and flung himself again on the warm bank.

"If a man did that wrong to me -- " he repeated.

4

Certainly, just or unjust, the Marquis could make himself infernally unpleasant. Having ridden over from head-quarters and settled the plans for the new assault, he returned to his main army and there demanded fifty volunteers from each of the fifteen regiments composing the First, Fourth, and Light Divisions -- men (as he put it) who could show other troops how to mount a breach. It may be guessed with what stomach the Fifth Division digested this; and among them not a man was angrier than their old general, Leith, who now, after a luckless absence, resumed command. The Fifth Division, he swore, could hold their own with any soldiers in the Peninsula. He was furious with the seven hundred and fifty volunteers, and, evading the Marquis's order, which was implicit rather than direct, he added an oath that these interlopers should never lead his men to the breaches.

Rage begets rage. During the misty morning hours of August 31st, the day fixed for the assault, these volunteers, held back and chafing with the reserves, could scarcely be restrained from breaking out of the trenches. "Why," they demanded, "had they been fetched here if not to show the way?" -- a question for which their officers were in no mood to provide a soft answer.

Yet their turn came. Sergeant Wilkes, that amateur in siege-operations, had rightly prophesied from the first that the waste of life at the breaches would be wicked and useless until the hornwork had been silenced and some lodgment made there. So as the morning wore on, and the sea-mists gave place to burning sunshine, and this again to heavy thunder-clouds collected by the unceasing cannonade, still more and more of the reserves of the Fifth Division were pushed up, until none but the volunteers and a handful of the 9th Regiment remained in the trenches. Them, too, at length Leith was forced to unleash, and they swept forward on the breaches yelling like a pack of hounds; but on the crest-line they fared at first no better than the regiments they had taunted. Thrice and four times they reached it only to topple back. The general, watching the fight from the batteries across the Urumea, now directed the gunners to fire over the stormers' heads; and again a cry went up that our men were being slaughtered by their own artillery. Undismayed by this, with no recollections of the first assault to daunt them, a company of the Light Division took advantage of the fire to force their way over the rampart on the right of the great breach and seize a lodgment in some ruined houses actually within the town. There for an hour or so these brave men were cut off, for the assault in general made no headway.

It must have failed, even after five hours" fighting, but for an accident. A line of powder-barrels collected behind the traverses by the great breach took fire and blew up, driving back all the French grenadiers but the nearest, whom it scattered in mangled heaps. As explosion followed explosion, the bright flame spread and ran along the high curtain. The British leapt after it, breaking through the traverse and swarming up to the curtain's summit. Almost at the same moment the Thirteenth and Twenty-fourth Portuguese, who had crossed the river by a lower ford, hurled themselves over the lesser breach to the right; and as the swollen heavens burst in a storm of rain and thunder, from this point and that the besiegers, as over the lip of a dam, swept down into the streets.

"Treat men like dogs, and they'll behave like dogs," grumbled Sergeant Wilkes, as he followed to prevent what mischief he might. But this, he well knew, would be little enough.

5

Corporal Sam Vicary, coming up to the edge of the camp-fire's light, stood there for a moment with a white face. The cause of it -- though it would have been a sufficient one -- was not the story to which the men around the fire had been listening; for the teller, at sight of the corporal, had broken off abruptly, knowing him to be a religious fellow after a fashion, with a capacity for disapproval and a pair of fists to back it up. So, while his comrades guffawed, he rather cleverly changed the subject.

"Oh, and by the way, talkin' of the convent" -- he meant the Convent of Santa Teresa, a high building under the very slope of the citadel, protected by its guns and still held by the enemy, after three days' fighting -- "do any of you know a small house to the left of it, with only a strip of garden between? Sort of a mud-nest it is, like a swallow's, stuck under overhang o' the cliff. No? Well, that's a pity, for I hear tell the general has promised five pounds to the first man who breaks into that house."

"But why, at all?" inquired a man close on his right. "I know the place," put in another; "a mean kind of building, with one window lookin" down the street, and that on the second floor, as you might say. It don't look to me the sort of house to hold five pounds' worth, all told -- let be that, to force it, a man must cross half the fire from the convent, and in full view. Five pounds be damned! Five pounds isn't so scarce in these times that a man need go there to fetch it for his widow."

The corporal was turning away. For three days San Sebastian had been a hell, between the flames of which he had seen things that sickened his soul. They sickened it yet, only in remembrance. Yes, and the sickness had more than once come nigh to be physical. His throat worked at the talk of loot, now that he knew what men did for it.

"The general ain't after the furnitcher," answered the first speaker. "It consarns a child."

"A child ain't no such rarity in San Sebastian that anybody need offer five pounds for one."

"What's this talk about a child?" asked Sergeant Wilkes, coming in from his rounds, and dropping to a seat by the blaze. He caught sight of Corporal Sam standing a little way back, and nodded.

"Well, it seems that, barring this child, every soul in the house has been killed. The place is pretty certain death to approach, and the crittur, for all that's known, has been left without food for two days and more. 'Tis a boy, I'm told -- a small thing, not above four at the most. Between whiles it runs to the window and looks out. The sentries have seen it more'n a dozen times; and one told me he"d a sight sooner look on a ghost."

"Then why don't the Frenchies help?" some one demanded. "There's a plenty of 'em close by, in the convent."

"The convent don't count. There's a garden between it and the house, and on the convent side a blank wall -- no windows at all, only loopholes. Besides which, there's a whole block of buildings in full blaze t'other side of the house, and the smoke of it drives across so that 'tis only between whiles you can see the child at all. The odds are, he'll be burnt alive or smothered before he starves outright; and, I reckon, put one against the other, 'twill be the mercifuller end."

"Poor little beggar," said the sergeant. "But why don't the general send in a white flag, and take him off?"

"A lot the governor would believe -- and after what you and me have seen these two days! A nice tenderhearted crew to tell him, 'If you please, we"ve come for a poor little three-year-old.' Why, he'd as lief as not believe we meant to eat him."

Sergeant Wilkes glanced up across the camp-fire to the spot where Corporal Sam had been standing. But Corporal Sam had disappeared.

6

Although the hour was close upon midnight, and no moon showed, Corporal Sam needed no lantern to light him through San Sebastian; for a great part of the upper town still burned fiercely, and from time to time a shell, soaring aloft from the mortar batteries across the river, burst over the citadel or against the rocks where the French yet clung, and each explosion flung a glare across the heavens.

He had passed into the town unchallenged. The fatigue parties, hunting by twos and threes among the ruins of the river-front for corpses to burn or bury, doubtless supposed him to be about the same business. At any rate, they paid him no attention.

Just within the walls, where the conflagration had burnt itself out, there were patches of black shadow to be crossed carefully. The fighting had been obstinate here, and more than one blazing house had collapsed into the thick of it. The corporal picked his way gingerly, shivering a little at the thought of some things buried, or half-buried, among the loose stones. Indeed, at the head of the first street his foot entangled itself in something soft. It turned out to be nothing more than a man's cloak, or poncho_, and he slipped it on, to hide his uniform and avoid explanations should he fall in with one of the patrols; but the feel of it gave him a scare for a moment.

The lad, in fact, was sick of fighting and slaughter -- physically ill at the remembrance and thought of them. The rage of the assault had burnt its way through him like a fever and left him weak, giddy, queasy of stomach. He had always hated the sight of suffering, even the suffering of dumb animals: and as a sportsman, home in England, he had learnt to kill his game clean, were it beast or bird. In thought, he had always loathed the trade of a butcher, and had certainly never guessed that soldiering could be -- as here in San Sebastian he had seen it -- more bestial than the shambles.

For some reason, as he picked his road, his mind wandered away from the reek and stink of San Sebastian and back to England, back to Somerset, to the slopes of Mendip. His home there had overlooked an ancient battle-field, and as a boy, tending the sheep on the uplands, he had conned it often and curiously, having heard the old men tell tales of it. The battle had been fought on a wide plain intersected by many water-dykes. Twice or thrice he had taken a holiday to explore it, half expecting that a close view would tell him something of its history; but, having no books to help him, he had brought back very little beyond a sense of awe that so tremendous a thing had happened just there, and (unconsciously) a stored remembrance of the scents blown across the level from the flowers

Corporal Sam Vicary

that lined the dykes -- scents of mint and meadow-sweet at home there, as the hawthorn was at home on the hills above.

He smelt them now, across the reek of San Sebastian, and they wafted him back to England -- to boyhood, dreaming of war but innocent of its crimes -- to long thoughts, long summer days spent among the unheeding sheep, his dog Rover beside him -- an almost thoroughbred collie, and a good dog, too, though his end had been tragic.... But why on earth should his thoughts be running on Rover just now?

Yet, and although, as he went, England was nearer to him and more real than the smoking heaps between which he picked his way, he steered all the while towards the upper town, through the square, and up the hill overlooked by the convent and the rocky base of the citadel. He knew the exact position of the house, and he chose a narrow street -- uninhabited now, and devastated by fire -- that led directly to it.

The house was untouched by fire as yet, though another to the left of it blazed furiously. It clung, as it were a swallow's nest, to the face of the cliff. A garden wall ran under the front; and, parallel with the wall, a road pretty constantly swept by musketry fire from the convent. At the head of the street Corporal Sam stumbled against a rifleman who, sheltered from bullets at the angle of the crossing, stood calmly watching the conflagration.

"Hallo!" said the rifleman cheerfully; "I wanted some more audience, and you're just in time."

"There's a child in the house, eh?" Panted Corporal Sam, who had come up the street at a run. The rifleman nodded. "Poor little devil! He'll soon be out of his pain, though."

"Why, there's heaps of time! The fire won't take hold for another half-hour. What's the best way in? ... You an' me can go shares, if that's what you're hangin' back for," added Corporal Sam, seeing that the man eyed him without stirring.

"Hi! Bill!" the rifleman whistled to a comrade, who came

slouching out of a doorway close by, with a clock in one hand, and in the other a lantern by help of which he had been examining the inside of this piece of plunder. "Here's a boiled lobster in a old woman's cloak, wants to teach us the way into the house yonder."

"Tell him to go home," said Bill, still peering into the works of the clock. "Tell him we"ve been there." He chuckled a moment, looked up, and addressed himself to Corporal Sam. "What regiment?"

"The Royals."

The two burst out laughing scornfully. "Don't wonder you cover it up," said the first rifleman.

Corporal Sam pulled off his poncho. "I'd offer to fight the both of you," he said, "but 'tis time wasted with a couple of white-livers that don't dare fetch a poor child across a roadway. Let me go by; you'll keep, anyway."

"Now look here, sonny -- " The first rifleman blocked his road. "I don't bear no malice for a word spoken in anger: so stand quiet and take my advice. That house isn't goin' to take fire. 'Cos why? 'Cos as Bill says, we've been there -- there and in the next house, now burnin' -- and we know. 'Cos before leavin' -- the night before last it was -- some of our boys set two barrels o' powder somewheres in the next house, on the ground floor, with a slow match. That's why we left; though, as it happened, the match missed fire. But the powder's there, and if you'll wait a few minutes now you'll not be disapp'inted."

"You left the child behind!"

"Well, we left in a hurry, as I tell you, and somehow in the hurry nobody brought him along. I'm sorry for the poor little devil, too." The fellow swung about. "See him there at the window, now! If you want him put out of his pain -- "

He lifted his rifle. Corporal Sam made a clutch at his arm to drag it down, and in the scuffle both men swayed out upon the roadway. And with that, or a moment later, he felt the rifleman slip down between his arms, and saw the blood gush from his mouth as he collapsed on the cobbles.

Corporal Sam heard the man Bill shout a furious oath, cast one puzzled look up the roadway towards the convent, saw the flashes jetting from its high wall, and raced across unscathed. A bullet sang past his ear as he found the gate and hurled himself into the garden. It was almost dark here, but dark only for a moment. . . . For as he caught sight of a flight of steps leading to a narrow doorway, and ran for them -- and even as he set foot on the lowest -- of a sudden the earth heaved under him, seemed to catch him up in a sheet of flame, and flung him backwards -- backwards and flat on his back, into a clump of laurels.

Slowly he picked himself up. The sky was dark now; but, marvellous to say, the house stood. The mass of it yet loomed over the laurels. Yes, and a light showed under the door at the head of the steps. He groped his way up and pushed the door open.

The light came through a rent in the opposite wall, and on the edge of this jagged hole some thin laths were just bursting into a blaze. He rushed across the room to beat out the flame, and this was easily done; but, as he did it, he caught sight of a woman's body, stretched along the floor by the fireplace, and of a child cowering in the corner, watching him.

"Come and help, little one," said Corporal Sam, still beating at the laths.

The child understood no English, and moreover was too small to help. But it seemed that the corporal's voice emboldened him, for he drew near and stood watching.

"Who did this, little one?" asked Corporal Sam, nodding towards the corpse, as he rubbed the charred dust from his hands.

For a while the child stared at him, not comprehending; but by-and-by pointed beneath the table and then back at its mother.

The corporal walked to the table, stooped, and drew from under it a rifle and a pouch half-filled with cartridges.

"Tell him we've been there." He seemed to hear the rifleman Bill's voice repeating the words, close at hand. He recognised the badge on the pouch.

He was shaking where he stood; and this, perhaps, was why the child stared at him so oddly. But, looking into the wondering young eyes, he read only the question, "What are you going to do?"

He hated these riflemen. Nay, looking around the room, how he hated all the foul forces that had made this room what it was! ...And yet, on the edge of resolve, he knew that he must die for what he meant to do . . . that the thing was unpardonable, that in the end he must be shot down, and rightly, as a dog.

He remembered his dog Rover, how the poor brute had been tempted to sheep-killing at night, on the sly; and the look in his eyes when, detected at length, he had crawled forward to his master to be shot. No other sentence was possible, and Rover had known it.

Had he no better excuse? Perhaps not. . . . He only knew that he could not help it; that this thing had been done, and by the consent of many . . . and that as a man he must kill for it, though as a soldier he deserved only to be killed.

With the child's eyes still resting on him in wonder, he set the rifle on its butt and rammed down a cartridge; and so, dropping on hands and knees, crept to the window.

7

Early next morning Sergeant Wilkes picked his way across the ruins of the great breach and into the town, keeping well to windward of the fatigue parties already kindling fires and collecting the dead bodies that remained unburied.

Within and along the sea-wall San Sebastian was a heap of burnt-out ruins. Amid the stones and rubble encumbering the streets, lay broken muskets, wrenched doors, shattered sticks of furniture -- mirrors, hangings, women's apparel, children's clothes -- loot dropped by the pillagers as valueless, wreckage of the flood. He passed a very few inhabitants, and these said nothing to him; indeed, did not appear to see him, but sat by the ruins of their houses with faces set in a stupid horror. Even the crash of a falling house near by would scarcely persuade them to stir, and hundreds during the last three days had been overwhelmed thus and buried.

The sergeant had grown callous to these sights. He walked on, heeding scarcely more than he was heeded, came to the great square, and climbed a street leading northwards, a little to the left of the great convent. The street was a narrow one, for half its length lined on both sides with fire-gutted houses; but the upper half, though deserted, appeared to be almost intact. At the very head, and close under the citadel walls, it took a sharp twist to the right, and another twist, almost equally sharp, to the left before it ended in a broader thoroughfare, crossing it at right angles and running parallel with the ramparts.

At the second twist the sergeant came to a halt; for at his feet, stretched across the causeway, lay a dead body.

He drew back with a start, and looked about him. Corporal Sam had been missing since nine o'clock last night, and he felt sure that Corporal Sam must be here or hereabouts. But no living soul was in sight.

The body at his feet was that of a rifleman; one of the volunteers whose presence had been so unwelcome to General Leith and the whole Fifth Division. The dead fist clutched its rifle; and the sergeant stooping to disengage this, felt that the body was warm.

"Come back, you silly fool!"

He turned quickly. Another rifleman had thrust his head out of a doorway close by. The sergeant, snatching up the weapon, sprang and joined him in the passage where he sheltered.

"I -- I was looking for a friend hereabouts."

"Fat lot of friend you'll find at the head of this street!" snarled the rifleman, and jerked his thumb towards the corpse. "That makes the third already this morning. These Johnnies ain't no sense of honour left -- firing on outposts as you may call it."

"Where are they firing from?"

"No 'they' about it. You saw that cottage -- or didn't you? -- right above there, under the wall; the place with one window in it? There's a devil behind it somewheres; he fires from the back of the room, and what's more, he never misses his man. You have Nick's own luck -- the pretty target you made, too; that is unless, like some that call themselves Englishmen and ought to know better, he's a special spite on the Rifles."

The sergeant paid no heed to the sneer. He was beginning to think.

"How long has this been going on?" he asked.

"Only since daylight. There was a child up yonder, last night; but it stands to reason a child can't be doing this. He never misses, I tell you. Oh, you had luck, just now!"

"I wonder," said Sergeant Wilkes, musing. "I'll try it again, anyway." And while the rifleman gasped he stepped out boldly into the road.

He knew that his guess might, likely enough, be wrong: that, even were it right, the next two seconds might see him a dead man. Yet he was bound to satisfy himself. With his eyes on the sinister window -- it stood half open and faced straight down the narrow street -- he knelt by the corpse, found its ammunition pouch, unbuckled the strap and drew out a handful of cartridges. Then he straightened himself steadily -- but his heart was beating hard -- and as steadily walked back and rejoined the rifleman in the passage.

"You have a nerve," said the rifleman, his voice shaking a little. "Looks like he don't fire on redcoats; but you have a nerve all the same."

Corporal Sam Vicary

"Or else he may be gone," suggested the sergeant, and on the instant corrected himself; "but I warn you not to reckon upon that. Is there a window facing on him anywhere, round the bend of the street?"

"I dunno."

The rifleman peered forth, turning his head sideways for a cautious reconnoitre. "Maybe he has gone, after all -- "

It was but his head he exposed beyond the angle of the doorway; and yet, on the instant a report cracked out sharply, and he pitched forward into the causeway. His own rifle clattered on the stones beside him, and where he fell he lay, like a stone.

Sergeant Wilkes turned with a set jaw and mounted the stairs of the deserted house behind him. They led him up to the roof, and there he dropped on his belly and crawled. Across three roofs he crawled, and lay down behind a balustrade overlooking the transverse roadway. Between the pillars of the balustrade he looked right across the roadway and into the half-open window of the cottage. The room within was dark save for the glimmer of a mirror on the back wall.

"Kill him I must," growled the sergeant through his teeth, "though I wait the day for it."

And he waited there, crouching for an hour - for two hours.

He was shifting his cramped attitude a little -- a very little -- for about the twentieth time, when a smur of colour showed on the mirror, and the next instant passed into a dark shadow. It may be that the marksman within the cottage had spied yet another rifleman in the street. But the sergeant had noted the reflection in the glass, that it was red. Two shots rang out together. But the sergeant, after peering through the parapet, stood upright, walked back across the roofs, and regained the stairway.

The street was empty. From one of the doorways a voice called to him to come back. But he walked on, up the street and across the roadway to a green-painted wicket. It opened upon a garden, and across the garden he came to a flight of steps with an open door above. Through this, too, he passed and stared into a small room. On the far side of it, in an armchair, sat Corporal Sam, leaning back, with a hand to his breast; and facing him, with a face full of innocent wonder, stood a child -- a small, grave, curly-headed child.

8

"I'm glad you done it quick," said Corporal Sam.

His voice was weak, yet he managed to get out the words firmly, leaning back in the wooden armchair, with one hand on his left breast, spread and covering the lower ribs.

The sergeant did not answer at once. Between the spread fingers he saw a thin stream welling, darker than the scarlet tunic which it discoloured. For perhaps three seconds he watched it. To him the time seemed as many minutes, and all the while he was aware of the rifle-barrel warm in his grasp.

"Because," Corporal Sam pursued with a smile that wavered a little, half wistfully seeking his eyes, "you'd 'a had to do it, anyway -- wouldn't you? And any other way it -- might -- 'a been hard."

"Lad, what made you?"

It was all Sergeant Wilkes could say, and he said it, wondering at the sound of his own voice. The child, who, seeing that the two were friends and not, after all, disposed to murder one another, had wandered to the head of the stairs to look down into the sunlit garden shining below, seemed to guess that something was amiss after all, and, wandering back, stood at a little distance, finger to lip.

"I don't know," the corporal answered, like a man with difficulty trying to collect his thoughts. "Leastways, not to explain to you. It must 'a been comin' on for some time."

"But what, lad -- what?"

"Ah -- 'what?' says you. That's the trouble, and I can't never make you see -- yes, make you see -- the hell of it. It began with thinkin' -- just with thinkin' -- that first night you led me home from the breach. And the things I saw and heard; and then, when I came here, only meanin' to save him -- "

He broke off and nodded at the child, who catching his eye, nodded back smiling.

He and the corporal had evidently made great friends.

But the corporal's gaze, wavering past him, had fixed itself on a trestle bed in the corner.

"There was a woman," he said. "She was stone cold; but the child told me -- until I stopped his mouth, and made a guess at the rest. I took her down and buried her in the garden. And with that it came over me that the whole of it -- the whole business -- was wrong, and that to put myself right I must kill, and keep on killing. Of course I knew what the end would be. But I never looked for such luck as your coming. . . . I was ashamed, first along, catching sight o' you -- not -- not ashamed, only I didn't want you to see. But when you took cover an' waited -- though I wouldn't 'a hurt you for worlds -- why then I knew how the end would be."

"Lad," said the sergeant, watching him as he panted, "I don't understand you, except that you're desperate wrong. But I saw you -- saw you by the lookin'-glass, behind there; and 'tis right you should know."

"O' course you saw me. . . . I'm not blamin', am I? You had to do it, and I had to take it. That was the easiest way. I couldn' do no other, an' you couldn' do no other, that bein' your duty. An' the child, there -- "

Sergeant Wilkes turned for a moment to the child, who met his gaze, round-eyed; then to his friend again. But the corporal's head had dropped forward on his chest. The sergeant touched his shoulder, to make sure; then, with one look behind him, but ignoring the child, reeled out of the room and down the stairs, as in a dream. In the sunny garden the fresh air revived him and he paused to stare at a rose-bush, rampant, covered with white blossoms against which the bees were humming. Their hum ran in his head so that he failed to notice that the sound of musketry had died down. An hour before it had been death to walk, as he did, under the convent wall and out into the street leading to the lesser breach. The convent had, in fact, surrendered, and its defenders were even now withdrawing up the hill to the citadel.

He found the lesser breach and climbed down it to the shore of the Urumea, beside the deserted ford across which the Portuguese had waded on the morning of the second assault. Beyond it shone the sandhills, hiding our batteries.

He sat down on the bank and pulled off boots and socks, preparing to wade; but turned at a slight sound.

The child had followed him and stood half-way down the ruins of the breach, wistful, uncertain.

In a rage, as one threatens off an importunate dog, Sergeant Wilkes waved an arm. The child turned and slunk away, back into San Sebastian.

Three Men of Badajos

1

You enter the village of Gantick between two round-houses set one on each side of the high road where it dips steeply towards the valley bottom. On the west of the opposite hill the road passes out between another pair of round-houses. And down in the heart of the village among the elms facing the churchyard lych-gate stands a fifth, alone.

The five, therefore, form an elongated St. Andrew's cross; but nobody can tell for certain who built them, or why. They are all alike; each, built of cob, circular, whitewashed, having pointed windows and a conical roof of thatch with a wooden cross on the apex. When I was a boy these thatched roofs used to be pointed out to me as masterpieces; and they still endure. But the race of skilled thatchers, once the peculiar pride of Gantick, has come to an end. What time has eaten modern and clumsy hands have tried to repair; yet a glance will tell you that the old sound work means to outwear the patches.

The last of these famous thatchers lived in the round-house on your right as you leave Gantick by the seaward road. His name was old Nat Ellery, or Thatcher Ellery, and his age (as I remember him) between seventy or eighty. Yet he clung to his work, being one of those lean men upon whom age, exposure, and even drink take a long while to tell. For he drank; not socially at the King of Bells, but at home in solitude with a black bottle at his elbow. He lived there alone; his neighbours, even of the round-house across the road, shunned him and were shunned by him: children would run rather than meet him on the road as he came along, striding swiftly for his age (the drink never affected his legs), ready greaved and sometimes gauntleted as if in haste for his job, always muttering to himself; and when he passed us with just a side-glance from his red eyes, we observed that his pale face did not cease to twitch nor his lips to work. We felt something like awe for the courage of Archie Passmore, who followed twenty paces behind with his tools and a bundle of spars or straw-rope, or perhaps at the end of a ladder which the two carried between them. Archie (aged sixteen) used to boast to us that he did not fear the old man a ha'penny; and the old man treated Archie as a Gibeonite, a hewer of wood, a drawer of water, never as an apprentice. Of his craft, except what he picked up by watching, the lad learned nothing.

What made him so vaguely terrible to us was the common rumour in the village that Thatcher Ellery had served once under his Majesty's colours, but had deserted and was still liable to be taken and shot for it. Now this was true and everyone knew it, though why and how he had deserted were questions answered among us only by dark and frightful guesses. He had outlived all risk of the law's revenge; no one, it was certain, would take the trouble to seize and execute justice upon a drunkard of seventy. But we children never thought of this, and for us as we watched him down the road there was always the thrilling chance that over the hedge or around the next corner would pop up a squad of redcoats. Some of us had even seen it, in dreams.

2

This is the story of Thatcher Ellery as it was told to me after his death, which happened one night a few weeks before I came home from school on my first summer holidays.

His father, in the early years of the century, had kept the mill

Three Men of Badajos

up at Trethake Water, two miles above Gantick. There were two sons, of whom Reub, the elder, succeeded to the mill. Nat had been apprenticed to the thatching. Accident of birth assigned to the two these different walks of life but by taking thought their parents could not have chosen more wisely, for Nat was born clever, with an ambition to cut a figure in man's eyes and just that sense of finish and the need of it which makes the good workman. Whereas his brother went the daily round at home as contentedly as a horse at a cider press. But Nat made the mistake of lodging under his father's roof, and his mother made the worse mistake of liking her first-born the better and openly showing it. Nat, jealous and sensitive by nature, came to imagine the whole world against him, and Reub, who had no vice beyond a large thick-witted selfishness, seemed to make a habit of treading on his corns. At length came the explosion: a sudden furious assault which sent Reub souse into the paternal mill-leat.

The mother cursed Nat forth from the door, and no doubt said a great deal more than she meant. The boy -- he was just seventeen -- carried his box down to the Ring of Bells. Next morning as he sat viciously driving in spars astride on a rick ridge, whence he could see far over the Channel, there came into sight round Derryman's Point a ship-of-war, running before the strong easterly breeze with piled canvas, white stunsails bellying, and a fine froth of white water running off her bluff bows. Another ship followed, and another -- at length a squadron of six. Nat watched them from time to time until they trimmed sails and stood in for Falmouth. Then he climbed down from the rick and put on his coat.

Two years later he landed at Portsmouth, heartily sick of the sea and all belonging to it. He drank himself silly that night and for ten nights following, and one morning found himself in the streets without a penny. Portsmouth just then (July, 1808) was filled with troops embarking under Sir John Moore for

Portugal. One regiment especially took Nat's eye -- the 4th or King's Own, and indeed the whole service contained no finer body of men. He sidled up to a corporal and gave a false name. Varcoe had been his mother's maiden name, and it came handy. The corporal took him to a recruiting sergeant and handed him over with a wink. The recruiting sergeant asked a few convenient questions, and within the hour Nat was a soldier of King George. To his disgust, however, they did not embark him for Portugal, but marched him up the length of England to Lancaster, to learn his drill with the second battalion.

Seventeen months later they marched him back through the length of England -- outwardly a made soldier -- and shipped him on a transport for Gibraltar. In the meanwhile he had found two friends, the only two real ones he ever found in his life. They were Dave McInnes and Teddy Butson, privates of the 4th Regiment of Foot, 2nd Battalion, C Company. Dave McInnes came from somewhere to the west of Perth and drank like a fish when he had the chance. Teddy Butson came from the Lord knew where, with a tongue that wagged about everything except his own past. It did indeed wag about that, but told nothing but lies which were understood and accepted for lies and by consequence didn't count. These two had christened Nat Ellery "Spuds." He had no secret from them but one.

He was the cleverest of the three, and they admired him for it. He admired them in return for possessing something he lacked. It seemed to him the most important, almost the only important, thing in the world.

For (this was his secret) he believed himself to be a coward. He was not really a coward, though he carried about in his heart the liveliest fear of death and wounds. He was always asking himself how he would behave under fire, and somehow he found the odds heavy against his behaving well. He put roundabout questions to Dave and Teddy with the aim of discovering what they felt about it. They answered in a careless, matter-of-fact way, as men to whom it had never occurred to have any doubt about themselves. Nat was desperately afraid they might guess his reason for asking. Just here, when their friendship might have been helpful, it failed altogether. He felt angry with them for not understanding, while he prayed that they might not understand. He took to observing other men in the regiment, and found them equally cheerful, concerned only with the moment. He became secretly religious after a fashion. He felt that he was the one and only coward in the King's Own, and prayed and planned his behaviour day and night to avoid being found out.

In this state of mind he landed at Gibraltar. When the order came for the 4th to move up to the front, he cheered with the rest, watching their faces.

3

At ten o'clock on the night of April 6th, 1812, our troops were to assault Badajos. It was now a few minutes past nine.

The night had closed in without rain, but cloudy and thick, with river fog. The moon would not rise for another hour or more. After the day's furious bombardment silence had fallen on besieged and besiegers; but now and then a light flitted upon the ramparts, and at intervals the British in the trenches could hear the call of a sentinel proclaiming that all was well in Badajos.

In the trenches a low continuous murmur mingled with the voices of running water. On the right by the Guadiana waited Picton's Third Division, breathing hard as the time drew nearer. Kempt commanded these for the moment. Picton was in camp attending to a hurt, but his men knew that before ten o'clock he would arrive to lead across the Rivillas by the narrow bridge and up to the walls of the Castle frowning over the river at the city's north-east corner.

In the centre and over against the wall to the left of the Castle were assembled Colville's and Barnard's men of the Fourth and Light Divisions. Theirs, according to the General's plan, was to be the main business to-night -- to carry the breaches hammered in the Trinidad and Santa Maria bastions and the curtain between; the Fourth told off for the Trinidad and the curtain, the Light Bobs for the Santa Maria -- heroes these of Moore's famous rear-guard, tried men of the 52nd Foot and the 95th Rifles, with the 43rd beside them, and destined to pay the heaviest price of all to-night for the glory of such comradeship. But, indeed, Ciudad Rodrigo had given the 43rd a title to stand among the best.

And far away to the left, on the lower slopes of the hills, Leigh's Fifth Division was halted in deep columns. A knoll separated his two brigades, and across the interval of darkness they could hear each other's movements. They were to operate independently; and concerning the task before the brigade on the right there could be no doubt: a dash across the gorge at their feet, and an assault upon the outlying Pardaleras, on the opposite slope. But the business before Walker's brigade, on the left, was by no means so simple. The storming party had been marching light, with two companies of Portuguese to carry their ladders, and stood discussing prospects: for as yet they were well out of earshot of the walls, and the moment for strict silence had not arrived.

"The Vincenty," grumbled Teddy Butson; "and by shot to me if I even know what it's like."

"Like!" McInnes' jaws shut on the word like a steel trap. "The scarp's thirty feet high, and the ditch accordin'. The last on the west side it will be -- over by the river. I know it like your face, and its uglier, if that's possible."

"Dick Webster was saying it's mined," put in Nat, commanding a firm voice.

"Eh? The glacis? I shouldn't wonder. Walker will know."

"But what'll he do?"

"Well, now" -- Dave seemed to be considering -- "it will not be for the likes of me to be telling the brigadier-general. But if Walker comes to me and says, 'Dave, there's a mine hereabouts. What will I be doing?' it's like enough I shall say: 'Your honour knows best; but the usual course is to walk round it.'"

Teddy Butson chuckled, and rubbed the back of his axe approvingly. Nat held his tongue for a minute almost, and then broke out irritably: "To hell with this waiting!"

His nerves were raw. Two minutes later a man on his right kicked awkwardly against his foot. It startled him, and he cursed furiously.

"Hold hard, Spuds, my boy," said the man cheerfully; "you ain't Lord Wellington, nor his next-of-kin, to be makin' all the noise."

Teddy Butson wagged his head solemnly at a light which showed foggily for a moment on the distant ramparts.

"All right," said he, "you -- -- town! Little you know 'tis Teddy's birthday."

"There will be wine," said Dave, dreamily.

"Lashins of it; wine and women, and loot things. I wonder how our boys are feeling on the right? What's that?" -- as a light shot up over the ridge to the eastward. "Wish I could see what's doing over there. My belief we're only put up for a feint."

"O hush it, you royal mill-clappers!" This came from the darkness behind -- from some man of the 30th, no doubt.

The voice was tense, with a note of nervousness in it, which Nat recognised at once. He turned with a sudden desire to see the speaker's face. Here was one who felt as he did, one who could understand him, but his eyes sought in vain among the lines of glimmering black shakos.

"Silence in the ranks!" Two officers came forward, talking together and pausing to watch the curious light now rising and sinking and rising again in the sky over the eastern ridges. "They must have caught sight of our fellows -- listen, wasn't that a cheer? What time is it?" The officer was Captain Hopkins commanding Nat's Company, but now in charge of the stormers. A voice hailed him, and he ran back. "Yes, sir, I think so decidedly," Nat heard him saying, and he came running clutching his sword sheath. "Silence men -- the brigade will advance."

The Portuguese picked up and shouldered their ladders: the orders were given, and the columns began to move down the slope. For a while they could hear the tramp of the other brigade moving parallel with them on the other side of the knoll, then fainter and fainter as it wheeled aside and down the gorge to the right. At the foot of the slope they opened a view up the gorge lit for a moment by a flare burning on the ramparts of the Pardaleras, and saw their comrades moving down and across the bottom like a stream of red lava pouring towards the foot. The flare died down and our brigade struck away to the left over the level country. On this side Badajos remained dark and silent.

They were marching quickly, yet the pace did not satisfy Nat. He wanted to be through with it, to come face to face with the worst and know it. And yet he feared it abominably. For two years he had contrived to hide his secret. He had marched, counter-marched, fed, slept, and fought with his comrades; had dodged with them behind cover, loaded, fired, charged with them; had behaved outwardly like a decent soldier, but almost always with a sickening void in the pit of the stomach. Once or twice in particularly bad moments he had caught himself blubbering, and with a deadly shame. He had not an idea that at least a dozen of his comrades -- among them Dave and Teddy -- had seen it, and thought nothing of it; still less did he imagine that those had been his most courageous moments. Soldiers fight differently. Teddy Butson, for instance, talked all the time until his tongue swelled, and then he barked like a dog. Dave shut his teeth and groaned. But these symptoms escaped Nat, whose habit was to think all the while of himself. Of one thing he felt sure, that he had never yet been anything but glad to hear the recall sounded.

Well, so far he had escaped. Heaven knew how he had managed it; he only knew that the last two years had been as long as fifty, and he seemed to have been living since the beginning of the world. But here he was, and actually keeping step with a storming party. He kept his eyes on Dave's long lean back immediately in front and trudged on, divided between an insane desire to know of what Dave was thinking, and an equally insane wonder what Dave's body might be worth to him as cover.

What was the silly word capering in his head? "Mill-clappers." Why on earth "Mill-clappers?" It put him in mind of home: but he had no silly tender thoughts to waste on home, or the folks there. He had never written to them. If they should happen on the copy of the Gazette -- and the chances were hundred to one against it -- the name of Nathaniel Varcoe among the killed or wounded would mean nothing to them. He tramped on, chewing his fancy, and extracted this from it: "A man with never a friend at home hasn't even an excuse to be a coward, curse it!"

Suddenly the column halted, in a bank of fog through which his ear caught the lazy ripple of water. He woke up with a start. The fog was all about them.

"What's this?" he demanded aloud; then, with a catch of his breath, "Mines?"

"Eh, be quiet," said Teddy Butson at his elbow; "listen to yonder." And the word was hardly out when an explosion split the sky and was followed by peal after peal of musketry. Nat had a swift vision of a high black wall against a background of flame, and then night came down again as you might close a shutter. But the musketry continued. "That will be at the breaches," Dave flung the words over his left shoulder. Then followed another flash and another explosion. This time, however, the light, though less vivid than the first flash, did not vanish. While he wondered at this Nat saw first of all the rim of the moon through the slant of an embrasure, and then Teddy's pale but cheerful face.

The head of the column had been halted a few yards only from a breastwork, with a stockade above it and a chevaux de frise on top of all. As far as knowledge of his whereabouts went, Nat might have been east, west, north or south of Badajos, or somewhere in another planet. But the past two years had somehow taught him to divine that behind this ugly obstruction lay a covered way with a guard house. And sure enough the men, keeping dead silence now, could hear the French soldiers chatting in that unseen guard house and laughing.

"Now's the time." Nat heard the word passed back by the young engineer officer who had crept forward to reconnoitre: and then an order given in Portuguese.

"Ay, bring up the ladders, you greasers, and let's put it through." This from Teddy Butson chafing by Nat's side.

The two Portuguese companies came forward with the ladders as the storming party moved up to the gateway. And just at that moment there the sentry let off his alarm shot. It set all within the San Vincente bastion moving and whirring like the works of a mechanical toy; feet came running along the covered way; muskets clinked on the stone parapet; tongues of fire spat forth from the embrasures; and then, as the musketry quickened, a flash and a roar lifted the glacis away behind, to the right of our column, so near that the wind of it drove our men sideways.

"All right, Johnny," Dave grunted, recovering himself as the clods of earth began to fall: "Blaze away, my silly ducks -- we're not there!"

But the Portuguese companies as the mine exploded cast down the ladders and ran. Half a dozen came charging back along the column's right flank, and our soldiers cursed and struck at them as they fled. But the curses were as nothing beside those of the Portuguese officers striving to rally their men.

"My word," said Teddy. "Hear them scandalous greasers! It's poor talk, is English."

"On with you, lads" -- it was Walker himself who shouted. "Pick up the ladders, and on with you!"

They hardly waited for the word, but, shouldering the ladders, ran forward through the dropping bullets to the gate, cheering and cheered by the rear ranks.

But they flung themselves in vain on the gate. On its iron-bound and iron-studded framework their axes made no impression. A dozen men charged it, using a ladder as a battering ram. "Aisy with that, ye blind ijjits!" yelled an Irish sergeant. "Ye'll be needin' them ladders prisintly!" Our three privates found themselves in the crowd surging towards the breastwork to the right of the gate. "Nip on my shoulders, Teddy lad," grunted McInnes, and Teddy nipped up and began hacking at the chevaux de frise with his axe. "That's av ut, bhoys," yelled the Irish sergeant again. "Lave them spikes an' go for the stockade. Good for you, little man -- whirro!" Nat by this time was on a comrade's back, and using his axe for dear life; one of twenty men hacking, ripping, tearing down the wooden stakes. But it was Teddy who wriggled through first with Dave at his heels. The man beneath Nat gave a heave with his shoulders and shot him through his gap, a splinter tearing his cheek open. He fell head foremost sprawling down the slippery slope of the ditch.

While he picked himself up and stretched out a hand to recover his axe a bullet struck the blade of it -- ping! He caught up the axe and ran his finger over it stupidly. Phut -- another bullet spat into the soft earth behind his shoulder. Then he understood. A fellow came tumbling through the gap, pitched exactly where Nat had been sprawling a moment before, rose to his knees, and then with a quiet bubbling sound lay down again.

"Ugh! he would be killed -- he must get out of this!" But there was no cover unless he found it across the ditch and close under the high stone curtain. They would be dropping stones, beams, fire barrels; but at least he would be out of the reach of the bullets. He forgot the chance -- the certainty -- of an enfilading fire from the two bastions. His one desire was to get across and pick some place of shelter.

But by this time the men were pouring in behind and fast filling the ditch. A fire-ball came crashing over the rampart, rolled down the grass slope and lay sputtering, and in the infernal glare he saw all his comrades' faces -- every detail of their dress down to the moulded pattern on their buttons. "Fourth! Fourth!" some one shouted, and then voice and vision were caught up and drowned together in a hell of musketry. He must win across or be carried he knew not where by the brute pressure of the crowd. A cry broke from him and he ran, waving his axe, plunged down the slope and across. On the further slope an officer caught him up and scrambled beside him. "Whirro, Spuds! After him, boys!" sang out Teddy Butson. But Spuds did not hear.

He and the officer were at the top of the turf -- at the foot of the curtain. "Ladders! Ladders!" He caught hold of the first as it was pushed up and helped -- now the centre of a small crowd -- to plant it against the wall. Then he fell back, mopping his forehead, and feeling his torn cheek. What the devil were they groaning at? Short? The ladder too short? He stared up foolishly. The wall was thirty feet high perhaps and the ladder ten feet short of that or more. "Heads!" A heavy beam crashed down, snapping the foot of the ladder like a cabbage stump. Away to the left a group of men were planting another. Half a dozen dropped while he watched them. Why in the world were they dropping like that? He stared beyond and saw the reason. The French marksmen in the bastion were sweeping the face of the curtain with their cross fire -- those cursed bullets again! And the ladder did not reach, after all. O it was foolishness -- flinging away men like this for no earthly good! Why not throw up the business and go home? Why didn't somebody stop those silly bugles sounding the Advance?

There they went again! It was enough to drive a man mad!

He turned and ran down the slope a short way. For the moment he held a grip on himself, but it was slackening, and in another half-minute he would have lost it and run in mere blind horror. But in the first group he blundered upon were Dave and Teddy, and a score of the King's Own, with a couple of ladders between them; and better still, they were listening to Captain Hopkins, who waved an arm and pointed to an embrasure to the left. Nat, pulling himself up and staring with the rest, saw that no gun stood in this embrasure, only a gabion. In a moment he was climbing the slope again; if a man must die, there's comfort at least in company. He bore a hand in planting the two ladders; a third was fetched -- heaven knew whence or how -- and planted beside them, and up the men swarmed, three abreast, Dave leading on the right-hand one, at the foot of which Nat hung back and swayed. He heard Dave's long sigh, the sigh, the sob almost, of desire answered at last. He watched him as he mounted. The ladders were still too short, and the leader on each must climb on the second man's shoulders to get hand-hold on the coping. In that moment he might be clubbed on the head, defenceless. On the middle ladder a young officer of the 30th mounted by Dave's side. Nat turned his head away, and as he did so a rush of men, galled by the fire from the bastion to the right, came on him like a wave, and swept him up the first four rungs.

He was in for it now. Go back he could not, and he followed the tall Royal ahead, whose heels scraped against his breast buttons, and once or twice bruised him in the face; followed up, wondering what face of death would meet him at the top, where men were yelling and jabbering in three languages -- French, English, and that tongue which belongs equally to men and brutes at close quarters and killing.

Something came sliding down the ladder. The man in front of Nat ducked his head; Nat ducked too; but the body slid sideways before it reached them and dropped plumb -- the inert lump which had been Dave McInnes. His shako, spinning straight down the ladder, struck Nat on the shoulder and leaped off it down into darkness.

He saw other men drop; he saw Teddy Butson parallel with him on the far ladder, and mounting with him step for step -- now earlier, now later, but level with him most of the time. They would meet at the embrasure; find together whatever waited for them there. Nat was sobbing by this time -- sweat and tears together running down the caked blood on his cheek -- but he did not know it.

He had almost reached the top when a sudden pressure above forced his feet off the rung and his body over the ladder's side; and there he dangled, hooked by his armpit. Someone grabbed his leg, and, pulling him into place, thrust him up over the shoulders of the tall Royal in front. He saw the leader on the middle ladder go down under a clubbed blow which burst through his japanned shako-cover, and then a hand came down to help him.

"Spuds, O Spuds!"

It was Teddy reaching down from the coping to help him, and he paid for it with his life. The two wriggled into the embrasure together, Nat's head and shoulders under Teddy's right arm. Nat did not see the bayonet thrust given, but heard a low grunt, as he and his friend's corpse toppled over the coping together and into Badajos.

He rose on his knees, caught a man by the leg, flung him, and

Three Men of Badajos

as the fellow clutched his musket, wrenched the bayonet from it and plunged it into his body. While the Frenchman heaved, he pulled out the weapon for another stab, dropped sprawling on his enemy's chest, and the first wave of the storming party broke over him, beating the breath out of him, and passed on.

Yet he managed to wriggle his body from under this rush of feet, and, by-and-bye, to raise himself, still grasping the sidearm. Men of the 4th were pouring thick and fast through the embrasure, and turning to the right in pursuit of the enemy now running along the curve of the ramparts. A few only pressed straight forward to silence the musketry jetting and crackling from the upper windows of two houses facing on the fortifications.

Nat staggered down after them, but turned as soon as he gained the roadway, and, passing to the right, plunged down a black side street. An insane notion possessed him of taking the two houses in the rear, and as he went he shouted to the 4th to follow him. No one paid him the smallest attention, and presently he was alone in the darkness, rolling like a drunkard, shaken by his sobs, but still shouting and brandishing his sidearm. He clattered against a high blank wall.

Still he lurched forward over uneven cobbles. He had forgotten his design upon the two houses, but a light shone at the end of this dark lane, and he made for it, gained it, and found himself in a wider street. And there the enchantment fell on him.

For the street was empty, utterly empty, yet brilliantly illuminated. Not a soul could he see: yet in house after house as he passed lights shone from every window, in the lower floors behind blinds or curtains which hid the inmates. It was as if Badajos had arrayed itself for a fête; and still, as he staggered forward a low buzz, a whisper of voices surrounded him, and now and again at the sound of his footstep on the cobbles a lattice would open gently and be as gently re-shut. Hundreds of eyes were peering at him, the one British soldier in a bewitched city; hundreds of unseen eyes, stealthy, expectant. And always ahead of him, faint and distant, sounded the bugles and the yells around the Trinidad and the breaches.

He stood alone in the great square. While he paused at the corner, his eyes following the rows of mysterious lights from house to house, from storey to storey, the regular tramp of feet fell on his ears and a company of Foot marched down into the moonlight patch facing him and grounded arms with a clatter. They were men of his own regiment, and they formed up in the moonlight like a company of ghosts. One or two shots were fired at them, low down, from the sills of a line of doorways to his right; but no citizen showed himself and no one appeared to be hit. And ever from the direction of the Trinidad came the low roar of combat and the high notes of the bugles.

He was creeping along the side of the square towards an outlet at its north-east corner, when the company got into motion again and came towards him. Then he turned up a narrow lane to the left and fled. He was sobbing no longer; the passion had died out of him, and he knew himself to be mad. In the darkness the silent streets began to fill; random shots whistled at every street corner; but he blundered on, taking no account of them. Once he ran against a body of Picton's men -- half a score of the 74th Regiment let loose at length from the captured Castle, and burning for loot. One man thrust the muzzle of his musket against his breast before he was recognized. Then two or three shook hands with him.

He was back in the square again and fighting -- Heaven knew why -- with an officer of the Brunswickers over a birdcage. Whence the birdcage came he had no clear idea, but there was a canary-bird inside, and he wanted it. A random shot smashed his left hand as he gripped the cage, and he dropped it as something with which he had no further concern. As he turned away, hugging his hand, and cursing the marksman, a second shot from another direction took the Brunswicker between the shoulders.

Three Men of Badajos

At dawn he found himself on the ramparts by the Trinidad breach, peering curiously among the slain. Across the top of the breach stretched a heavy beam studded with sword blades, and all the bodies on this side of it were French. Right beneath it lay one red-coat whose skull had been battered out of shape as he attempted to wriggle through. All the upper blades were stained, and on one fluttered a strip of flannel shirt. Powder blackened every inch of the rampart hereabouts, and as Nat passed over he saw the bodies piled in scores on the glacis below -- some hideously scorched -- -among beams, gabions, burnt out fire-pots, and the wreckage of ladders. A horrible smell of singed flesh rose on the morning air; and, beyond the stench and the sullen smoke, birds sang in dewy fields, and the Guadiana flowed between grey olives and green promise of harvest.

Below, a single British officer, wrapped in a dark cape, picked his way among the corpses. Behind, intermittent shots and outcries told of the sack in progress. Save for Nat and the dead, the Trinidad was a desert. Yet he talked incessantly, and, stooping to pat the shoulder of the red-coat beneath the chevaux de frise, spoke to Dave McInnes and Teddy Butson to come and look. He never doubted they were beside him. "Pretty mess they've made of this chap." He touched the man's collar: "48th, a corporal! Ugh, let's get out of this!" In imagination he linked arms with two men already stiffening, one at the foot and the other on the summit of the San Vincent's bastion "King's Own all friends in the King's Own!" he babbled as he retraced his way into the town.

He had a firelock in his hands ... he was fumbling with it, very clumsily, by reason of his shattered fingers. He had wandered down a narrow street, and was groping at an iron-studded door. "Won't open," he told the ghosts beside him. "Must try the patent key." He put the muzzle against the lock and fired, flung himself against the door, and as it broke before him, stood swaying, staring across a whisp of smoke into a mean room, where a priest knelt in one corner by a straw pallet, and a girl rose from beside him and slowly confronted the intruder. As she rose she caught at the edge of a deal table, and across the smoke she too seemed to be swaying.

4

Seventeen years later Nat Ellery walked down the hill into Gantick village, and entered the King of the Bells.

"I've come," said he, "to inquire about a chest I left here, one time back along." And he told his name and the date.

The landlord, Joshua Martin -- son of old Joshua, who had kept the inn in 1806 -- rubbed his double chin. "So you be Nat Ellery? I can just mind'ee as a lad. As for the chest -- come to think, father sent it back to Trethake Water. Reckon it went in the sale."

"What sale?"

"Why, don't 'ee know? When Reub sold up. That would be about five years after the old folks died. The mill didn' pay after the war, so Reub sold up and emigrated."

"Ah! What became of him?"

"I did hear he was dead too," said Joshua Martin, "out in Canady somewhere. But that may be lies," he added cheerfully.

Nat made no further comment, but paid for his gin-and-water, picked up his carpet bag, and went out to seek for a cottage. On his way he eyed the thatched roofs critically. "Old Thatcher Hockaday will be dead," he told himself. "There's work for me here." He felt certain of it in Farmer Sprague's rick-yard. Farmer Sprague owned the two round-houses at the seaward end of the village, and wanted a tenant for one of them. Nat applied for it, and declared his calling.

"Us can't afford to pay the old prices these times," said the farmer.

Nat's eyes had wandered off to the ricks. "You'll find you can when you've seen my work," he answered.

Thus he became tenant of the round-house, and lived in it to the day of his death. No one in my day knew when or how the story first spread that he had been in the army and deserted. Perhaps he let slip the secret in his cups; for at first he spent his Saturday evenings at the King of Bells, dropping this habit when he found that every soul there disliked him. Perhaps some discharged veteran of the 4th, tramping through Gantick in search of work, had recognised him and let fall a damning hint. Long before I can remember the story had grown up uncontradicted, believed in by everyone. Beneath it the man lived on and deteriorated; but his workmanship never deteriorated, and no man challenged its excellence.

About a month before his death (I have this from the postmistress) he sat down and wrote a letter, and ten days later a visitor arrived at the round-house. This visitor the Jago family (who lived across the road) declare to have been Satan himself; they have assured me so again and again, and I cannot shake their belief. But that is nonsense. The man was a grizzled artizan looking fellow well over fifty; extraordinarily like the old Thatcher, though darker of skin -- yellow as a guinea, said Gantick; in fact and beyond doubt, the old man's son. He made no friends, no acquaintances ever, but confined himself to nursing the Thatcher, now tied to his chair by rheumatism. One thing alone gives colour to the Jagos' belief; the Thatcher who had sent for him could not abide the sight of him. The Jago children, who snatched a fearful joy by stealing after dark into the unkempt garden and peering through the uncurtained lattice windows, reported that as the pair sat at table with the black bottle between them, the Thatcher's eyes would be drawn to fix themselves on the other's with a stealthy shrinking terror -- or, as they put it, "vicious when he wasna' lookin' and afeared when he was."

They would sit (so the children reported) half an hour, or maybe an hour, at a time, without a word spoken between them; but, indeed, the yellow stranger troubled few with his speech. His only visits were paid to the postmistress, who kept a small grocery store, where he bought arrowroot and other spoon-food for the invalid, and the Ring of Bells, where he went nightly to have the black bottle refilled with rum. On the doctor he never called.

It was on July 12th that the end came. The fine weather, after lasting for six weeks, had broken up two days before into light thunderstorms, which did not clear the air as usual. Ky Jago (short for Caiaphas), across the way, prophesied a big thunderstorm to come, but allowed he might be mistaken when on the morning of the 12th the rain came down in sheets. This torrential rain lasted until two in the afternoon, when the sky cleared and a pleasant northwesterly draught played up the valley. At six o'clock Ky Jago, who, in default of the Thatcher, was making shift to cover up Farmer Sprague's ricks, observed dense clouds massing themselves over the sea and rolling up slowly against the wind, and decided that the big storm would happen after all. At nine in the evening it broke.

It broke with such fury that the Stranger, with the black bottle under his arm, paused on the threshold as much as to ask his father, "Shall I go?" But the old man was clamouring for drink, and he went. He was half-way down the hill when with a crack the heavens opened and the white jagged lightning fairly hissed by him. Crack followed crack, flash and peal together, or so quick on each other, that no mortal could distinguish the rattle of one discharge from the bursting explosion of the other. No such tempest, he decided, could last for long, and he fled down to the Ring of Bells for shelter until the worst should be over. He waited there perhaps twenty minutes, and still the infernal din grew worse instead of better, until his anxiety for the old man forced him out in the teeth of it and up the hill, where the gutters had overflowed upon the roadway, and the waters raced over his ankles. The first thing he saw at the top in one lurid instant was the entire Jago family gathered by their garden gate -- six of them -- and all bareheaded under the deluge.

The next flash revealed why they were there. Against the round-house opposite a ladder rested, and above it on the steep roof clung a man -- his father. He had clamped his small ladder into the thatch, and as the heaven opened and shut, now silhouetting the round-house, now wrapping it in white flames -- they saw him climbing up, and still up, towards the cross at the top.

"Help, there!" shouted the Stranger. "Come down! O help, you! -- we must get him down!" The women and children screamed. A fresh explosion drowned shout and screams.

Jago and the Stranger reached the ladder together. The Stranger mounted first; but as he did so, the watchers in one blinding moment saw the old Thatcher's hand go up and grip the cross. The shutters of darkness came to with a roar, but above it rose a shrill, a terribly human cry.

"Dave!" cried the voice. "Ted!"

Silence followed, and then a heavy thud. They waited for the next flash. It came. There was no one on the roof of the round-house, but a broken stump where the cross had been.

5

This was the story the yellow Stranger told to the Coroner. And the Coroner listened and asked:

"Can you account for conduct of deceased? Had he been drinking that evening?"

"He had," answered the witness, and for a moment, while the Coroner took a note, it seemed he had said all. Then he seemed to think better of it, and added "My father suffered from delusions sir."

"Hey? What sort of delusions?" The Coroner glanced at the jury, who sat impassive.

"Well, sir, my father in his young days had served as a soldier."

Here the jurymen began to show interest suddenly. One or two leaned forward. "He belonged to the 4th Regiment, and was at the siege of Badajos. During the sack of the city he broke into a house, and -- and -- after that he was missing."

"Go on," said the Coroner, for the witness had paused.

"That was where he first met my mother, sir. It was her house, and she and a priest kept him hidden till the English had left. After that he married her. There were three children -- all boys. My brothers came first: they were twins. I was born two years later."

"All born in Badajos?"

"All in Badajos, sir. My brothers will be there still, if they're living."

"But these delusions -- "

"I'm coming to them. My father must have been hurt, somehow hurt in his head. He would have it that my two brothers -- twins, sir, if you'll be pleased to mark it -- were no sons of his, but of two friends of his, soldiers of the 4th Regiment who had been killed, the both, that evening by the San Vincente bastion. So you see he must have been wrong in his head."

"And you?"

"O, there couldn't be any mistake about me. I was his very image, and -- perhaps I ought to say, sir -- he hated me for it. When my mother died -- she had been a fruit-seller -- he handed the business over to my brothers, taking only enough to carry him back to England and me with him. The day after we landed in London he apprenticed me to a brassworker. I was just turned fifteen, and from that day until last Wednesday three weeks we never set eyes on each other."

"Let me see," said the Coroner, turning back a page or two. "At the last moment just before he fell, you say -- and the other witnesses confirm it -- that he called out twice -- uttered two names, I think."

"They were the names by which he used to call my brothers, sir -- the names of his two mates in the storming party."

The Two Scouts

[Chapters from the Memoirs of Manuel (or Manus) McNeill, an agent in the Secret Service of Great Britain during the campaigns of the Peninsula (1808-1813). A Spanish subject by birth, and a Spaniard in all his upbringing, he traces in the first chapter of his Memoirs his descent from an old Highland family through one Manus McNeill, a Jacobite agent in the Court of Madrid at the time of the War of Succession, who married and settled at Aranjuez. The authenticity of these Memoirs has been doubted, and according to Napier the name of the two scouts whom Marmont confused together (as will appear in a subsequent chapter) was not McNeill, but Grant: which is probable enough, but not sufficient to stamp the Memoirs as forgeries. Their author may have chosen McNeill as a nom de guerre, and been at pains to deceive his readers on this point while adhering to strictest truth in his relation of events. And this I conceive to be the real explanation of a narrative which itself clears up, and credibly, certain obscurities in Napier. -- Q.]

1: The Ford of the Tormes

In the following chapters I shall leave speaking of my own adventures and say something of a man whose exploits during the campaigns of 1811-1812 fell but a little short of mine. I do so the more readily because he bore my own patronymic, and was after a fashion my kinsman; and I make bold to say that in our calling Captain Alan McNeill and I had no rival but each other. The reader may ascribe what virtue he will to the parent blood of a family which could produce at one time in two distinct branches two men so eminent in a service requiring the rarest conjunction of courage and address.

I had often heard of Captain McNeill, and doubtless he had as often heard of me. At least thrice in attempting a coup d'espionage upon ground he had previously covered -- albeit long before and on a quite different mission -- I had been forced to take into my calculations the fame left behind by "the Great McNeill," and a wariness in our adversaries whom he had taught to lock the stable door after the horse had been stolen. For while with the Allies the first question on hearing of some peculiarly daring feat would be "Which McNeill?" the French supposed us to be one and the same person; which, if possible, heightened their grudging admiration.

Yet the ambiguity of our friends upon these occasions was scarcely more intelligent than our foes' complete bewilderment; since to anyone who studied even the theory of our business the Captain's method and mine could have presented but the most superficial resemblance. Each was original, and each carried even into details the unmistakable stamp of its author. My combinations, I do not hesitate to say, were the subtler. From choice I worked alone; while the Captain relied for help on his servant José (I never heard his surname), a Spanish peasant of remarkable quickness of sight, and as full of resource as of devotion. Moreover I habitually used disguises, and prided myself in their invention, whereas it was the Captain's vanity to wear his conspicuous scarlet uniform upon all occasions, or at most to cover it with his short dark-blue riding cloak. This, while to be sure it enhanced the showiness of his exploits, obliged him to carry them through with a suddenness and dash foreign to the whole spirit of my patient work. I must always maintain that mine were the sounder methods; yet if I had no other reason for my admiration I could not withhold it from a man who, when

I first met him, had been wearing a British uniform for three days and nights within the circuit of the French camp. I myself had been living within it in a constant twitter for hard upon three weeks.

It happened in March, 1812, when Marmont was concentrating his forces in the Salamanca district, with the intent (it was rumoured) of marching and retaking Ciudad Rodrigo, which the Allies had carried by assault in January. This stroke, if delivered with energy, Lord Wellington could parry; but only at the cost of renouncing a success on which he had set his heart, the capture of Badajos. Already he had sent forward the bulk of his troops with his siege-train on the march to that town, while he kept his headquarters to the last moment in Ciudad Rodrigo as a blind. He felt confident of smashing Badajos before Soult with the army of the south could arrive to relieve it; but to do this he must leave both Almeida and Ciudad Rodrigo exposed to Marmont, the latter with its breaches scarcely healed and its garrison disaffected. He did not fear actual disaster to these fortresses; he could hurry back in time to defeat that, for he knew that Marmont had no siege guns, and could only obtain them by successfully storming Almeida and capturing the battering train which lay there protected by 3,000 militia. Nevertheless a serious effort by Marmont would force him to abandon his scheme.

All depended therefore (1) on how much Marmont knew and (2) on his readiness to strike boldly. Consequently, when that General began to draw his scattered forces together and mass them on the Tormes before Salamanca, Wellington grew anxious; and it was to relieve that anxiety or confirm it that I found myself serving as tapster of the Posada del Rio in the village of Huerta, just above a ford of the river, and six miles from Salamanca. Neither the pay it afforded nor the leisure had attracted me to the Posada del Rio. Pay there was little, and leisure there was none, since Marmont's lines came down to the river here, and we had a battalion of infantry quartered about the village -- sixteen under our roof -- and all extraordinarily thirsty fellows for Frenchmen; besides a squadron of cavalry, vedettes of which constantly patrolled the farther bank of the Tormes. The cavalry officers kept their chargers -- six in all -- in the ramshackle stable in the court-yard facing the inn; and since (as my master explained to me the first morning) it was a tradition of the posada to combine the duties of tapster and ostler in one person, I found all the exercise I needed in running between the cellar and the great kitchen, and between the kitchen and the stable, where the troopers had always a job for me, and allowed me in return to join in their talk. They seemed to think this an adequate reward, and I did not grumble.

Now, beside the stable, and divided from it by a midden-heap, there stood at the back of the inn a small outhouse with a loft. This in more prosperous days had accommodated the master's own mule, but now was stored with empty barrels, strings of onions, and trusses of hay -- which last had been hastily removed from the larger stable when the troopers took possession. Here I slept by night, for lack of room indoors, and also to guard the fodder -- an arrangement which suited me admirably, since it left me my own master for six or seven hours of the twenty-four. My bedroom furniture consisted of a truss of hay, a lantern, a tinder-box, and a rusty fowling piece. For my toilet I went to the bucket in the stable yard.

On the fifth night, having some particular information to send to headquarters, I made a cautious expedition to the place agreed upon with my messenger -- a fairly intelligent muleteer, and honest, but new to the business. We met in the garden at the rear of his cottage, conveniently approached by way of the ill-kept cemetery which stood at the end of the village. If surprised, I was to act the nocturnal lover, and he the angry defender of his sister's reputation -- a foolish but not ill-looking girl, to whom

I had confided nothing beyond a few amorous glances, so that her evidence (if unluckily needed) might carry all the weight of an obvious incapacity to invent or deceive.

These precautions proved unnecessary. But my muleteer, though plucky, was nervous, and I had to repeat my instructions at least thrice in detail before I felt easy. Also he brought news of a fresh movement of battalions behind Huerta, and of a sentence in the latest General Order affecting my own movements, and this obliged me to make some slight alteration in my original message. So that, what with one thing and another, it wanted but an hour of dawn when I regained the yard of the Posada del Rio and cautiously re-entered the little granary.

Rain had fallen during the night -- two or three short but heavy showers. Creeping on one's belly between the damp graves of a cemetery is not the pleasantest work in the world, and I was shivering with wet and cold and an instant want of sleep. But as I closed the door behind me and turned to grope for the ladder to my sleeping loft, I came to a halt, suddenly and painfully wide awake. There was someone in the granary. In the pitch darkness my ear caught the sound of breathing -- of someone standing absolutely still and checking his breath within a few paces of me -- perhaps six, perhaps less.

I, too, stood absolutely still, and lifted my hand towards the hasp of the door. And as I did so -- in all my career I cannot recall a nastier moment -- as my hand went up, it encountered another. I felt the fingers closing on my wrist, and wrenched loose. For a moment our two hands wrestled confusedly; but while mine tugged at the latch the other found the key and twisted it round with a click. (I had oiled the lock three nights before.) With that I flung myself on him, but again my adversary was too quick, for as I groped for his throat my chest struck against his uplifted knee, and I dropped on the floor and rolled there in intolerable pain.

No one spoke. As I struggled to raise myself on hands and

knees, I heard the chipping of steel on flint, and caught a glimpse of a face. As its lips blew on the tinder this face vanished and reappeared, and at length grew steady in the blue light of the sulphur match. It was not the face, however, on which my eyes rested in a stupid wonder, but the collar below it -- the scarlet collar and tunic of a British officer.

And yet the face may have had something to do with my bewilderment. I like, at any rate, to think so; because I have been in corners quite as awkward, yet have never known myself so pitifully demoralised. The uniform might be that of a British officer, but the face was that of Don Quixote de la Mancha, and shone at me in that blue light straight out of my childhood and the story-book. High brow, high cheek-bone, long pointed jaw, lined and patient face -- I saw him as I had known him all my life, and I turned up at the other man, who stooped over me, a look of absurd surmise.

He was a Spanish peasant, short, thick-set and muscular, but assuredly no Sancho: a quiet quick-eyed man, with a curious neat grace in his movements. Our tussle had not heated him in the least. His right fist rested on my back, and I knew he had a knife in it; and while I gasped for breath he watched me, his left hand hovering in front of my mouth to stop the first outcry. Through his spread fingers I saw Don Quixote light the lantern and raise it for a good look at me. And with that in a flash my wits came back, and with them the one bit of Gaelic known to me.

"Latha math leat" I gasped, and caught my breath again as the fingers closed softly on my jaw, "O Alan mhic Neill!"

The officer took a step and swung the lantern close to my eyes -- so close that I blinked.

"Gently, José." He let out a soft pleased laugh while he studied my face. Then he spoke a word or two in Gaelic -- some question which I did not understand.

"My name is McNeill," said I; "but that's the end of my mother tongue."

The Captain laughed again. "We've caught the other one, José," said he. And José helped me to my feet -- respectfully, I thought. "Now this," his master went on, as if talking to himself, "this explains a good deal."

I guessed. "You mean that my presence has made the neighbourhood a trifle hot for you!"

"Exactly; there is a General Order issued which concerns one or both of us."

I nodded. "In effect it concerns us both; but, merely as a matter of history, it was directed against me. Pardon the question, Captain, but how long have you been within the French lines?"

"Three days," he answered simply; "and this is the third night."

"What? In that uniform?"

"I never use disguises," said he -- a little too stiffly for my taste.

"Well, I do. And I have been within Marmont's cantonments for close, on three weeks. However, there's no denying you're a champion. But did you happen to notice the date on the General Order?"

"I did; and I own it puzzled me. I concluded that Marmont must have been warned beforehand of my coming."

"Not a bit of it. The order is eight days old. I secured a copy on the morning it was issued; and the next day, having learnt all that was necessary in Salamanca, I allowed myself to be hired in the market-place of that city by the landlord of this damnable inn."

"I disapprove of swearing," put in Captain McNeill, very sharp and curt.

"As well as of disguises? You seem to carry a number of scruples into this line of business. I suppose," said I, nettled, "when you read in the General Order that the notorious McNeill was lurking disguised within the circle of cantonments, you took it that Marmont was putting a wanton affront on your character, just for the fun of the thing?"

"My dear sir," said the Captain, "if I have expressed myself rudely, pray pardon me: I have heard too much of you to doubt your courage, and I have envied your exploits too often to speak slightingly of your methods. As a matter of fact, disguise would do nothing, and worse than nothing, for a man who speaks Spanish with my Highland accent. I may, perhaps, take a foolish pride in my disadvantage, but," and here he smiled, "so, you remember, did the fox without a tail."

"And that's very handsomely spoken," said I; "but unless I'm mistaken, you will have to break your rule for once, if you wish to cross the Tormes this morning."

"It's a case of must. Barring the certainty of capture if I don't, I have important news to carry -- Marmont starts within forty-eight hours."

"Since it seems that for once we are both engaged on the same business, let me say at once, Captain, and without offence, that my news is as fresh as yours. Marmont certainly starts within forty-eight hours to assault Ciudad Rodrigo, and my messenger is already two hours on his way to Lord Wellington."

I said this without parade, not wishing to hurt his feelings. Looking up I found his mild eyes fixed on me with a queer expression, almost with a twinkle of fun.

"To assault Ciudad Rodrigo? I think not."

"Almeida, then, and Ciudad Rodrigo next. So far as we are concerned the question is not important."

"My opinion is that Marmont intends to assault neither."

"But, my good sir," I cried, "I have seen and counted the scaling-ladders!"

"And so have I. I spent six hours in Salamanca itself," said the Captain quietly.

"Well, but doesn't that prove it? What other place on earth can he want to assault? He certainly is not marching south to join Soult." I turned to José, who had been listening with an impassive face.

"The Captain will be right. He always is," said José, perceiving that I appealed to him.

"I will wager a month's pay -- "

"I never bet," Captain McNeill interrupted, as stiffly as before. "As you say, Marmont will march upon the Agueda, but in my opinion he will not assault Ciudad Rodrigo."

"Then he will be a fool."

"H'm! As to that I think we are agreed. But the question just now is how am I to get across the Tormes? The ford, I suppose, is watched on both sides." I nodded. "And I suppose it will be absolutely fatal to remain here long after daybreak?"

"Huerta swarms with soldiers," said I, "we have sixteen in the posada and a cavalry picket just behind. A whole battalion has eaten the village bare, and is foraging in all kinds of unlikely places. To be sure you might have a chance in the loft above us, under the hay."

"Even so, you cannot hide our horses."

"Your horses?"

"Yes, they're outside at the back. I didn't know there was a cavalry picket so close, and José must have missed it in the darkness."

José looked handsomely ashamed of himself.

"They are well-behaved horses," added the Captain. "Still, if they cannot be stowed somewhere, it is unlikely they can be explained away, and of course it will start a search."

"Our stable is full."

"Of course it is. Therefore you see we have no choice -- apart from our earnest wish -- but to cross the ford before daybreak. How is it patrolled on the far side?"

"Cavalry," said I; "two vedettes."

"Meeting, I suppose, just opposite the ford? How far do they patrol?"

"Three hundred yards maybe: certainly not more."

The Captain pursed up his lips as if whistling.

"Is there good cover on the other side? My map shows a wood of fair size."

"About half a mile off; open country between. Once there, you ought to be all right; I mean that a man clever enough to win there ought to make child's-play of the rest."

He mused for half a minute. "The stream is two wide for me to hear the movements of the patrols opposite. José has a wonderful ear."

"Yes, Captain, I can hear the water from where we stand," José put in.

"He is right," said I, "it's not a question of distance, but of the noise of the water. The ford itself will not be more than twenty yards across."

"What depth?"

"Three feet in the middle, as near as can be. I have rubbed down too many horses these last three days not to know. The river may have fallen an inch since yesterday. They have cleared the bottom of the ford, but just above and below there are rocks, and slippery ones."

"My horse is roughed. Of course the bank is, watched on this side?"

"Two sentries by the ford, two a little up the road, and the guard-house not twenty yards beyond. Captain, I think you'll have to put on a disguise for once in your life."

"Not if I can help it."

"Then, excuse me, but how the devil do you propose to manage?"

He frowned at the oath, recovered himself, and looked at me again with something like a twinkle of fun in his solemn eyes.

"Do you know," said he, "it has just occurred to me to pay you a tremendous compliment -- McNeill to McNeill, you understand? I propose to place myself entirely in your hands."

"Oh, thank you!" I pulled a wry face. "Well, it's a compliment if ever there was one -- an infernally handsome compliment. Your man, I suppose, can look after himself?" But before he could reply I added, "No; he shall go with me: for if you do happen to get across, I shall have to follow, and look sharp about it." Then, as he seemed inclined to protest, "No inconvenience at all -- my work here is done, and you are pretty sure to have picked up any news I may have missed. You had best be getting your horse at once; the dawn will be on us in half an hour. Bring him round to the door here. José will find straw -- hay -- anything -- to deaden his footsteps. Meanwhile I'll ask you to excuse me for five minutes."

The Spaniard eyed me suspiciously.

"Of course," said I, reading his thoughts, "if your master doubts me -- "

"I think, Señor McNeill, I have given you no cause to suspect it," the Captain gravely interrupted. "There is, however, one question I should like to ask, if I may do so without offence. Is it your intention that I should cross in the darkness or wait for daylight?"

"We must wait for daylight; because although it increases some obvious dangers -- "

"Excuse me; your reasons are bound to be good ones. I will fetch around my horse at once, and we shall expect you back here in five minutes."

In five minutes time I returned to find them standing in the darkness outside the granary door. José had strewn a space round about with hay; but at my command he fetched more and spread it carefully, step by step, as Captain McNeill led his horse forward. My own arms were full; for I had spent the five

The Two Scouts

minutes in collecting a score of French blankets and shirts off the hedges, where the regimental washermen had spread them the day before to dry.

The sketch on the following page will explain my plan and our movements better than a page of explanation: --

The reader will observe that the Posada del Rio, which faces inwards upon its own courtyard, thrusts out upon the river at its rear a gable which overhangs the stream and flanks its small waterside garden from view of the village street. Into this garden, where the soldiers were used to sit and drink their wine of an evening, I led the Captain, whispering him to keep silence, for eight of the Frenchmen slept behind the windows above. In the corner by the gable was an awning, sufficient, when cleared of stools and tables, to screen him and his horse from any eyes looking down from these windows, though not tall enough to allow him to mount. And at daybreak, when the battalion assembled at its alarm-post above the ford, the gable itself would hide him. But of course the open front of the garden -- where in two places the bank shelved easily down to the water -- would leave him in full view of the troopers across the river. It was for this that I had brought the blankets. Across the angle by the gable there ran a clothes line on which the house-servant, Mercedes, hung her dish-clouts to dry. Unfastening the inner end, I brought it forward and lashed it to a post supporting a dovecote on the river wall. To fasten it high enough I had to climb the post, and this set the birds moving uneasily in the box overhead. But before their alarm grew serious I had slipped down to earth again, and now it took José and me but a couple of minutes to fling the blankets over the line and provide the Captain with a curtain, behind which, when day broke, he could watch the troopers and his opportunity. Already, in the village behind us, a cock was crowing. In twenty minutes the sun would be up and the bugles sounding the reveille. "Down the bank by the gable,"

I whispered. "It runs shallow there, and six or seven yards to the right you strike the ford. When the vedettes are separated -- just before they turn to come back -- that's your time."

I took José by the arm. "We may as well be there to see. How were you planning to cross?"

"Oh," said he, "a marketer -- with a raw-boned Galician horse and two panniers of eggs -- for Arapiles -- "

"That will do; but you must enter the village at the farther end and come down the road to the ford. Get your horse" -- we crept back to the granary together -- "but wait a moment, and I will show you the way round."

When I rejoined him at the back of the granary he had his horse ready, and we started to work around the village. But I had miscalculated the time. The sky was growing lighter, and scarcely were we in the lane behind the courtyard before the bugles began to sound.

"Well," said I, "that may save us some trouble after all."

Across the lane was an archway leading into a wheelwright's yard. It had a tall door of solid oak studded with iron nails; but this was unlocked and unbolted, and I knew the yard to be vacant, for the French farriers had requisitioned all the wheelwright's tools three days before, and the honest man had taken to his bed and proposed to stay there pending compensation.

To this archway we hastily crossed, and had barely time to close the door behind us before the soldiers, whose billets lay farther up the lane, came running by in twos and threes for the alarm-post, the later ones buckling their accoutrements as they ran halting now and then, and muttering as they fumbled with a strap or a button. José at my instruction had loosened his horse's off hind shoe just sufficiently to allow it to clap; and as soon as he was ready I opened the door boldly, and we stepped out into the lane among the soldiers, cursing the dog's son of a smith who would not arise from his lazy bed to attend to two poor marketers pressed for time.

Now it had been dim within the archway, but out in the lane there was plenty of light, and it did me good to see José start when his eyes fell on me. For a couple of seconds I am sure he believed himself betrayed: and yet, as I explained to him afterwards, it was perhaps the simplest of all my disguises and -- barring the wig -- depended more upon speech and gait than upon any alteration of the face. (For a particular account of it I must refer the reader back to my adventure in Villafranca. On this occasion, having proved it once, I felt more confident; and since it deceived José, I felt I could challenge scrutiny as an aged peasant travelling with his son to market.)

A couple of soldiers passed us and flung jests behind them as we hobbled down the lane, the loose shoe clacking on the cobbles, José tugging at his bridle, and I limping behind and swearing volubly, with bent back and head low by the horse's rump, and on the near side, which would be the unexposed one when we gained the ford. And so we reached the main street and the river, José turning to point with wonder at the troops as we hustled past. One or two made a feint to steal an egg from our panniers. José protested, halting and calling in Spanish for protection. A sergeant interfered; whereupon the men began to bait us, calling after us in scraps of camp Spanish. José lost his temper admirably; for me, I shuffled along as an old man dazed with the scene; and when we came to the water's edge felt secure enough to attempt a trifle of comedy business as José hoisted my old limbs on to the horse's back behind the panniers. It fetched a shout of laughter. And then, having slipped off boots and stockings deliberately, José took hold of the bridle again and waded into the stream. We were safe.

I had found time for a glance at the farther bank, and saw that the troopers were leisurely riding to and fro. They met and parted just as we entered the ford. Before we were half-way across they had come near to the end of their beat, with about three hundred yards between them, and I was thinking this a fair opportunity for the Captain when José whispered, "There he goes," very low and quick, and with a souse, horse and rider struck the water behind us by the gable of the inn. As the stream splashed up around them we saw the horse slip on the stony bottom and fall back, almost burying his haunches, but with two short heaves he had gained the good gravel and was plunging after us. The infantry spied him first -- the two vedettes were in the act of wheeling about and heard the warning before they saw. Before they could put their charges to the gallop Captain McNeill was past us and climbing the bank between them. A bullet or two sang over us from the Huerta shore. Not knowing of what his horse was capable, I feared he might yet be headed off; but the troopers in their flurry had lost their heads and their only chance unless they could drop him by a fluking shot. They galloped straight for the ford-head, while the Captain slipped between, and were almost charging each other before they could pull up and wheel at right angles in pursuit.

"Good," said José simply. A shot had struck one of our panniers, smashing a dozen eggs (by the smell he must have bought them cheap), and he halted and gesticulated in wrath like a man in two minds about returning and demanding compensation. Then he seemed to think better of it, and we moved forward; but twice again before we reached dry land he turned and addressed the soldiers in furious Spanish across the babble of the ford. José had gifts.

For my part I was eager to watch the chase which the rise of the bank hid from us, though we could hear a few stray shots. But José's confidence proved well grounded, for when we struck the high road there was the Captain half a mile away within easy reach of the wood, and a full two hundred yards ahead of the foremost trooper.

"Good!" said José again. "Now we can eat!" and he pulled out a loaf of coarse bread from the injured pannier, and trimming off an end where the evil-smelling eggs had soaked it, divided it in two. On this and a sprig of garlic we broke our fast, and were munching and jogging along contentedly when we met the returning vedettes. They were not in the best of humours, you may be sure, and although we drew aside and paused with crusts half lifted to our open mouths to stare at them with true yokel admiration, they cursed us for taking up too much of the roadway, and one of them even made a cut with his sabre at the near pannier of eggs.

"It's well he broke none," said I as we watched them down the road. "I don't deny you and your master any reasonable credit, but for my taste you leave a little too much to luck."

Our road now began to skirt the wood into which the Captain had escaped, and we followed it for a mile and more, José all the while whistling a gipsy air which I guessed to carry a covert message; and sure enough, after an hour of it, the same air was taken up in the wood to our right, where we found the Captain dismounted and seated comfortably at the foot of a cork tree.

He was good enough to pay me some pretty compliments, and, after comparing notes, we agreed that -- my messenger being a good seven hours on his way with all the information Lord Wellington could need for the moment -- we would keep company for a day or two, and a watch on the force and disposition of the French advance. We had yet to discover Marmont's objective. For though in Salamanca the French officers had openly talked of the assault on Ciudad Rodrigo, there was still a chance (though neither of us believed in it) that their general meant to turn aside and strike southward for the Tagus. Our plan, therefore, was to make for Tammames where the roads divided, where the hills afforded good cover, and to wait.

So towards Tammames (which lay some thirty miles off) we turned our faces, and arriving there on the 27th, encamped for two days among the hills. Marmont had learnt on the 14th that none of Wellington's divisions were on the Algueda, and we agreed, having watched his preparations, that on the 27th he would be ready to start. These two days, therefore, we spent at ease, and I found the Captain, in spite of his narrow and hide-bound religion, an agreeable companion. He had the McNeills' genealogy at his finger ends, and I picked up more information from him concerning our ancestral home in Ross and our ancestral habits than I have ever been able to verify. Certainly our grandfathers, Manus of Aranjuez and Angus (slain at Sheriff-muir), had been first cousins. But this discovery had no sooner raised me to a claim on his regard than I found his cordiality chilled by the thought that I believed in the Pope or (as he preferred to put it) Antichrist. My eminence as a genuine McNeill made the shadow of my error the taller. In these two days of inactivity I felt his solicitude growing until, next to the immediate movements of Marmont, my conversion became for him the most important question in the Peninsula, and I saw that, unless I allowed him at least to attempt it, another forty-eight hours would wear him to fiddle-strings.

Thus it happened that mid-day of the 30th found us on the wooded hill above the cross-roads; found me stretched at full length on my back and smoking, and the Captain (who did not smoke) seated beside me with his pocket Testament, earnestly sapping the fundamental errors of Rome, when José, who had been absent all the morning reconnoitring, brought news that Marmont's van (which he had been watching, and ahead of which he had been dodging since ten o'clock) was barely two miles away. The Captain pulled out his watch, allowed them thirty-five minutes, and quietly proceeded with his exposition. As the head of the leading column swung into sight around the base of the foot-hills, he sought in his haversack and drew out a small volume -- the Pilgrim's Progress -- and having dog's-eared a page of it inscribed my name on the fly-leaf, "from his kinsman, Alan McNeill."

"It is a question," said he, as I thanked him, "and one often debated, if it be not better that a whole army, such as we see approaching, should perish bodily in every circumstance of horror than that one soul, such as yours or mine, should fail to find the true light. For my part" -- and here he seemed to deprecate a weakness -- "I have never been able to go quite so far; I hope not from any lack of intellectual courage. Will you take notes while I dictate?"

So on the last leaf of the Pilgrim's Progress I entered the strength of each battalion, and noted each gun as the great army wound its way into Tammames below us, and through it for the cross-roads beyond, but not in one body, for two of the battalions enjoyed an hour's halt there before setting forward after their comrades, by this time out of sight. They had taken the northern road.

"Ciudad Rodrigo!" said I. "And there goes Wellington's chance of Badajos."

The Captain beckoned to José and whispered in his ear, then opened his Testament again as the sturdy little Spaniard set off down the hill with his leisurely, lopping gait, so much faster than it seemed. The sun was setting when he returned with his report.

"I thought so," said the Captain. "Marmont has left three-fourths of his scaling ladders behind in Tammames. Ciudad Rodrigo he will not attempt; I doubt if he means business with Almeida. If you please," he added, "José and I will push after and discover his real business, while you carry to Lord Wellington a piece of news it will do him good to hear."

2: The Barber-Surgeon of Sabugal

So, leaving my two comrades to follow up and detect the true object of Marmont's campaign, I headed south for Badajos. The roads were heavy, the mountain torrents in flood, the only procurable horses and mules such as by age or debility had escaped the strictest requisitioning. Nevertheless, on the 4th of April I was able to present myself at Lord Wellington's headquarters before Badajos, and that same evening started northwards again with his particular instructions. I understood (not, of course, by direct word of mouth) that disquieting messages had poured in ahead of me from the allied commanders scattered in the north, who reported Ciudad Rodrigo in imminent peril; that my news brought great relief of mind; but that in any case our army now stood committed to reduce Badajos before Soult came to its relief. Our iron guns had worked fast and well, and already three breaches on the eastern side of the town were nearly practicable. Badajos once secured, Wellington would press northward again to teach Marmont manners; but for the moment our weak troops opposing him must even do the best they could to gain time and protect the magazines and stores.

At six o'clock then in the evening of the 4th, on a fresh mount, I turned my back on the doomed fortress, and crossing the Guadiana by the horse ferry above Elvas, struck into the Alemtejo.

On the 6th I reached Castello Branco and found the position of the Allies sufficiently serious. Victor Alten's German cavalry were in the town -- 600 of them -- having fallen back before Marmont without striking a blow, and leaving the whole country four good marches from Rodrigo exposed to the French marauders. They reported that Rodrigo itself had fallen (which I knew to be false, and, as it turned out, Marmont had left but one division to blockade the place); they spoke openly of a further retreat upon Vilha Velha. But I regarded them not. They had done mischief enough already by scampering southward and allowing Marmont to push in between them and the weak militias on whom it now depended to save Almeida with its battering train, Celorico and Pinhel with their magazines, and even

Ciudad Rodrigo itself; and while I listened I tasted to myself the sarcastic compliments they were likely to receive from Lord Wellington when he heard their tale.

Clearly there was no good to be done in Castello Branco, and the next morning I pushed on. I had no intention of rejoining Captain McNeill; for, as he had observed on parting -- quoting some old Greek for his authority -- "three of us are not enough for an army, and for any other purpose we are too many," and although pleased enough to have a kinsman's company he had allowed me to see that he preferred to work alone with José, who understood his methods, whereas mine (in spite of his compliments) were unfamiliar and puzzling. I knew him to be watching Marmont, and even speculated on the chances of our meeting, but my own purpose was to strike the Coa, note the French force there and its disposition, and so make with all serviceable news for the north, where Generals Trant and Wilson with their Portuguese militia were endeavouring to cover the magazines.

Travelling on mule-back now as a Portuguese drover out of work, I dodged a couple of marauding parties below Penamacor, found Marmont in force in Sabugal at the bend of the Coa, on the 9th reached Guarda, a town on the top of a steep mountain, and there found General Trant in position with about 6,000 raw militiamen. To him I presented myself with my report -- little of which was new to him except my reason for believing Ciudad Rodrigo safe for the present; and this he heard with real pleasure, chiefly because it confirmed his own belief and gave it a good reason which it had hitherto lacked.

And here I must say a word on General Trant. He was a gallant soldier and a clever one, but inclined (and here lay his weakness) to be on occasion too clever by half. In fact, he had a leaning towards my own line of business, and naturally it was just here that I found him out. I am not denying that during the past fortnight his cleverness had served him well. He had with a handful of untrained troops to do his best for a group of small towns and magazines, each valuable and each in itself impossible of defence. His one advantage was that he knew his weakness and the enemy did not, and he had used this knowledge with almost ludicrous success.

For an instance; immediately on discovering the true line of Marmont's advance he had hurried to take up a position on the lower Coa, but had been met on his march by an urgent message from Governor Le Mesurier that Almeida was in danger and could not resist a resolute assault. Without hesitation Trant turned and pushed hastily with one brigade to the Cabeça Negro mountain behind the bridge of Almeida, and reached it just as the French drew near, driving 200 Spaniards before them across the plain. Trant, seeing that the enemy had no cavalry at hand, with the utmost effrontery and quite as if he had an army behind him, threw out a cloud of skirmishers beyond the bridge, dressed up a dozen guides in scarlet coats to resemble British troopers, galloped with these to the glacis of Almeida, spoke the governor, drew off a score of invalid troopers from the hospital in the town, and at dusk made his way back up the mountain, which in three hours he had covered with sham bivouac fires.

These were scarcely lit when the governor, taking his cue, made a determined sortie and drove back the French light troops, who in the darkness had no sort of notion of the numbers attacking them. So completely hoaxed, indeed, was their commander that he, who had come with two divisions to take Almeida, and held it in the hollow of his hand, decamped early next morning and marched away to report, the fortress so strongly protected as to be unassailable.

Well this, as I say, showed talent. Artistically conceived as a ruse de guerre, in effect it saved Almeida. But a success of the kind too often tempts a man to try again and overshoot his mark. Now

Marmont, with all his defects of vanity, was no fool. He had a strong army moderately well concentrated; he had, indeed, used it to little purpose, but he was not likely, with his knowledge of the total force available by the Allies in the north, to be seriously daunted or for long by a game of mere impudence. In my opinion Trant, after brazening him away from Almeida, should have thanked Heaven and walked humbly for a while. To me even his occupation of Guarda smelt of dangerous bravado, for Guarda is an eminently treacherous position, strong in itself, and admirable for a force sufficient to hold the ridges behind it, but capable of being turned on either hand, affording bad retreat, and, therefore, to a small force as perilous as it is attractive. But I was to find that Trant's enterprise reached farther yet.

To my description of Marmont's forces he listened (it seemed to me) impatiently, asking few questions and checking off each statement with "Yes, yes," or "Quite so." All the while his fingers were drumming on the camp table, and I had no sooner come to an end than he began to question me about the French marshal's headquarters in Sabugal. The town itself and its position he knew as well as I did, perhaps better. I had not entered it on my way, but kept to the left bank of the Coa. I knew Marmont to be quartered there, but in what house or what part of the town I was ignorant. "And what the deuce can it matter?" I wondered.

"But could you not return and discover?" the general asked at length.

"Oh, as for that," I answered, "it's just as you choose to order."

"It's risky of course," said he.

"It's risky to be sure," I agreed; "but if the risk comes in the day's work I take it I shall have been in tighter corners."

"Excuse me," he said with a sort of deprecatory smile, "but I was not thinking of you; at least not altogether." And I saw by his face that he held something in reserve and was in two minds about confiding it.

"I beg that you won't think of me," I said simply, for I have always made it a rule to let a general speak for himself and ask no questions which his words may not fairly cover. Outside of my own business (the limits of which are well defined) I seek no responsibility, least of all should I seek it in serving one whom I suspect of over-cleverness.

"Look here," he said at length, "the Duke of Ragusa is a fine figure of a man."

"Notoriously," said I. "All Europe knows it, and he certainly knows it himself."

"I have heard that his troops take him at his own valuation."

"Well," I answered, "he sits his horse gallantly; he has courage. At present he is only beginning to make his mistakes; and soldiers, like women, have a great idea of what a warrior ought to look like."

"In fact," said General Trant, "the loss of him would make an almighty difference."

Now he had asked me to be seated and had poured me out a glass of wine from his decanter. But at these words I leapt up suddenly, jolting the table so that the glass danced and spilled half its contents.

"What the dickens is wrong?" asked the general, snatching a map out of the way of the liquor. "Good Lord, man! You don't suppose I was asking you to assassinate Marmont!"

"I beg your pardon," said I, recovering myself. "Of course not; but it sounded -- "

"Oh, did it?" He mopped the map with his pocket handkerchief and looked at me as who should say "Guess again."

I cast about wildly. "This man cannot be wanting to kidnap him!" thought I to myself.

"You tell me his divisions are scattered after supplies. I hear that the bulk of his troops are in camp above Penamacor; that at the outside he has in Sabugal under his hand but 5,000. Now

Silveira should be here in a couple of days; that will make us roughly 12,000."

"Ah!" said I, "a surprise?" He nodded. "Night?" He nodded again. "And your cavalry?" I pursued.

"I could, perhaps, force General Bacellar to spare his squadron of dragoons from Celorico. Come, what do you think of it?"

"I do as you order," said I, "and that I suppose is to return to Sabugal and report the lie of the land. But since, general, you ask my opinion, and speaking without local knowledge, I should say -- "

"Yes?"

"Excuse me, but I will send you my opinion in four days' time." And I rose to depart.

"Very good, but keep your seat. Drink another glass of wine."

"Sabugal is twenty miles off, and when I arrive I have yet to discover how to get into it," I protested.

"That is just what am going to tell you."

"Ah," said I, "so you have already been making arrangements?"

He nodded while he poured out the wine. "You come opportunely, for I was about to rely on a far less rusé hand. The plan, which is my own, I submit to your judgment, but I think you will allow some merit in it."

Well, I was not well-disposed to approve of any plan of his. In truth he had managed to offend me seriously. Had an English gentleman committed my recent error of supposing him to hint at assassination, General Trant (who can doubt it?) would have flamed out in wrath; but me he had set right with a curt carelessness which said as plain as words that the dishonouring suspicion no doubt came natural enough to a Spaniard. He had entertained me with a familiarity which I had not asked for, and which became insulting the moment he allowed me to see that it came from cold condescension. I have known a dozen combinations spoilt by English commanders who in this way have combined extreme offensiveness with conscious affability; and I have watched their allies -- Spaniards and Portuguese of the first nobility -- raging inwardly, while ludicrously impotent to discover a peg on which to hang their resentment.

I listened coldly, therefore, leaving the general's wine untasted and ignoring his complimentary deference to my judgment. Yet the neatness and originality of his scheme surprised me. He certainly had talent.

He had found (it seemed) an old vine-dresser at Bellomonte, whose brother kept a small shop in Sabugal, where he shaved chins, sold drugs, drew teeth, and on occasion practised a little bone-setting. This barber-surgeon or apothecary had shut up his shop on the approach of the French and escaped out of the town to his brother's roof. As a matter of fact he would have been safer in Sabugal, for the excesses of the French army were all committed by the marauding parties scattered up and down the country-side and out of the reach of discipline, whereas Marmont (to his credit) sternly discouraged looting, paid the inhabitants fairly for what he took, and altogether treated them with uncommon humanity.

It was likely enough, therefore, that the barber-surgeon's shop stood as he had left it. And General Trant proposed no less than that I should boldly enter the town, take down the shutters, and open business, either personating the old man or (if I could persuade him to return) going with him as his assistant. In either case the danger of detection was more apparent than real, for so violently did the Portuguese hate their invaders that scarcely an instance of treachery occurred during the whole of this campaign. The chance of the neighbours betraying me was small enough, at any rate, to justify the risk, and I told the General promptly that I would take it.

Accordingly I left Guarda that night, and reaching Bellomonte a little after daybreak, found the vine-dresser and presented Trant's letter.

He was on the point of starting for Sabugal, whither he had perforce to carry a dozen skins of wine, and with some little trouble I persuaded the old barber-surgeon to accompany us, bearing a petition to Marmont to be allowed peaceable possession of his shop. We arrived and were allowed to enter the town, where I assisted the vine-dresser in handling the heavy wine skins, while his brother posted off to headquarters and returned after an hour with the marshal's protection. Armed with this, he led me off to the shop, found it undamaged, helped me to take down the shutters, showed me his cupboards, tools, and stock in trade, and answered my rudimentary questions in the art of compounding drugs -- in a twitter all the while to be gone. Nor did I seek to delay him (for if my plans miscarried, Sabugal would assuredly be no place for him). Late in the afternoon he left me and went off in search of his brother, and I fell to stropping my razors with what cheerfulness I could assume.

Before nightfall my neighbours on either hand had looked in and given me good evening. They asked few questions when I told them I was taking over old Diego's business for the time, and kept their speculations to themselves. I lay down to sleep that night with a lighter heart.

The adventure itself tickled my humour, though I had no opinion at all of the design -- Trant's design -- which lay at the end of it. This, however, did not damp my zeal in using eyes and ears; and on the third afternoon, when the old vine-dresser rode over with more wine skins, and dropped in to inquire about business and take home a pint of rhubarb for the stomach-ache, I had the satisfaction of making up for him, under the eyes of two soldiers waiting to be shaved, a packet containing a compendious account of Marmont's dispositions with a description of his headquarters. My report concluded with these words: --

"With regard to the enterprise on which I have had the honour to be consulted I offer my opinion with humility. It is, however, a fixed one. You will lose two divisions; and even a third, should you bring it."

On the whole I had weathered through these three days with eminent success. The shaving I managed with something like credit (for a Portuguese). My pharmaceutics had been (it was vain to deny) in the highest degree empirical, but if my patients had not been cured they even more certainly had not died -- or at least their bodies had not been found. What gravelled me was the phlebotomy. Somehow the chance of being called upon to let blood had not occurred to me, and on the second morning when a varicose sergeant of the line dropped into my operating chair and demanded to have a vein opened, I bitterly regretted that I had asked my employer neither where to insert the lancet nor how to stop the bleeding. I eyed the brawn in the chair, so full of animal life and rude health -- no, strike at random I could not! I took his arm and asked insinuatingly, "Now, where do you usually have it done?" "Sometimes here, sometimes there," he answered. Joy! I remembered a bottle of leeches on the shelf. I felt the man's pulse and lifted his eyelids with trembling fingers. "In your state," said I, "it would be a crime to bleed you. What you want is leeches." "You think so?" he asked -- "how many?" "Oh, half-a-dozen -- to begin with." In my sweating hurry I forgot (if I had ever known) that the bottle contained but three. "No," said I, "we'll start with a couple and work up by degrees." He took them on his palm and turned them over with a stubby forefinger. "Funny little beasts!" said he and marched out of the shop into the sunshine. To this day when recounting his Peninsular exploits he omits his narrowest escape.

I can hardly describe the effect of this ridiculous adventure upon my nerves. My heart sank whenever a plethoric customer entered the shop, and I caught fright or snatched relief even from the weight of a footfall or the size of a shadow in my doorway. A dozen times in intervals of leisure I reached down the bottle from its shelf and studied my one remaining leech. A horrible suspicion possessed me that the little brute was dead. He remained at any rate completely torpid, though I coaxed him almost in agony to show some sign of life. Obviously the bottle contained nothing to nourish him; to offer him my own blood would be to disable him for another patient. On the fourth afternoon I went so far as to try him on the back of my hand. I waited five minutes; he gave no sign. Then, startled by a footstep outside, I popped him hurriedly back in his bottle.

A scraggy, hawk-nosed trooper of hussars entered and flung himself into my chair demanding a shave. In my confusion I had lathered his chin and set to work before giving his face any particular attention. He had started a grumble at being overworked (he was just off duty and smelt potently of the stable), but sat silent as men usually do at the first scrape of the razor. On looking down I saw in a flash that this was not the reason. He was one of the troopers whose odd jobs I had done at the Posada del Rio in Huerta, an ill-conditioned Norman called Michu -- Pierre Michu. Since our meeting, with the help of a little walnut juice, I had given myself a fine Portuguese complexion with other small touches sufficient to deceive a cleverer man. But by ill-luck (or to give it a true name, by careless folly) I had knotted under my collar that morning a yellow-patterned handkerchief which I had worn every day at the Posada del Rio, and as his eyes travelled from this to my face I saw that the man recognised me.

There was no time for hesitating. If I kept silence, no doubt he would do the same; but if I let him go, it would be to make straight for headquarters with his tale. I scraped away for a second or two in dead silence, and then holding my razor point I said, sharp and low, "I am going to kill you."

He turned white as a sheet, opened his mouth, and I could feel him gathering his muscles together to heave himself out of the chair; no easy matter. I laid the flat of the razor against his flesh, and he sank back helpless. My hand was over his mouth. "Yes, I shall have plenty of time before they find you." A sound in his throat was the only answer, something between a grunt and a sob. "To be sure" I went on, "I bear you no grudge. But there is no other way, unless -- "

"No, no," he gasped. "I promise. The grave shall not be more secret."

"Ah," said I, "but how am I to believe that?"

"Parole d'honneur."

"I must have even a little more than that." I made him swear by the faith of a soldier and half-a-dozen other oaths which occurred to me as likely to bind him if, lacking honour and religion, he might still have room in his lean body for a little superstition. He took every oath eagerly, and with a pensive frown I resumed my shaving. At the first scrape he winced and tried to push me back.

"Indeed no," said I; "business is business," and I finished the job methodically, relentlessly. It still consoles me to think upon what he must have suffered.

When at length I let him up he forced an uneasy laugh. "Well, comrade, you had the better of me I must say. Eh! but you're a clever one -- and at Huerta, eh?" He held out his hand. "No rancour though -- a fair trick of war, and I am not the man to bear a grudge for it. After all war's war, as they say. Some use one weapon, some another. You know," he went on confidentially, "it isn't as if you had learnt anything out of me. In that case -- well, of course, it would have made all the difference."

I fell to stropping my razor. "Since I have your oath -- " I began.

"That's understood. My word, though, it is hard to believe!"

The Two Scouts

"You had best believe it, anyway," said I; and with a sort of shamefaced swagger he lurched out of the shop.

Well, I did not like it. I walked to the door and watched him down the street. Though it wanted an hour of sunset I determined to put up my shutters and take a stroll by the river. I had done the most necessary part of my work in Sabugal; tomorrow I would make my way back to Bellomonte, but in case of hindrance it might be as well to know how the river bank was guarded. At this point a really happy inspiration seized me. There were many pools in the marsh land by the river -- pools left by the recent floods. Possibly by hunting among these and stirring up the mud I might replenish my stock of leeches. I had the vaguest notion how leeches were gathered, but the pursuit would at the worst give me an excuse for dawdling and spying out the land.

I closed the shop at once, hunted out a tin box, and with this and my bottle (to serve as evidence, if necessary, of my good faith) made my way down to the river side north of the town. The bank here was well guarded by patrols, between whom a number of peaceful citizens sat a-fishing. Seen thus in line and with their backs turned to me they bore a ludicrous resemblance to a row of spectators at a play; and gazing beyond them, though dazzled for a moment by the full level rays of the sun, I presently became aware of a spectacle worth looking at.

On the road across the river a squadron of lancers was moving northward.

"Hallo!" thought I, "here's a reconnaissance of some importance." But deciding that any show of inquisitiveness would be out of place under the eyes of the patrols, I kept my course parallel with the river's, at perhaps 300 yards distance from it. This brought me to the first pool, and there I had no sooner deposited my bottle and tin box on the brink than beyond the screen of the town wall came pushing the head of a column of infantry.

Decidedly here was something to think over. The column unwound itself in clouds of yellow dust -- a whole brigade; then an interval, then another dusty column -- two brigades! Could Marmont be planning against Trant the very coup which Trant had planned against him? Twenty miles -- it could be done before daybreak; and the infantry (I had seen at the first glance) were marching light.

I do not know to this day if any leeches inhabit the pools outside Sabugal. It is very certain that I discovered none. About a quarter of a mile ahead of me and about the same distance back from the river there stood a ruinous house which had been fired, but whether recently or by the French I could not tell; once no doubt the country villa of some well-to-do townsman, but now roofless, and showing smears of black where the flames had licked its white outer walls. Towards this I steered my way cautiously, that behind the shelter of an outbuilding I might study the receding brigades at my leisure.

The form of the building was roughly a hollow square enclosing a fair-sized patio, the entrance of which I had to cross to gain the rearward premises and slip out of sight of the patrols. The gate of this entrance had been torn off its hinges and now lay jammed aslant across the passage; beyond it the patio lay heaped with bricks and rubble, tiles, and charred beams. I paused for a moment and craned in for a better look at the débris.

And then the sound of voices arrested me -- a moment too late. I was face to face with two French officers, one with a horse beside him. They saw me, and on the instant ceased talking and stared; but without changing their attitudes, which were clearly those of two disputants. They stood perhaps four paces apart. Both were young men, and the one whose attitude most suggested menace I recognised as a young lieutenant of a line regiment (the 102nd) whom I had shaved that morning. The other wore the uniform of a staff officer, and at the first glance I read a touch of superciliousness in his indignant face. His left hand held his horse's bridle, his other he still kept tightly clenched while he stared at me.

"What the devil do you want here?" demanded the lieutenant roughly in bad Portuguese. "But, hallo!" he added, recognising me, and turned a curious glance on the other.

"Who is it?" the staff officer asked.

"It's a barber; and I believe something of a surgeon. That's so, eh?" He appealed to me.

"In a small way," I answered apologetically.

The lieutenant turned again to his companion. "He might do for us; the sooner the better, unless -- "

"Unless," interrupted the staff officer with cold politeness, "you prefer the apology you owe me."

The lieutenant swung round again with a brusque laugh. "Look here, have you your instruments about you?"

For answer I held up my bottle with the one absurd leech dormant at the bottom. He laughed again just as harshly.

"That is about the last thing to suit our purpose. Listen" -- he glanced out through the passage -- "the gates won't be shut for an hour yet. It will take you perhaps twenty minutes to fetch what is necessary. You understand? Return here, and don't keep us waiting. Afterwards, should the gates be shut, one of us will see you back to the town."

I bowed without a word and hurried back across the water meadow. Along the river bank between the patrols the anglers still sat in their patient row. And on the road to the north-west the tail of the second brigade was winding slowly out of sight.

Once past the gate and through the streets, I walked more briskly, paused at my shop door to fit the key in the lock, and was astonished when the door fell open at the push of my hand.

Then in an instant I understood. The shop had been ransacked -- by that treacherous scoundrel Michu, of course. Bottles, herbs, shaving apparatus all was topsy-turvy. Drawers stood half-open; the floor was in a litter.

I had two consolations: the first that there were no incriminating papers in the, house; the second that Michu had clearly paid me a private visit before carrying his tale to headquarters. Otherwise the door would have been sealed and the house under guard. I reflected that the idiot would catch it hot for this unauthorised piece of work. Stay! he might still be in the house rummaging the upper rooms. I crept upstairs.

No, he was gone. He had left my case of instruments, too, after breaking the lock and scattering them about the floor. I gathered them together in haste, descended again, snatched up a roll of lint, and pausing only at the door for a glance up and down the street, made my escape post haste for the water meadow.

In the patio I found the two disputants standing much as I had left them, the staff officer gently and methodically smoothing his horse's crupper, the lieutenant with a watch in his hand.

"Good," said he, closing it with a snap, "seventeen minutes only. By the way, do you happen to understand French?"

"A very little," said I.

"Because, as you alone are the witness of this our little difference, it will be in order if I explain that I insulted this gentleman."

"Somewhat grossly," put in the staff officer.

"Somewhat grossly, in return for an insult put upon me -- somewhat grossly -- in the presence of my company, two days ago, in the camp above Penamacor, when I took the liberty to resent a message conveyed by him to my colonel -- as he alleges upon the authority of the marshal, the Duke of Ragusa."

"An assertion," commented the staff officer, "which I am able to prove on the marshal's return and with his permission, provided always that the request be decently made."

They had been speaking in French and meanwhile removing their tunics. The staff officer had even drawn off his riding boots. "Do you understand?" asked the lieutenant.

"A little," said I; "enough to serve the occasion."

"Excellent barber-surgeon! Would that all your nation were no more inquisitive!" He turned to the staff officer. "Ready? On guard, then, monsieur!"

The combat was really not worth describing. The young staff officer had indeed as much training as his opponent (and that was little), but no wrist at all. He had scarcely engaged before he attempted a blind cut over the scalp. The lieutenant, parrying clumsily, but just in time, forced blade and arm upward until the two pointed almost vertically to heaven, and their forearms almost rubbed as the pair stood close and chest to chest. For an instant the staff officer's sword was actually driven back behind his head; and then with a rearward spring the lieutenant disengaged and brought his edge clean down on his adversary's left shoulder and breast, narrowly missing his ear. The cut itself, delivered almost in the recoil, had no great weight behind it, but the blood spurted at once, and the wounded man, stepping back for a fresh guard, swayed foolishly for a moment and then toppled into my arms.

"Is it serious?" asked the lieutenant, wiping his sword and looking, it seemed to me, more than a little scared.

"Wait a moment," said I, and eased the body to the ground. "Yes, it looks nasty. And keep back, if you please; he has fainted."

Being off my guard I said it in very good French, which in his agitation he luckily failed to remark.

"I had best fetch help," said he.

"Assuredly."

"I'll run for one of the patrols; we'll carry him back to the town."

But this would not suit me at all. "No," I objected, "you must fetch one of your surgeons. Meanwhile I will try to stop the bleeding; but I certainly won't answer for it if you attempt to move him at once."

I showed him the wound as he hurried into his tunic. It was a long and ugly gash, but (as I had guessed) neither deep nor dangerous. It ran from the point of the collar-bone aslant across the chest, and had the lieutenant put a little more drag into the stroke it must infallibly have snicked open the artery inside the upper arm. As it was, my immediate business lay in frightening him off before the bleeding slackened, and my heart gave a leap when he turned and ran out of the patio, buttoning his tunic as he went.

It took me ten minutes perhaps to dress the wound and tie a rude bandage; and perhaps another four to pull off coat and shoes and slip into the staff officer's tunic, pull on his riding boots over my blue canvas trousers -- at a distance scarcely discernible in colour from his tight-fitting breeches -- and buckle on his sword-belt. I had some difficulty in finding his cap, for he had tossed it carelessly behind one of the fallen beams, and by this time the light was bad within the patio. The horse gave me no trouble, being an old campaigner, no doubt, and used to surprises. I untethered him and led him gently across the yard, picking my way in a circuit which would take him as far as possible from his fallen master. But glancing back just before mounting, to my horror I saw that the wounded man had raised himself on his right elbow and was staring at me. Our eyes met; what he thought -- whether he suspected the truth or accepted the sight as a part of his delirium -- I shall never know. The next instant he fell back again and lay inert.

I passed out into the open. The warning gun must have sounded without my hearing it, for across the meadow the townspeople were retracing their way to the town gate, which closed at sunset.

At any moment now the patrols might be upon me; so swinging myself into the saddle I set off at a brisk trot towards the gate.

My chief peril for the moment lay in the chance of meeting the lieutenant on his way back with the doctor; yet I must run this risk and ride through the town to the bridge gate, the river being unfordable for miles to the northward and trending farther and farther away from Guarda; and Guarda must be reached at all costs, or by to-morrow Trant's and Wilson's garrisons would have ceased to exist. My heart fairly sank when on reaching the gate I saw an officer in talk with the sentry there, and at least a score of men behind him. I drew aside; he stepped out and called an order to his company, which at once issued and spread itself in face of the scattered groups of citizens returning across the meadow.

"Yes, captain," said the sentry, answering the question in my look," they are after a spy, it seems, who has been practising here as a barber. They say even the famous McNeill."

I rode through the gateway and spurred my horse to a trot again, heading him down a side street to the right. This took me some distance out of my way, but anything was preferable to the risk of meeting the lieutenant, and I believed that I had yet some minutes to spare before the second gunfire.

In this I was mistaken. The gun boomed out just as I came in sight of the bridge gate, and the lieutenant of the guard appeared clanking out on the instant to close the heavy doors. I spurred my horse and dashed down at a canter, hailing loudly: --

"A spy! -- a barber fellow; here, hold a minute!"

"Yes, we have had warning half an hour ago. Nobody has passed out since."

"At the gate below," I panted, "they sighted him; and he made for the river -- tried to swim it. Run out your men and bring them along to search the bank!"

He began to shout orders. I galloped through the gate and

hailed the sentry at the tête du pont. "A spy!" I shouted -- "in the river. Keep your eyes open if he makes the bank!"

The fellow drew aside, and I clattered past him with a dozen soldiers at my heels fastening their belts and looking to their muskets as they ran. Once over the bridge I headed to the right again along the left bank of the river.

"This way! This way! Keep your eyes open!"

I was safe now. In the rapidly falling dusk, still increasing the distance between us, I led them down past the town and opposite the astonished patrols on the meadow bank. Even then, when I wheeled to the left and galloped for the high road, it did not occur to them to suspect me, nor shall I ever know when first it dawned on them that they had been fooled. Certainly not a shot was sent after me, and I settled down for a steady gallop northward, pleasantly assured of being at least twenty minutes ahead of any effective pursuit.

I was equally well assured of overtaking the brigades, but my business, of course, was to avoid and get ahead of them. And with this object, after an hour's brisk going, I struck a hill-track to the left which, as I remembered (having used it on my journey from Badajoz), at first ran parallel with the high road for two miles or more and then cut two considerable loops which the road followed along the valley bottom.

Recent rains had unloosed the springs on the mountain side and set them chattering so loudly that I must have reined up at least a score of times before I detected the tramp of the brigades in the darkness below me. Of the cavalry, though I rode on listening for at least another two miles, I could hear no sound. Yet, as I argued, they could not be far distant; and I pushed forward with heart elate at the prospect of trumping Marmont's card, for I remembered the staff officer's words, "on the marshal's return." I knew that Marmont had been in Sabugal no longer ago than mid-day; and irregular and almost derogatory as it might be

The Two Scouts

thought for a marshal of France to be conducting a night surprise against a half-disciplined horde of militia, I would have wagered my month's pay that this was the fact.

And then, with a slip of my horse on the stony track, my good fortune suddenly ended, and smash went my basket of eggs while I counted the chickens. The poor brute with one false step came down heavily on his near side. Quick as I was in flinging my foot from the stirrup, I was just a moment too late; I fell without injury to bone, but his weight pinned me to earth by the boot, and when I extricated myself it was with a wrenched ankle. I managed to get him to his feet, but he had either dislocated or so severely wrung his near shoulder that he could scarcely walk a step. It went to my heart to leave him there on the mountain side, but it had to be done, for possibly the fate of the garrison at Guarda depended on it.

I left him, therefore, and limped forward along the track until it took an abrupt turn around a shoulder of the mountain. Immediately below me, unless I erred in my bearings, a desolate sheep farm stood but a short distance above the high road. Towards this I descended, and finding it with no great difficulty, knocked gently at the back door. To my surprise the shepherd opened it almost at once. He was fully dressed in spite of the lateness of the hour, and seemed greatly perturbed; nor, I can promise you, was he reassured when, after giving him the signal arranged between Trant and the peasantry, I followed him into his kitchen and his eyes fell on my French uniform.

But it was my turn to be perturbed when, satisfied with my explanation, he informed me that a body of cavalry had passed along the road towards Guarda a good twenty minutes before. It was this had awakened him. "No infantry?" I asked.

He shook his head positively. He had been on the watch ever since. And this, while it jumped with my own conviction that the infantry was at least a mile behind me, gave me new hope. I could

The Two Scouts

not understand this straggling march, but it was at least reasonable to suppose that Marmont's horse would wait upon his foot before attempting such a position as Guarda.

"I must push on," said I, and instructed him where to seek for my unfortunate charger.

He walked down with me to the road. My ankle pained me cruelly.

"See here," said he, "the señor had best let me go with him. It is but six miles, and I can recover the horse in the morning."

He was in earnest, and I consented. It was fortunate that I did, or I might have dropped in the road and been found or trodden on by the French column behind us.

As it was I broke down after the second mile. The shepherd took me in his arms like a child and found cover for me below a bank to the left of the road beside the stream in the valley bottom. I gave him my instructions and he hurried on.

Lying there in the darkness half an hour later I heard the tramp of the brigade approaching, and lay and listened while they went by.

I have often, in writing these memoirs, wished I could be inventing instead of setting down facts. With a little invention only, how I could have rounded off this adventure! But that is the way with real events. All my surprising luck ended with the casual stumble of a horse, and it was not I who saved Guarda, nor even my messenger, but Marmont's own incredible folly.

When my shepherd reached the foot of the ascent to the fortress he heard a drum beaten suddenly in the darkness above. This single drum kept rattling (he told me) for at least a minute before a score of others took up the alarm. There had been no other warning, not so much as a single shot fired; and even after the drums began there was no considerable noise of musketry until the day broke and the shepherd saw the French cavalry retiring slowly down the hill scarcely 500 yards ahead of the Portuguese militia, now pouring forth from the gateway. These were at once checked and formed up in front of the town, the French still retiring slowly, with a few English dragoons hanging on their heels. A few shots only were exchanged, apparently without damage. The man assured me that the whole 400 or 500 troopers passed within a hundred yards of him and so down the slope and out of his sight.

What had happened was this: Marmont, impatient at the delay of his two brigades of infantry (which by some bungle in the starting did not reach the foot of the mountain before daylight), had pushed his horsemen up the hill and managed to cut off and silence the outposts without their firing a shot. Encouraged by this he pressed on to the very gates of the town, and had actually entered the street when the alarm was sounded -- and by whom? By a single drummer whom General Trant, distrusting the watchfulness of his militia, had posted at his bedroom door! Trant's servant entering with his coffee at daybreak brought a report that the French were at the gates; the drummer plied his sticks like a madman; other drummers all over the town caught up their sticks and tattooed away without the least notion of what was happening; the militia ran helter-skelter to their alarm post; and the French marshal, who might have carried the town at a single rush and without losing a man, turned tail! Such are the absurdities of war.

But in fancy I sometimes complete the picture and see myself, in French staff officer's dress, boldly riding up to the head of the French infantry column and in the name of the, Duke of Ragusa commanding its general to halt. True, I did not know the password -- which might have been awkward. But a staff officer can swagger through some small difficulties, as I had already proved twice that night. But for the stumble of a horse -- who knows? The possibility seems to me scarcely more fantastic than the accident which actually saved Guarda.

3: The Parole

Marmont's night attack on Guarda, though immediately and even absurdly unsuccessful, did, in fact, convince Trant that the hill was untenable, and he at once attempted to fall back upon Celorico across the river Mondego, where lay Lord Wellington's magazines and very considerable stores, for the moment quite unprotected.

Marmont had from four to six thousand horsemen and two brigades of infantry. The horse could with the utmost ease have headed Trant off and trotted into Celorico while the infantry fell on him, and but for the grossest blundering the militia as a fighting force should have been wiped out of existence. But blunders dogged Marmont throughout this campaign. Trant and Wilson marched their men (with one day's provisions only) out of Guarda and down the long slopes toward the river. Good order was kept for three or four miles, and the head of the column was actually crossing by a pretty deep ford when some forty dragoons (which Trant had begged from Bacellar to help him in his proposed coup upon Sabugal, and which had arrived from Celorico but the day before) came galloping down through the woods with a squadron of French cavalry in pursuit, and charging in panic through the rearguard flung everything into confusion. The day was a rainy one, and the militia, finding their powder wet, ran for the ford like sheep. The officers, however, kept their heads and got the men over, though with the loss of two hundred prisoners. Even so, Marmont might have crossed the river on their flank and galloped into Celorico ahead of them. As it was, he halted and allowed the rabble to save themselves in the town. While blaming his head I must do justice to his heart and add that, finding what poor crea-

The Two Scouts

tures he had to deal with, he forbade his horsemen to cut down the fugitives, and not a single man was killed.

Foreseeing that Trant must sooner or later retreat upon Celorico -- though ignorant, of course, of what was happening -- I was actually crossing the river at the time by a ford some four miles above, not in the French staff officer's uniform which I had worn out of Sabugal, but in an old jacket lent me by my friend the shepherd. By the time I reached the town Wilson had swept in his rabble and was planting his outposts, intending to resist and, if this became impossible, to blow up the magazines before retiring. Trant and Bacellar with the bulk of the militia were continuing the retreat meanwhile towards Lamego.

I need only say here that Wilson's bold front served its purpose. Once, when the French drove in his outposts, he gave the order to fire the powder, and a part of the magazine was actually destroyed when Marmont (who above all things hated ridicule, and was severely taxing the respect of his beautiful army by these serio-comic excursions after a raw militia) withdrew his troops and retired in an abominable temper to Sabugal.

How do I know that Marmont's temper was abominable? By what follows.

On March 30th I had left my kinsman, Captain Alan McNeill, with his servant José at Tammanies. They were to keep an eye on the French movements while I rode south and reported to Lord Wellington at Badajoz. It was now April 16th, and in the meanwhile a great deal had happened; but of my kinsman's movements I had heard nothing. At first I felt sure he must be somewhere in the neighbourhood of Marmont's headquarters; but even in Sabugal itself no hint of him could I hear, and at length I concluded that having satisfied himself of the main lines of Marmont's campaign he had gone off to meet and receive fresh instructions from Wellington, now posting north to save the endangered magazines.

The Two Scouts

On the evening of the 16th General Wilson sent for me.

"Here is a nasty piece of news," said he. "Your namesake is a prisoner."

"Where?"

"In Sabugal; but it seems he was brought there from the main camp above Penamacor. Trant tells me that you are not only namesakes but kinsmen. Would you care to question the messenger?"

The messenger was brought in -- a peasant from the Penamacor district. Out of his rambling tale one or two certainties emerged. McNeill -- the celebrated McNeill -- was a prisoner; he had been taken on the 14th somewhere in the pass above Penamacor, and conveyed to Sabugal to await the French marshal's return. His servant was dead -- killed in trying to escape, or to help his master's escape. So much I sifted out of the mass of inaccuracies. For, as usual, the two McNeills had managed to get mixed up in the story, a good half of which spread itself into a highly coloured version of my own escape from Sabugal on the evening of the 13th; how I had been arrested by a French officer in a back shop in the heart of the town; how, as he overhauled my incriminating papers, I had leapt on him with a knife and stabbed him to the heart, while my servant did the same with his orderly; how, having possessed ourselves of their clothes and horses, we had ridden boldly through the gate and southward to join Lord Wellington; and a great deal more equally veracious. As I listened I began to understand how legends grow and demigods are made.

It was flattering; but without attempting to show how I managed to disengage the facts, I will here quote the plain account of them, sent to me long afterwards by Captain Alan himself:

Captain Alan McNeill's Statement

"You wish, for use in your Memoirs, an account of my capture in the month of April, 1811, and the death of my faithful servant, José. I imagine this does not include an account of all our movements from the time you left us at Tammames (though this, too, I shall be happy to send if desired), and so I come at once to the 14th, the actual date of the capture.

"The preceding night we had spent in the woods below the great French camp, and perhaps a mile above the mouth of the pass opening on Penamacor. All through the previous day there had been considerable stir in the camp, and I believed a general movement to be impending. I supposed Marmont himself to be either with the main army or behind in his headquarters at Sabugal, and within easy distance. It never occurred to me -- nor could it have occurred to any reasonable man -- to guess, upon no evidence, that a marshal of France had gone gallivanting with six thousand horse and two brigades of infantry in chase of a handful of undrilled militia.

"My impression was that his move, if he made one, would be a resolute descent through Penamacor and upon Castello Branco. As a matter of fact, although Victor Alten had abandoned that place to be held by Lecor and his two thousand five hundred militiamen, the French (constant to their policy of frittering away opportunities) merely sent down two detachments of cavalry to menace it, and I believe that my capture was the only success which befel them.

"Early on the 14th, and about an hour before these troops (dragoons for the most part) began to descend the pass, I had posted myself with José on one of the lower ridges and (as I imagined) well under cover of the dwarf oaks which grew thickly there. They did indeed screen us admirably from the squadrons I was watching, and they passed unsuspecting within fifty yards of us. Believing them to be but an advance guard, and that we should soon hear the tramp of the main army, I kept my shelter for another ten minutes, and was prepared to keep it for another hour, when José -- whose eyes missed nothing -- caught me by the arm and pointed high up the hillside behind us.

"'Scouts!' he whispered. 'They have seen us, sir!'

"I glanced up and saw a pair of horsemen about two gunshots away galloping down the uneven ridge towards us, with about a dozen in a cluster close behind. We leapt into saddle at once, made off through the oaks for perhaps a couple of hundred yards, and then wheeling sharply struck back across the hillside towards Sabugal. We were still in good cover, but the enemy had posted his men more thickly than we had guessed, and by-and-by I crossed a small clearing and rode straight into the arms of a dragoon. Providentially I came on him with a suddenness which flurried his aim, and though he fired his pistol at me point-blank he wounded neither me nor my horse. But hearing shouts behind him in answer to the shot, we wheeled almost right-about and set off straight down the hill.

"This new direction did not help us, however; for almost at once a bugle was sounded above, obviously as a warning to the dragoons at the foot of the pass, who halted and spread themselves along the lower slopes to cut us off. Our one chance now lay in abandoning our horses and crawling deep into the covert of the low oaks where cavalry would have much ado to follow. This we promptly did, and for twenty minutes we managed to elude them, so that my hopes began to grow. But unhappily a knot of officers on the ridge above had watched this manoeuvre through their telescopes, and now detached small parties of infantry down either side of the pass to beat the covers. Our hiding place quickly became too hot, and as we broke cover and dashed across another small clearing we were spied again by those on the ridge, who shouted to the soldiers and directed the chase by waving their caps. For another ten minutes we baffled them, and then crawling on hands and knees from a thicket where we could hear our enemies not a dozen yards away beating the bushes with the flat of their swords, we came face to face with a second party advancing straight upon us. I stood up straight and was on the point of making a last desperate run for it when I saw José sink on his face exhausted.

"'Do not shoot!' I called to the officer. 'We have hurt no man, monsieur.' -- For it is, as you know, a fact that in our business I strongly disapprove of bloodshed, and in all our expeditions together José had never done physical injury to a living creature.

"But I was too late. The young officer fired, and though the ball entered my poor servant's skull and killed him on the instant, a hulking fellow beside him had the savagery to complete what was finished with a savage bayonet-thrust through the back.

"I stood still, fully expecting to be used no more humanely, but the officer lowered his pistol and curtly told me I was his prisoner. By this time the fellows had come up from beating the thicket behind and surrounded me. I therefore surrendered, and was marched up the hill to the camp with poor José's body at my heels borne by a couple of soldiers.

"In all the hurry and heat of this chase I had found time to wonder how our pursuers happened to be so well posted. For a good fortnight and more -- in fact, since my escape across the ford at Huerta -- I could remember nothing that we had done to give the French the slightest inkling that we were watching them or, indeed, were anywhere near. And yet the affair suggested no casual piece of scouting, but a deliberate plan to entrap somebody of whose neighbourhood they were aware.

"Nor was this perplexity at all unravelled by the general officer to whose tent they at once conveyed me -- a little round white-headed man, Ducrôt by name. He addressed me at once as Captain McNeill, and seemed vastly elated at my capture.

"'So we have you at last!' he said, regarding me with a jocular smile and a head cocked on one side, pretty much after the fashion of a thrush eyeing a worm. 'But, excuse me, after so much finesse it was a blunder -- hein?'

"Now finesse is not a word which I should have claimed at any time for my methods,[A] and I cast about in my memory for the exploit to which he could be alluding.

(**Note by Manuel McNeill**: Here the captain, in his hurry to pay me a compliment, does himself some injustice. Finesse, to be sure, was not generally characteristic of his methods, but he used it at times with amazing dexterity, as, for instance, the latter part of this very adventure will prove, if I can ever prevail on him to narrate it. On the whole I should say that he disapproved of finesse much as he disapproved of swearing, but had a natural aptitude for both.)

"'It is the mistake of clever men,' continued General Ducrôt sagely, 'to undervalue their opponents; but surely after yesterday the commonest prudence might have warned you to put the greatest possible distance between yourself and Sabugal.'

"'Sabugal?' I echoed.

"'Oh, my dear sir, we know. It was amusing -- eh! -- the barber's shop? I assure you I laughed. It was time for you to be taken; for really, you know, you could never have bettered it, and it is not for an artist to wind up by repeating inferior successes.'

"For a moment I thought the man daft. What on earth (I asked myself) was this nonsense about Sabugal and a barber's shop? I had not been near Sabugal; as for the barber's shop it sounded to me like a piece out of the childish rigmarole about cutting a cabbage leaf to make an apple pie. Some fleeting suspicion I may have had that here was another affair in which you and I had again managed to get confused; but if so the suspicion occurred only to be dismissed. A fortnight before you had left me on your way south to Badajoz, and you will own that to connect you with something which apparently had happened yesterday in a barber's shop in Sabugal was to overstrain guessing. Having nothing to say, I held my tongue; and General Ducrôt put on a more magisterial air. He resented this British phlegm in a prisoner with whom he had been graciously jocose and fell back on his national belief that we islanders, though occasionally funny, are so by force of eccentricity rather than by humour.

"'I do not propose to deal with you myself,' he announced. 'At one time and another, sir, you have done our cause an infinity of mischief, and I prefer that the Duke of Ragusa should decide your fate. I shall send you therefore to Sabugal to await his return.'

"This gave me my first intimation that Marmont was neither in Sabugal nor with his main army. That same afternoon they marched me off to the town and set me under guard in a house next door to his headquarters.

"Marmont returned from Celorico (if my memory serves me) on the afternoon of the 17th. I was taken before him at once. He treated me with the greatest apparent kindness, hoped I had suffered no ill-usage, and wound up by inviting me to dinner. A couple of hours later I was escorted to headquarters, where, on entering the room where he received his guests, I found him in conversation with a young staff officer who wore his arm in a sling.

"The marshal turned to me at once, and very gaily. 'I understand,' said he with a smile, 'that I have no need to introduce you to Captain de Brissac.'

"I looked from him to the young officer in some bewilderment, and saw in a moment that Captain de Brissac was certainly not less bewildered than I.

"'But Monsieur le Maréchal -- but this is not the man!'

"'Not the man?'

"'Most decidedly not. The man of whom I spoke was dark and not above middle height. He spoke Portuguese like a native, and belonged to a class altogether different. It would be impossible for this gentleman to disguise himself so.'

"For a moment Marmont seemed no less puzzled than we. Then he broke out laughing again.

"'Ah! of course; that will have been Captain McNeill's servant -- the poor fellow who was killed,' he added more gravely. 'I am told, sir, that this servant shared and furthered most of your adventures?'

"'He did indeed, M. le Maréchal,' said I; 'but excuse me if I am at a loss -- '

"The Duke interrupted me by laughing again and laying a hand on my shoulder as an orderly announced dinner. 'Rest easy, my friend, we know of all your little tricks.' And at table he amused himself and more and more befogged me by a precise account of my haunts and movements. How I had kept a barber's shop in Sabugal under his very nose; what disguises I used (and you know that I never used a disguise in my life); how my servant had assisted M. de Brissac in a duel and afterwards escaped in his uniform -- with much more, and all of it news to me. My astonished face merely excited his laughter; he set it down to my eccentricity. But after dinner, when M. de Brissac had taken his departure, Marmont crossed his handsome legs and came to business.

"'Sir,' said he, 'I am going to pay you a compliment. We have suffered heavily through your cleverness; and although Lord Wellington may choose to call you a scouting officer, you must be aware (and will forgive me for reminding you) that I might well be excused for calling you by an uglier name.'

"You may be sure I did not like this. You may also remember how at Huerta on the occasion of our first meeting the question of disguise came up between us, and how I assured you that to me, with my Scottish face and accent, a disguise would be worse than useless. Well, that was true enough so far as it went; but I fear that in my anxiety not to offend your feelings I spoke less than the whole truth, for I have always held that in our business as soon as a man resorts to disguise his work ceases to be legitimate scouting. It may be no less justifiable and even more useful, but it is no longer scouting. I admit the distinction to be a nice one;[A] and I have sometimes asked myself, when covering my uniform with my dark riding cloak, 'What, after all, is a disguise?' Nevertheless, I had always observed it, and standing before Marmont now in His Majesty's scarlet, which (as I might have told him) I had never discarded either to further a plan or to avoid a danger, I put some constraint on myself to listen in silence on the merest off-chance that my silence might help an affair with which the marshal assumed my perfect acquaintance, while I could only surmise that somehow you were mixed up in it, and therefore presumably it aimed at some advantage to our arms. I did keep silence, however, though without so much as a bow to signify that I assented.

[**Note by Manuel McNeill**: I should think so indeed! To me the moral difference, say, between hiding in a truss of hay and hiding under a wig is not worth discussing outside a seminary.]

"'But you are a gentleman,' Marmont continued, 'and I propose to treat you as one. You will be sent in safe custody to France, and beyond this I propose to take no revenge on you -- but upon one condition.'

"I waited.

"'The condition is you give me your parole that on your journey through Spain to France you not only make no effort to escape, but will not consent to be rescued should the attempt be made by any of the partidas in hope of reward.'

"I considered this for a moment. 'That is not a small thing to require, since Wellington may be reasonably expected to offer a round price for my recapture.'

"The marshal laughed not too pleasantly. 'Truly,' said he, 'I have heard that Scotsmen are hard bargainers. But considering that I could have you shot out of hand for a spy, I believed I was offering you generous terms.'

"Well, that was unfortunately true; so after a few seconds' pause I answered, 'Monsieur le Duc, by imposing these terms on me you at any rate pay me a handsome compliment. I accept it and give you my word.'

"Upon this parole, then, on the 19th I began my journey towards France and captivity, escorted only by M. Gérard, a young lieutenant of dragoons, and one trooper. The rest you know."

(Conclusion of Captain McNeill's Statement.)

The Two Scouts

As I have said, the bare news of my kinsman's capture and of poor José's death reached me at Celorico on the 16th, late in the evening. Knowing that Lord Wellington was by this time well on his way northward, and believing that for more than one reason the captain's fate would concern him deeply -- feeling, moreover, some compunction at the toils I had all innocently helped to wind about an honest man -- I at once sought and obtained leave from General Wilson to ride southward to meet the Commander-in-Chief with the tidings, and if necessary solicit his help in a rescue. The captain (on this point the messenger was precise) had been taken to Sabugal to await Marmont's return. I did not know that Marmont was actually at that moment on his way thither, but I thought him at least likely to be returning very soon. To be sure he might decide to shoot Captain Alan out of hand. My recent performances gave him a colourable excuse, unless the prisoner could disassociate himself from these and prove an alibi, which under the circumstances and without the help of José's evidence he could scarcely hope to do. I built, however, some faith on Marmont's known humanity, of which in his pursuit of the militia he had just given striking proof. The longer I weighed the chances the more certain I became that Marmont would treat him as an ordinary prisoner of war and send him up to France under escort.

Why, then (the reader may ask), did I lose time in seeking Lord Wellington instead of making my way at once to the north and doing my best to incite the partidas to attempt a rescue somewhere on the road north of Burgos, or even between Valladolid and Burgos? My answer is that such an affair would certainly turn on the question of money. The French held the road right away to the Pyrenees, not so strongly perhaps as to forbid hope, but strongly enough to make an attempt upon it risky in the extreme. The bands of Mendizabal, Mina, and Merino were kept busy by Generals Bonnet and Abbé; for a big convoy they might be counted on to exert themselves, but for a single prisoner they as certainly had no time to spare without the incitement of such a reward as only the Commander-in-Chief could offer.

Accordingly I made my way south to Castello Branco and reached it on the 18th, to find Lord Wellington arrived there and making ready to push on as soon as overtaken by the bulk of his troops. I had always supposed him to cherish a peculiar liking for my kinsman, but was fairly astonished by the emotion he showed.

"Rescued? Of course he must be rescued!" He broke off to use (I must confess) some very strong words upon Trant's design against Marmont and the tomfoolery, as he called it, which had taken me into Sabugal, and left a cloud of suspicion hanging over "the best scouting officer in my service; the only man of the lot, sir, who knows his business." Lord Wellington could, when he lost his temper, be singularly unjust. I strove to point out that my "tomfoolery" in Sabugal had as a matter of fact put a stop to the very scheme of General Trant's which he condemned. He cut me short by asking if I proposed to argue with him.

"Ride back, sir. Choose the particular blackguard who can effect your purpose, and inform him that on the day he rescues Captain McNeill I am his debtor for twelve thousand francs."

The speech was ungracious enough, but the price more than I had dared to hope for. Feeling pretty sure that in his lordship's temper a word of thanks would merely invite him to consign my several members to perdition, I bowed and left him. Twenty minutes later I was on the road and galloping north again.

Before starting from Celorico I had sent the peasant who brought news of Captain Alan's plight back to Sabugal with instructions to discover what more he could, and bring his report to Bellomonte on my northward road not later than the 20th. On the afternoon of the 19th when I rode into that place I could hear no news of him. But late in the evening he arrived with word that "the great McNeill" had been sent off under escort towards Salamanca. Of the strength of that escort he could tell me nothing, and had very wisely not stayed to inquire; he had picked up the news from camp gossip and brought it at once, rightly judging that time was more valuable to me just now than detailed information.

His news was doubly cheering; it assured me that my kinsman still lived, and also that by riding to secure Lord Wellington's help I had not missed my opportunity. Yet there was need to hurry, for I had not only to fetch a long circuit by difficult paths before striking the road to the Pyrenees, -- I had to find the partidas, persuade them, and get them on to the road ahead of their quarry.

I need not describe my journey at length. I rode by Guarda, Almeida, Ledesma, keeping to the north of the main road, and travelling, not by day only, but through the better part of each night. Beyond the ford of Tordesillas, left for the while unguarded, I was in country where at any moment I might stumble on the guerilla bands, or at least get news of them. The chiefs most likely for my purpose were "the three M's" -- the curate Merino, Mina and Mendizabal. Of these, the curate was about the biggest scoundrel in Spain. I learned on my way that having lately taken about a hundred prisoners near Aranda, he had hanged the lot, sixty to avenge three members of the local junta put to death by the French, and the rest in proportion of ten for every soldier of his lost in the action. From dealing with such a blackguard I prayed to be spared. And by all accounts Mina ran him close for brutal ferocity. I hoped, therefore, for Mendizabal, but at Sedano I heard that Bonnet, after foiling an attack by him on a convoy above Burgos, had beaten him into the Asturias, where his scattered bands were now shifting as best they could among the hills. Merino was in no better case, and my only hope rested on Mina, who after a series of really brilliant operations, helped out by some lucky escapes, had on the 7th with five thousand men planted himself in ambush behind Vittoria, cut up a Polish regiment, and mastered the same enormous convoy which had escaped the curate and Mendizabal at Burgos, releasing no less than four hundred Spanish prisoners and enriching himself to the tune of a million francs, not to speak of carriages, arms, stores, and a quantity of church plate.

This was no cheerful hearing, since so much in his pocket must needs lessen the attractiveness of my offer of twelve thousand francs. And, indeed, when I found him in his camp above the road a little to the east of Salvatierra his first answer was to bid me go to the devil. Although for months he had only supported his troops on English money conveyed through Sir Howard Douglas, this ignorant fellow snapped his dirty fingers at the mention of Wellington and, flushed with a casual triumph, had nothing but contempt for the allied troops who were saving his country while he and his like wasted themselves on futile raids. I can see him now as he sat smoking and dangling his legs on a rock in the midst of his unwashed staff officers.

"For an Englishman," he scoffed, "I won't say but twelve thousand francs is a high price to pay. Unfortunately, it is no price for my troops to earn. Here am I expecting at any moment a convoy which is due from the Valencia side, and Lord Wellington asks me to waste my men and miss my chance for the sake of a single redcoat. He must be a fool."

Said I, nettled, "For a Spaniard you have certainly acquired a rare suit of manners. But may I suggest that their rarity will scarcely prove worth the cost when your answer comes to Lord Wellington's ears."

He glared at me for a moment, during which no doubt he weighed the temptation of shooting me against the probable risk. Then his features relaxed into a grin, and withdrawing the chewed cigarette from his teeth he spat very deliberately on the ground. "The interview," he announced, "is ended."

I took my way down the hillside in no gay mood. I had trav-

The Two Scouts

elled far; my nerves were raw with lack of sleep. I judged myself at least a day ahead of any convoy with which the captain could be travelling, even though it had moved with the minimum of delay. But where in the next two days was I to find the help which Mina had refused? To be sure I had caught up at Sedano a flying rumour that the curate Merino had eluded Bonnet, broken out of the Asturias, and was again menacing the road above Burgos. I had come across no sign of him on my way, yet could hit on no more hopeful course than to hark back along the road on the chance of striking the trail of a man who as likely as not was a hundred miles away.

It was about nine in the morning when Mina gave me his answer, and at three in the afternoon I was scanning the road towards Miranda de Ebro from a hill about a mile beyond Arinez (the same hill, in fact, where General Gazan's centre lay little more than a year afterwards on the morning of the battle of Vittoria). I had been scanning the road perhaps for ten minutes when my heart gave a jump and my hand, I am not ashamed to confess, shook on the small telescope. To the south-west, between me and Nanclares three horsemen were advancing at a walk, and the rider in the middle wore a scarlet jacket.

It took me some seconds to get my telescope steady enough for a second look, and with that I wheeled my horse, struck spur and posted back towards Salvatierra as fast as the brute would carry me through the afternoon heat.

I reached Mina's camp again at nightfall, and found the chief seated exactly as I had left him, still smoking and still dangling his legs. Were it not that he now wore a cloak against the night air I might have supposed him seated there all day without stirring, and the guard who led me to him promised with a grin that I was dangerously near one of those peculiar modes of death which his master passed his amiable leisure in inventing.

At the sight of me Mina's eyebrows went up and he chuckled, "Indeed," said he, "it has been a dull day, and I have been regretting that I let you off so easily this morning."

"This morning," I said, "I made you an offer of twelve thousand francs. You replied that you considered it too little for the services of your army. Perhaps it was; but you will admit it to be pretty fair pay for the services of a couple of men."

"Hullo!" He eyed me sharply. "What has happened?"

"That," I answered, "is my secret. Lend me a couple of men, say, for forty-eight hours. In return, on producing this paper, you receive twelve thousand francs; that is, as soon as Lord Wellington has assured himself on my report that you received the paper from me and did as I requested."

"Two men? This begins to look like business."

"It is business," said I curtly. "To your patriotism I should not have troubled to appeal a second time."

He warned me to keep a civil tongue in my head; but I knew my man, and within half-an-hour I rode out of his camp with two of his choicest ruffians, one beside me and one ahead to guide me through the darkness.

Now at Vittoria the road towards Irun and the frontier runs almost due north for some distance and then bends about in a rough arc towards the east. Another road runs almost due east from Vittoria to Pamplona. The first road would certainly be taken by my kinsman and his escort: Mina's camp lay above the second: but, a little way beyond, at Alsasua, a third road of about five leagues joins the two, and by this short cut I was certain of heading off our quarry.

There was no call to hurry. If, as I judged likely, the party meant to sleep the night at Vittoria, I had almost twenty-four hours in hand. So we rode warily, on the look-out for French vedettes, and reaching Beasain a little before two in the morning took up a comfortable position on the hillside above the junction of the roads.

The Two Scouts

At dawn we shifted into better shelter -- a shepherd's hut, dilapidated and roofless -- and eked out a long day with tobacco and a greasy pack of cards. A few bullock carts passed along the road below us, the most of them bound westward, and perhaps half-a-dozen peasants on mule-back. At about four in the afternoon a French patrol trotted by. As the evening drew on I began to feel anxious.

A little before sunset I sent off one of my ruffians -- Alonso something-or-other (I forget his magnificent surname) -- to scout along the road. He had been gone half-an-hour when his fellow, Juan Gallegos, flung down his cards in the dusk -- the more readily perhaps because he held a weak hand -- and pricked up his ears.

"Horses!" he whispered, and after a pause nodded confidently. "Three horses!"

We picked up our muskets and crept down towards the road. Halfway down we met Alonso ascending with the news. Yes, there were three horsemen on this side of Zumarraga and coming at a trot. One of them wore a red coat.

"Be careful, then, how you pick them off. The man in red must not be hurt; the money depends on that."

They nodded. Night was now falling fast, yet not so fast but that as the horsemen came up I could distinguish Captain Alan. He was riding on the left beside the young French officer, the orderly about six yards behind. As they came abreast of us Juan let fly, and the orderly's horse pitched forward at once and fell, flinging his man, who struck the road and lay either stunned or dead. At the noise of the report the other horses shied violently and separated, thus giving us our chance without danger to the prisoner. Alonso and I fired together, and rushed out upon the officer, who groaned in the act of wheeling upon us. One of the bullets had shattered his sword arm. Within the minute we had him prisoner, the captain not helping us at all.

"What is this?" he demanded in Spanish, peering at me out of the dusk and breaking off to quiet his frightened horse. "What is this, and who are you?"

"Well, it looks like a rescue," said I; "and I am your kinsman, Manus McNeill, and have been at some pains to effect it."

"You!" he peered at me. "I thank you," said he, "but you have done a bad evening's work. I am on parole, as a man so clever as you might have guessed by the size of my escort."

"We will talk of that later," I answered, and sent Juan and Alonso off to examine the fallen trooper. "Meanwhile the man here has fainted. Oblige me by helping him a little way up the hill, or by leading his horse while I carry him. The road here is not healthy."

Captain Alan followed in silence while I bore my burden up to the hut. Having tethered the horses outside, he entered and stood above me while I lit a lantern and examined the young officer's wound.

"Nothing serious," I announced, "a fracture of the forearm and maybe a splintered bone. I can fix this up in no time."

"You had better leave it to me and run," my kinsman answered. "This M. Gérard is an amiable young man and a friend of mine, and I charge myself to see him safe to Tolosa to-night. What are you doing?"

"Searching for his papers."

"I forbid it."

"Alain mhic Neill," said I, "you are not yet the head of our clan." And I broke the seal of a letter addressed to the Governor of Bayonne. "Ah! I thought as much," I added, having glanced over the missive. "It seems, my dear kinsman, that my knowledge of the Duke of Ragusa goes a bit deeper than yours. Listen to this: 'The prisoner I send you herewith is one Captain McNeill, a spy and a dangerous one, who has done infinite mischief to our arms. I have not executed him on the spot out of respect

The Two Scouts

to something resembling an uniform which he wears. But I desire you to place him at once in irons and send him up to Paris, where he will doubtless suffer as he deserves' ..."

Captain Alan took the paper from me and perused it slowly, biting his upper lip the while. "This is very black treachery," said he.

"It acquits you at any rate."

"Of my parole?" He pondered for a moment; then, "I cannot see that it does," he said. "If the Duke of Ragusa chooses to break an implied bond with me it does not follow that I can break an explicit promise to him."

"No? Well, I should have thought it did."

At once my kinsman put on that stiff pedantic tone which had irritated me at Huerta. "I venture to think," said he, "that no McNeill would say so unless he had been corrupted by traffic with the Scarlet Woman."

"Scarlet grandmother!" I broke out. "You seem to forget that I have ridden a hundred leagues to effect this rescue, for which, by the way, Lord Wellington offers twelve thousand francs. I have promised them to the biggest scoundrel in Spain; but because he happens to be even a bigger scoundrel than the Duke of Ragusa must I break my bond with him and let you go to be shot for the sake of your silly punctilio?"

I spoke with heat, and bent over the groaning officer. My kinsman rubbed his chin. "What you say," he replied, "demands a somewhat complicated answer, or rather a series of answers. In the first place, I thank you sincerely for what you have done, and not the less sincerely because I am going to nullify it. I shall, perhaps, not cheat myself by believing that a clansman's spirit went some way to help your zeal" -- here I might well have blushed in truth, for it had not helped my zeal a peseta. "I thank Lord Wellington, too, for the extravagant price he has set upon my services, and I beg you to convey my gratitude to him. As for being shot, I might answer that my parole extends only to the Pyrenees; but I consider myself to have extended it tacitly to my young friend here, who has treated me with all possible consideration on the journey; and I shall go to Bayonne."

He spoke quietly and in the most matter-of-fact voice. But I have often thought since of his words; and often when I call up the figure of Marmont in exile at Venice, where, as he strode gloomily along the Riva dei Schiavoni, the very street urchins pointed and cried after him, "There goes the man who betrayed Napoleon!" I call up and contrast with it the figure of this humble gentleman of Scotland in the lonely hut declining simply and without parade to buy his life at the expense of a scruple of conscience.

"But," he continued, "I fancy I may persuade M. Gérard at least to delay the delivery of that letter, in which case I see my way at least to a chance of escape. For the rest, these partidas have been promised twelve thousand francs for a service which they have duly rendered. My patrimony is not a rich one, but I can promise that this sum, whether I escape or not, shall be as duly paid. Hush!" he ended as I sprang to my feet, and Juan and Alonso appeared in the doorway supporting the trooper, who had only been stunned after all.

"We did not care to kill him," Juan explained blandly, "until we had the señor's orders."

"You did rightly," I answered, and glanced at my kinsman. His jaw was set. I pulled out a couple of gold pieces for each. "An advance on your earnings," said I. "My orders are that you leave the trooper here with me, ride back instantly to your chief, report that your work has been well done and successfully, and the money for which he holds an order shall be forwarded as soon as I return and report to Lord Wellington in Beira."

The Lamp and the Guitar

[From the memoirs of Manuel, or Manus, MacNeill, an agent in the secret service of Great Britain during the Peninsular Campaigns of 1808 - 13.]

I have not the precise date in 1811 when Fuentes and I set out for Salamanca, but it must have been either in the third or fourth week of July.

In Portugal just then Lord Wellington was fencing, so to speak, with the points of three French armies at once. On the south he had Soult, on the north Dorsenne, and between them Marmont's troops were scattered along the valley of the Tagus, with Madrid as their far base. Being solidly concentrated, by short and rapid movements he could keep these three armies impotent for offence; but *en revanche*, he could make no overmastering attack upon any one of them. If he advanced far against Soult or against Dorsenne he must bring Marmont down on his flank, left or right; while, if he reached out and struck for the Tagus Valley, Marmont could borrow from right and left without absolutely crippling his colleagues, and roll up seventy thousand men to bar the road on Madrid. In short, the opposing armies stood at a deadlock, and there were rumours that Napoleon, who was pouring troops into Spain from the north, meant to follow and take the war into his own hands.

Now, the strength and the weakness of the whole position lay with Marmont; while the key of it, curiously enough, was Ciudad Rodrigo, garrisoned by Dorsenne — as in due time appeared. For the present, Wellington, groping for the vital spot, was learning all that could be learnt about Marmont's strength, its disposition,

The Lamp and the Guitar

and (a matter of first importance) its victualling, Spain being a country where large armies starve. How many men were being drafted down from the north? How was Marmont scattering his cantonments to feed them? What was the state of the harvest? What provisions did Salamanca contain? And what stores were accumulating at Madrid, Valladolid, Burgos?

I had just arrived at Lisbon in a *chassemaree* of San Sebastian, bringing a report of the French troops, which for a month past had been pouring across the bridge of Irun: and how I had learnt this is worth telling. There was a cobbler, Martinez by name — a little man with a green shade over his eyes — who plied his trade in a wooden hutch at the end of the famous bridge. While he worked he counted every man, horse, standard, wagon, or gun that passed, and forwarded the numbers without help of speech or writing (for he could not even write his own name). He managed it all with his hammer, tapping out a code known to our fellows who roamed the shore below on the pretence of hunting for shellfish, but were prevented by the French cordon from getting within sight of the bridge. As for Martinez, the French Generals themselves gossipped around his hutch while he cobbled industriously at the soldiers' shoes.

I had presented my report to Lord Wellington, who happened to be in Lisbon quarrelling with the Portuguese Government and re-embarking (apparently for Cadiz) a battering train of guns and mortars which had just arrived from England: and after two days' holiday I was spending an idle morning in a wine-shop by the quay, where the proprietor, a fervid politician, kept on file his copies of the Government newspaper, the *Lisbon Gazette*. A week at sea had sharpened my appetite for news; and I was wrapped in study of the *Gazette* when an orderly arrived from headquarters with word that Lord Wellington requested my attendance there at once.

I found him in conference with a handsome, slightly built

The Lamp and the Guitar

man — a Spaniard by his face — who stepped back as I entered, but without offering to retire. Instead, he took up his stand with his back to one of the three windows overlooking the street, and so continued to observe me, all the while keeping his own face in shade.

The General, as his habit was, came to business at once.

"I have sent for you," said he, "on a serious affair. Our correspondents in Salamanca have suddenly ceased to write."

"If your Excellency's correspondents are the same as the Government's," said I, "'tis small wonder," and I glanced at the newspaper in his hand — a copy of the same *Gazette* I had been reading.

"Then you also think this is the explanation?" He held out the paper with the face of a man handling vermin.

"The Government publishes its reports, the English newspapers copy them: these in turn reach Paris; the Emperor reads them: and," concluded I, with a shrug, "your correspondents cease to write, probably for the good reason that they are dead."

"That is just what I want you to find out," said he.

"Your Excellency wishes me to go to Salamanca? Very good. And, supposing these correspondents to be dead?"

"You will find others."

"That may not be easy: nevertheless, I can try. Your Excellency, by the way, will allow me to promise that future reports are not for publication?"

Wellington smiled grimly, doubtless from recollection of a recent interview with Silveira and the Portuguese Ministry. "You may rest assured of that," said he; and added: "There may be some delay, as you suggest, in finding fresh correspondents: and it is very necessary for me to know quickly how Salamanca stands for stores."

"Then I must pick up some information on my own account."

"The service will be hazardous------"

"Oh, as for that------" I put in, with another shrug.

"——and I propose to give you a companion," pursued Wellington, with a half-turn toward the man in the recess of the window. " This is Senor Fuentes. You are not acquainted, I believe? — as you ought to be."

Now from choice I have always worked alone: and had the General uttered any other name I should have been minded to protest, with the old Greek, that two were not enough for an army, while for any other purpose they were too many. But on hearsay the performances of this man Fuentes and his methods and his character had for months possessed a singular fascination for me. He was at once a strolling guitar-player and a licentiate of the University of Salamanca, a consorter with gypsies, and by birth a pure-blooded Castilian hidalgo. Some said that patriotism was a passion with him; with a face made for the love of women, he had a heart only for the woes of Spain. Others averred that hatred of the French was always his master impulse; that they, by demolishing the colleges of his University, and in particular his own beloved College of San Lorenzo, had broken his heart and first driven him to wander. Rewards he disdained; dangers he laughed at: his feats in the service had sometimes a touch of high comedy and always a touch of heroic grace. In short, I believe that if Spain had held a poet in those days, Fuentes would have passed into song and lived as one of his country's demigods.

He came forward now with a winning smile and saluted me cordially, not omitting a handsome compliment on my work. You could see that the man had not an ounce of meanness in his nature.

"We shall be friends," said he, turning to the Commander-in-Chief. "And that will be to the credit of both, since Senor MacNeill has an objection to comrades."

The Lamp and the Guitar

"I never said so."

"Excuse me, but I have studied your methods."

"Well, then," I replied, "I had the strongest objection, but you have made me forget it — as you have forgotten your repugnance to visit Salamanca." For although Fuentes flitted up and down and across Spain like a will-o'-the-wisp, I had heard that he ever avoided the city where he had lived and studied.

His fine eyes clouded, and he muttered some Latin words as it were with a voice indrawn.

"I beg your pardon?" put in Wellington sharply.

"*Cecidit, cecidit Salmantica ilia fortis*," Fuentes repeated.

"'*Cecidit*' — ah! I see — a quotation. Yes, they are knocking the place about: as many as fifteen or sixteen colleges razed to the ground." He opened the newspaper again and ran his eyes down the report. "You'll excuse me: in England we have our own way of pronouncing Latin, and for the moment I didn't quite catch------Yes, sixteen colleges; a clean sweep! But before long, Senor Fuentes, we'll return the compliment upon their fortifications."

"That must be my consolation, your Excellency," Fuentes made answer with a smile which scarcely hid its irony.

The General began to discuss our route: our precautions he left to us. He was well aware of the extreme risk we ran, and once again made allusion to it as he dismissed us.

"If that were all your Excellency demanded!"

Fuentes' gaiety returned as we found ourselves in the street. "We shall get on together like a pair of schoolboys," he assured me. "We understand each other, you and I. But oh, those islanders!"

We left Lisbon that same evening on muleback, taking the road for Abrantes. So universally were the French hated that the odds were we might have dispensed with precautions at this stage, and indeed for the greater part of the journey. The frontier once passed we should be travelling in our native country — Fuentes as a gypsy and I as an Asturian, moving from one harvest-job to another. We carried no compromising papers: and if the French wanted to arrest folks on mere suspicion they had the entire population to practise on. Nevertheless, having ridden north-east for some leagues beyond Abrantes — on the direct road leading past Ciudad Rodrigo to Salamanca — we halted at Amendoa, bartered one of our mules for a couple of skins of wine and ten days' provisions, and, having made our new toilet in a chestnut grove outside the town, headed back for the road leading east through Villa Velha into the Tagus valley.

Beyond the frontier we were among Marmont's cantonments: but these lay scattered, and we avoided them easily. Keeping to the hill-tracks on the northern bank of the river, and giving a wide berth to the French posts in front of Alcantara, we struck away boldly for the north through the Sierras: reached the Alagon, and, following up its gorges, crossed the mountains in the rear of Bejar, where a French force guarded the military pass.

So far we had travelled unmolested, if toilsomely; and a pleasanter comrade than Fuentes no man could ask for. His gaiety never failed him: yet it was ever gentle, and I suspected that it covered either a native melancholy or some settled sorrow — sorrow for his country, belike — but there were depths he never allowed me to sound. He did everything well, from singing a love-song to tickling a trout and cooking it for our supper: and it was after such a supper, as we lay and smoked on a heathery slope beyond Bejar, that he unfolded his further plans.

"My friend," said he, "there were once two brothers, students of Salamanca, and not far removed in age. Of these the elder was given to love-making and playing on the guitar; while the other stuck to his books — which was all the more creditable because his eyes were weak. I hope you are enjoying this story?"

"It begins to be interesting."

"Yet these two brothers — they were nearly of one height, by the way — obtained their bachelor's degrees, and in time their licentiates, though as rewards for different degrees of learning. They were from Villacastin, beyond Avila in Old Castille: but their father, a hidalgo of small estates there, possessed also a farm and the remains of a castle across the frontier in the kingdom of Leon, a league to the west of Sal-vatierra on the Tormes. It had come to him as security for a loan which was never paid: and, dying, he left this property to his younger son Andrea. Now when the French set a Corsican upon the throne of our kingdoms, these two brothers withdrew from Salamanca; but while Andrea took up his abode on his small heritage, and gave security for his good behaviour, Eugenio, the elder, turned his back on the paternal home (which the French had ravaged), and became a rebel, a nameless, landless man and a wanderer, with his guitar for company. You follow me?"

"I follow you, Senor Don Eugenio------"

"Not 'de Fuentes,'" he put in with a smile. "The real name you shall read upon certain papers and parchments of which I hope to possess myself tonight. In short, my friend, since we are on the way to Salamanca, why should I not apply there for my doctor's degree?"

"It requires a thesis, I have always understood."

"That is written."

"May I ask upon what subject?"

"The fiend take me if I know yet! But it is written, safe enough."

"Ah, I see! We go to Salvatierra? Yes, yes, but what of me, who know scarcely any Latin beyond my *credo*?"

"Why, that is where I feel a certain delicacy. Having respect to your rank, caballero, I do not like to propose that you should become my servant."

"I am your servant already, and for a week past I have been an Asturian. It will be promotion."

He sprang up gaily. "What a comrade is mine!" he cried, flinging away the end of his cigarette. "To Salvatierra, then — Santiago, and close Spain!"

Darkness overtook us as we climbed down the slopes: but we pushed on, Fuentes leading the way boldly. Evidently he had come to familiar ground. But it was midnight before he brought me, by an abominable road, to a farmstead the walls of which showed themselves ruinous even in the starlight — for moon there was none. At an angle of the building, which ohce upon a time had been whitewashed, rose a solid tower, with a doorway and an iron-studded door, and a narrow window overlooking it. In spite of the hour, Fuentes advanced nonchalantly and began to bang the door, making noise enough to wake the dead. The window above was presently opened — one could hear, with a shaking hand. "Who is there?" asked a man's voice no less tremulous. "Who are you, for the love of God?"

"*Gente de paz*, my dear brother! — not your friends the French. I hope, by the way, you are entertaining none."

"I have been in bed these four hours or five. 'Peace,' say you? I wish you would take your own risks and leave me in peace! What is it you want, this time?"

"'Tis a good six weeks, brother, since my last visit: and, as you know, I never call without need."

"Well, what is it you need?"

"I need," said Fuentes with great gravity, "the loan of your spectacles."

"Be serious, for God's sake! And do not raise your voice so: the French may be following you------"

"Dear Andrea, and if the French were to hear it, surely mine is an innocent request. A pair of spectacles!"

"The French------" began Don Andrea and broke off, peering down short-sightedly into the courtyard. "Ah, there, is someone else! Who is it? Who is it you have there in the darkness?"

"*Dios*! A moment since you were begging for silence, and now you want me to call out my_ friend's name — to who knows what ears? He has a mule, here, and I — oh yes, beside the spectacles I shall require a horse: a horse, and — let me see — a treatise."

"Have you been drinking, brother?"

"No: and, since you mention it, a cup of wine, too, would not come amiss. Is this a way to treat the *caballero* my friend? For the honour of the family, brother, step down and open the door."

Don Andrea closed the window, and by-and-by we heard the bolts withdrawn, one by one — and they were heavy. The door opened at length, and a thin man in a nightcap peered out upon us with an oil-lamp held aloft over the hand shading his eyes.

"You had best call Juan," said his brother easily, "and bid him stable the mule. For the remainder of the night we are your guests; and, to ensure our sleeping well, you shall fetch out the choicest of the theses you have composed for your doctorate and read us a portion over our wine."

We lay that night, after a repast of thin wine and chestnuts, in a spare chamber, and on beds across the feet of which the rats scudded. I did not see Don Andrea again: but his brother, who had risen betimes, awakened me from uneasy slumber and showed me his spoil. Sure enough it included a pair of spectacles and a bulky roll of manuscript, a leathern jerkin, a white shirt, and a pair of velvet-fustian breeches, tawny yellow in hue and something the worse for wear. Below-stairs, in the courtyard, we found a white-haired retainer waiting, with his grip on the bridles of my mule and a raw-boned grey mare.

"The *caballero* will bring them back when he has done with them?" said this old man as I mounted. The request puzzled me for a moment until I met his eyes and found them fastened wistfully on my breeches.

Assuredly Fuentes was an artist. Besides the spectacles, which in themselves transformed him, he had borrowed a broad-brimmed hat and a rusty black sleeveless *mancha*, which, by the way he contrived it to hang, gave his frame an extraordinary lankiness. But his final and really triumphant touch was simply a lengthening of the stirrups, so that his legs dangled beneath the mare's belly like a couple of ropes with shoes attached. If Don Andrea watched us out of sight from his tower — as I doubt not he did — his emotions as he recognised his portrait must have been lively.

In this guise we ambled steadily all day along the old Roman road leading to Salamanca, and came within sight of the city as the sun was sinking. It stood on the eastern bank of the river, fronting the level rays, its walls rising tier upon tier, its towers and cupolas of cream-coloured stone bathed in gold, with recesses of shadowy purple. A bridge of twenty-five or six arches spanned the cool river-beds, and towards this we descended between cornfields, of which the light swept the topmost ears while the stalks stood already in twilight. Truly it was a noble city yet, and so I cried aloud to Fuentes. But his eyes, I believe, saw only what the French had marred or demolished.

A group of their soldiery idled by the bridge-end, waiting for the guard to be relieved, and lolled against the parapet watching the bathers, whose shouts came up to me from the chasm below. But instead of riding up and presenting our passes, Fuentes, a furlong from the bridge, turned his mare's head to the left and reined up at the door of a small riverside tavern.

The innkeeper — a brisk, athletic man, with the air of a

The Lamp and the Guitar

retired servant — appeared at the door as we dismounted. He scanned Fuentes narrowly, while giving him affable welcome. Plainly he recognised him as an old patron, yet plainly the recognition was imperfect.

"Eh, my good Bartolome, and so you still cling above the river? I hope custom clings here too?"

"But — but can it be the Senor Don------"

"Eugenio, my friend. The spectacles puzzle you: they belong to my brother, Don Andrea, and I may tell you that after a day's wear I find them trying to the eyes. But, you understand, there are reasons . . . and so you will suppose me to be Don Andrea, while bringing a cup of wine, and another for my servant, to Don Eugenio's favourite seat, which was at the end of the garden beyond the mulberry-tree, if you remember."

"Assuredly this poor house is your Lordship's, and all that belongs to it. The wine shall be fetched with speed. But as for the table at the end of the garden, I regret to tell your Lordship that it is occupied for a while. If for this evening, I might recommend the parlour------" The innkeeper made his excuse with a certain quick trepidation which Fuentes did not fail to note.

"What is this? Your garden full? It appears then, my good Bartolome, that your custom has not suffered in these bad times."

"On the contrary, Senor, it has fallen off woefully! My garden has been deserted for months, and is empty now, save for two gentlemen, who, as luck will have it, have chosen to seat themselves in your Lordship's favourite corner. Ah, yes, the old times were the best! and I was a fool to grumble, as I sometimes did, when my patrons ran me off my legs."

"But steady, Bartolome: not so fast! Surely there used to be three tables beyond the mulberry-tree, or my memory is sadly at fault."

"Three tables? Yes, it is true there are three tables. Nevertheless------"

"I cannot see," pursued Fuentes with a musing air — "no, for the life of me I cannot see how two gentlemen should require three tables to drink their wine at."

"Nor I, Senor. It must, as you say, be a caprice: nevertheless they charged me that on all accounts they were to have that part of the garden to themselves."

"A very churlish caprice, then! They are Frenchmen, doubtless?"

"No, indeed, your Lordship: but two lads of good birth, gentlemen of Spain, the one a bachelor, the other a student of the University."

"All the more, then, they deserve a lesson. Bartolome, you will tell your tapster to bring my wine to the vacant table beyond the mulberry-tree."

"But, Senor ------" As Fuentes moved off, the inn-keeper put forth a hand to entreat if not to restrain him.

"Eh?" Fuentes halted as if amazed at his impudence. "Ah, to be sure, I am Don Andrea: but do not forget, my friend, that Don Eugenio used to be quick-tempered, and that in members of one family these little likenesses crop up in the most unexpected fashion." He strode away down the shadowy garden-path over which in the tree-tops a last beam or two of sunset lingered: and I, having hitched up our beasts, followed him, carrying the saddle-bags and his guitar-case.

Three tables, as he had premised, stood in the patch of garden beyond the mulberry-tree, hedged in closely on three sides, giving a view in front upon the towers and fortifications across the river; a nook secluded as a stage-box facing a scene that might have been built and lit up for our delectation. The tables, with benches alongside, stood moderately close together — two by the river-wall, the third in the rear, where the hedge formed an angle: and the two gentlemen so jealous of their privacy were seated at the nearer of the two tables overlooking the river, and on the same bench — though at the extreme ends of it and something more than a yard apart.

They stared up angrily at our intrusion, and for the moment the elder of the pair seemed about to demand our business. But Fuentes walked calmly by, took his seat at the next table, pulled out his bundle of manuscript, adjusted his spectacles, and began to read. Having deposited my baggage, I took up a respectful position behind him, ignoring — somewhat ostentatiously perhaps — the strangers' presence, yet not without observing them from the corner of my eye.

They were young: the elder, maybe, three-and-twenty, short, thick-set, with features just now darkened by his ill-humour, but probably sullen enough at the best of times: the younger, tall and nervous and extraordinarily fair for a Spaniard, with a weak, restless mouth and restless, passionate eyes. Indeed, either this restlessness was a disease with him or he was suffering just now from an uncontrollable agitation. Eyes, mouth, feet, fingers — the whole man seemed to be twitching. I set down his age at eighteen. On the table stood a large flask of wine, from which he helped himself fiercely, and beside the flask lay a long bundle wrapped in a cloak.

This young man, having drained his glass at a gulp, let out an oath and sprang up suddenly with a glare upon Fuentes, who had stretched out his legs and was already absorbed in his reading.

"Senor Stranger," he began impetuously, "we would have you to know, if the innkeeper has not already told you------"

"Gently!" interposed his comrade. "You are going the wrong way to work. My friend, Sir" — he addressed Fuentes, who looked up with a mild surprise — "my friend, Sir, was about to suggest that the light is poor for reading."

"Oh," answered Fuentes, smiling easily, "for a minute or two — until they bring my wine. Moreover, I wear excellent glasses."

"But the place is not too well chosen."

The Lamp and the Guitar

Fuentes appeared to digest this for a moment, then turned around upon me with a puzzled air.

"My good Pedro, you have not misled me, I hope? I am short-sighted, gentlemen; and if we have strayed into a private garden I offer you my profoundest apologies." He gathered his manuscript into a roll and stood up.

"To be plain with you, Sir," said the dark man sullenly, "this is not precisely a private garden, and yet we desire privacy."

"Oho?" After a glance around, Fuentes fixed his eyes on the bundle lying on the table. "And at the point of the sword — eh?"

The two young men started and at once began to eye each other suspiciously.

"No, no," Fuentes assured them, smiling; "this is no trap, believe me, but a chance encounter; and I am no *alguacil* in disguise, but a poor scholar returning to Salamanca for his doctorate. Nor do I seek to know the cause of your quarrel. But here comes the wine!" He waited until the tapster had set flask and glasses on the table and withdrawn. "In the interval before your friends arrive you will not grudge me, Sirs, the draining of a glass to remembrance in a garden where I too have loved my friends, and quarrelled with them, in days gone by — days older now than I care to reckon." He raised the wine and held it up for a moment against the sunset. "Youth — youth!" he sighed.

"You are welcome, Sir," said the younger man a trifle more graciously; "but we expect no seconds, and, believe me, we shall presently be pressed for time."

Fuentes raised his eyebrows. "You surprise and shock me, Sirs. In the days to which I drank just now it was not customary for gentlemen of the University of Salamanca to fight without witnesses. We left that to porters and grooms."

"And pray," sneered the darker young man, "may we know

the name of him who from the height of his years and experience presumes to intrude this lecture on us?"

"You may address me, if you will, as Don Andrea Galazza de Villacastin, a licentiate of your University------"

To my astonishment the younger man stopped him with a short offensive laugh. "You may spare us the rest, Sir. Don Andrea Galazza is known to us and to all honest patriots by repute: we can supply the rest of his titles for ourselves, beginning with *renegado*------"

"Hist!" interposed his comrade, at the same time catching up the swords from the table. "Don't be a fool, Sebastian — speak lower, for God's sake! — the very soldiers at the bridge will hear you!"

"Ay, Sir," chimed in Fuentes gravely; "listen to your friend's advice, and do not increase the peril of your remarks by the foolishness of shouting them."

But the youngster, flushed with wine and overstrung, had lost for the moment all self-control. "I accept that risk," cried he, "for the pleasure of telling Don Andrea Galazza what kind of man he passes for among honourable folk. He, the brother of Don Eugenio — of our hero, the noble Fuentes! He, that signed his peace while that noble heart preferred to break! He spat in furious contempt.

Fuentes turned to me quietly. "Behold one of the enthusiasts we came to seek," he murmured; "and one who will not fear risks. But these testimonials are embarrassing, and this fame of mine swells to a nuisance." He faced his accuser. "Nevertheless," answered he aloud, "you make a noise that must disconcert your friend, who is in two minds about assassinating me. Why spoil his game by arousing the neighbourhood?"

"Senor Don Andrea, you know too much — thanks to my friend here," said the dark man slowly.

"But we are not assassins," put in the youngster. "Renegade though you be, Don Andrea, I give you your chance." He snatched the foil from his senior's hand and presented it solemnly, hilt foremost, to Fuentes.

"Youth — youth!" murmured Fuentes with an appreciative laugh, as he tucked the foil under his arm, took off his spectacles and rubbed them, laughing again. He readjusted them carefully and, saluting, fell on guard. "I am at your service, Sir."

The youth stepped forward hotly, touched blades, and almost immediately lunged. An instant later his sword, as though it had been a bird released from his hand, flew over his shoulder into the twilight behind.

"That was ill-luck for you, Senor," said Fuentes lowering his point. "But who can be sure of himself in this confounded twilight?" He swung half-about towards the river-wall, with a glance across at the city, where already a few lights began to twinkle in the dusk. And, so turning, he seemed on a sudden to catch his breath.

And almost on that instant the youngster, who had fallen back disconcerted, sprang forward in a fresh fury and gripped his comrade by the arm, pointing excitedly towards a group of houses above the fortifications, whence from a high upper storey, deeply recessed between flanking walls, a light redder than the rest twinkled across to us.

"The proof!" cried he. "She knew you would be here, and that is the proof! You at least I will kill before I leave this garden, as I came to kill you tonight."

In his new gust of fury he seemed to have forgotten his discomfiture — to have forgotten even the existence of Fuentes, who now faced them both with a smile which (unless the dusk distorted it) had some bitterness in its raillery.

"If I mistake not, Sirs, the light you were discussing signals to us from an upper chamber in the Lesser Street of the Virgins. It can only be seen from this garden and from the far end of it, where we now stand. I will not ask you who lights it now: but she who lit it in former days was named Luisa. Oh yes, she was circumspect — a good maid then, and no doubt a good maid now: in that street of the Virgins there was at least one prudent. Youth flies, *ay de mi!* But youth also, as I perceive to-night, repeats itself; and Luisa — who was always circumspect, though a conspirator — apparently repeats herself too."

"Luisa? What do you know of Luisa?" stammered the younger man. The name seemed to have fallen on him like the touch of an enchanter's wand, stiffening him to stone. Like a statue he stood there, peering forward with a white face.

"My friend" — Fuentes turned to me — "be so good as to unstrap the case yonder and hand me my guitar."

He laid his foil on the table, took the guitar from me, and, having seated himself on the bench, tried the strings softly, all the while looking up with grave raillery at the two young men.

"What do I know of Luisa? Listen!" Under his voice he began a light-hearted little song, which in English might run like this, or as nearly as I can contrive —

My love, she lives in Salamanca
All up a dozen flights of stairs;
There with the sparrows night and morning
Under the roof she chirps her prayers.
They say her wisdom comes from heaven —
So near the clouds and chimneys meet —
I rather think Luisa's sparrows
Fetch it aloft there from the street!

What would you have? In la Verdura
All the day long she keeps a stall:
Students, bachelors buy her nosegays,
Given with a look and — well, that's all!
Go, silly boy, believe you first with her —

Twenty at once she'll entertain.
Why love a mistress and be curst with her?
Copy Luisa — love all Spain!"

He paused, still eyeing them. "You recognise the tune, Sirs? Does she play it yet? Well, then, I made it for her."

"*You?* How came you to make her that tune?" The younger man had found his voice at length. "No, Sir; coquette she may be, but that she ever was friends with such a one as Andrea Galazza I will not yet believe."

"And you are right. Sirs, you have not yet told me your names: but in your generous heat you have given me your secret — that you are two lovers of Spain, and even such a pair as my friend and I have travelled some distance to seek. In return you shall have mine. I tricked you just now. I am not Don Andrea, but his brother Eugenio — or, as some call him, Fuentes."

"Fuentes! *You!*"

"Upon my honour, yes." He pulled off his spectacles, meeting their incredulity with a frank laugh. "What proof can I give you?" The guitar still lay across his knees: he picked it up as if to play, but set it down after a moment with another laugh, hard and bitter. "Let us go together, gentlemen, to the Street of the Virgins, and ask Luisa if she remembers me."

It was agreed that the young men — who gave their names as Diego de Ribalta and Sebastian Paz — should not accompany us into the city, but wend their way back across the bridge, while we finished our wine and mounted our beasts at leisure. The officer at the bridge-end made no bother about our passports (borrowed, I need scarcely say, from the estimable Don Andrea, who, as his brother explained, was a careful man, and zealous in all dealings with the authorities); and by-and-by we were clattering up-hill through the ill-lighted streets of Salamanca. At the head of the first street our two friends stepped out of the shadow and joined us in silence. In silence, too, Fuentes regreeted them, and led the way — to an inn first, the Four Crowns, standing almost under the shadow of the Old Cathedral, where we stabled mare and mule; then, on foot, through a maze of zigzagging lanes and alleys, back into the depths of a waterside quarter. Once he was at fault — the lane we followed ending abruptly in an open space strewn with rubble-heaps, a broad area where the French had lately been at work. Among these heaps he blundered for a while in the darkness, and then, retracing his steps, took up the scent again and led us down one narrow street, across another; turned to the right, counting the houses as he went, and knocked at the twelfth door without hesitation. The knock was a peculiar one — five quick taps, followed, after a pause, by one distinct and heavy.

"But I must ask these gentlemen to do what remains," said he, turning and addressing our companions. "Luisa has doubtless changed the password since my time."

"Willingly, Senor Fuentes," agreed de Ribalta.

"You will not, of course, object to be blindfolded? — a formality, merely, in your case."

The porter, having received the password in a whisper through the grille, unbolted to us, and opened the door upon a pitch-dark passage. Here we submitted to have our eyes bandaged, and Sebastian Paz took my hand to guide me. Eight flights of stairs we mounted before the hubbub of many voices and the tinkle of a guitar saluted my ears; two more, and the hubbub grew louder; another, and it grew obstreperous, deafening. At the head of the twelfth flight one of our guides rapped on a door; the noise died down suddenly; a bolt was shot back and the bandage dragged from my eyes.

I found myself blinking and staring across a room filled with tobacco-smoke, and upon a company which at first glance I took for a crew of demons. They were, in fact, a students' chorus — young men in black, with black silk masks covering the upper half of their faces. All wore the same uniform — black tunic, short black cloak, knee-breeches, and stockings. Some squatted on the floor, two lolled on a divan by the window — each with a guitar across his knees. The man who had opened to us held a tambourine, and he alone wore a little round cap. The others wore black cocked hats, or had flung them off for better ease. In a deep armchair beside the fireplace sat a stiff-backed, middle-aged woman in black — a duenna evidently — who regarded us with eyes like large black beads, but did not interrupt her knitting. In the corner behind the door stood a bed, with a crucifix above it: and on the bed, between two crates, the one of them heaped with flowers, sat a young woman dangling a pretty pair of feet and smoking a cigarette while she made up a posy.

In spite of their masks one could tell that all the men were young—mere lads, indeed. And if this were Luisa, Fuentes had slandered her sorely. She seemed scarcely eighteen—-and we had taken her, too, at unawares, when a woman forgets for a moment her endless vigilant parry against Time. She tossed her posy into the half-filled basket, clapped her hands, and sprang off the bed.

"Two new recruits! Bravo, Sebastianillo!"

With that, as she stepped gaily forward, her eyes fell on Fuentes, and she swayed and fell back a pace, catching at the foot of the bed.

"Don Eugenio!"

"Your servant, Senorita." He bowed elaborately and coldly. "You keep the lamp burning, and I accepted its invitation. Your cheeks, too, Senorita, keep the old colour. I congratulate you — and you, Dona Isabel." He bowed to the old lady. "To live with youth — that is the way to live always young."

She had moved forward again, as if to take him by both hands: but faltered. "Yes, we have kept the lamp burning, Don

Eugenio," she answered with a voice curiously strained. "My friends" — she turned to the young men — "rise and salute our guest of guests, Don Eugenio Fuentes!"

"Fuentes!"

"What are you telling us, Luisa? *The* Fuentes? But it is impossible!"

"Impossible! Fuentes comes no more to Salamanca."

Nevertheless all had sprung to their feet, and Fuentes comprehended them all in an ironical bow.

"That is the name by which I call myself, Sirs, since leaving the University."

Luisa made a dumb signal, and one of the youths handed him a guitar. He struck but one chord to assure himself of its tune —

> "*There's one that lives in Salamanca*
> *All up a dozen flights of stairs;*
> *There with the sparrows, night and morning,*
> *Under the roof she chirps her prayers.*
> *They say her wisdom comes from heaven —*

Will you not take a guitar, Senorita, and help me with the old song?

> *So near the clouds and chimneys meet —*
> *I rather think Luisa's sparrows*
> *Fetch it aloft there from the street!*"

Above all things women suspect and fear irony: it is not one of their weapons. Luisa glanced at Fuentes doubtfully, I could see, and with some pain in her doubt. But it was the old song, after all, and he was singing it *de bon coeur*. She caught up a guitar and chimed in with the second verse, taking up the soprano's part, while he at once obeyed and dropped from treble to alto —

> "*Which will you have? In la Verdura*
> *Pretty Luisa keeps a stall:*
> *Hands you a rose for your peseta,*

Nothing to pay but a thorn — that's all!
King of her love, with no Prime Minister,
Lord of an attic blithe I'd reign.
But ay de mi!! *from here to Finisterre*
Pretty Luisa loves all Spain."

His eyes, as he sang, were fastened on young Sebastian Paz, and she, noting them, played the verse to its ringing close, turned abruptly, and laid the guitar on the bed between the flower-baskets.

"But I think it is business brings you here, Don Eugenio."

He had stepped to the open lattice, and with an upward glance at the lamp, burning steadily in the windless air, leaned on the sill and looked out over the city. Somewhere below by the waterside a dull noise sounded — the thud of a falling beam. The French down there were working by lantern-light, clearing away the houses from their fortifications.

"Yes, I come on business, and from Lord Wellington. The good citizens in Salamanca have ceased to write."

"And small blame to them," one of the young men answered.

"Small blame to them, I agree. And yet they must send news — this time to Lord Wellington, who knows better than to print it."

His eyes interrogated Luisa, who raised hers at length to meet them.

"That will not be easy," said she, with a pucker of her pretty forehead. "They are scared and afraid for their heads: nevertheless, Don Eugenio might bring back their confidence, if only we can bring him face to face with them." She seated herself on the bed's edge and mused awhile with her hands in her lap.

"You know where to find them?" asked Fuentes, addressing the company in general.

"Oh, yes, Senior — assuredly we know where to find them!" answered one or two.

"Then the whole thing is very simple. You must let me join your choir, gentlemen."

"Yes, yes, *that* is simple enough," put in Luisa impatiently: "the more so, as our chorus is popular not only in the taverns, but at the French officers' messes. But these spies of ours are slow and dull to a degree: I think sometimes it takes a quite special clumsiness to be a clerk of the arsenal or to swindle the country in the military stores. We can get you into communication with them, Don Eugenio: but how are they to pass their information to *you*? They are born bunglers, and the French begin to use their eyes." She pursed her lips for a moment. "Is your friend new to this work?" she asked, suddenly turning toward me a gaze of frank inspection.

Fuentes smiled. "You would not say so, Senorita, were I free to tell you his name."

"As for that," said I, "where Senor Don Eugenio entrusts his secret I may not hesitate to entrust mine. My name is Manuel MacNeill, Senorita, and I kiss your hands and am at your service."

Luisa rose and dropped me a very stately curtsey. "Happy were I, Don Manuel MacNeill, to welcome you, even if you did not solve our difficulty. You are clever at disguises, I have been told. Well, I have a disguise for you — though not, to be sure, a pleasant one."

"I take the downs with the ups," said I.

"Well, then, Don Diego here is an artist. He can paint you a bunch of grapes so that the birds come to peck at it: moreover, he has studied at the hospital. We must find you a suit of rags, Sir, and Don Diego shall paint you as full of sores as Lazarus."

"And after that?"

"After that you will go to the porch of the New Cathedral, to the shady side of it — look you how I study your comfort — facing on the Square of the Old College: and there you shall collect the alms of the charitable. Many things, I am told, find their way into a beggar's hat."

"Senorita," said Fuentes gravely, with a glance up at the lamp, "it was a good star that led us here to-night."

"The star, as you call it, has not failed in all these years," she answered, with a look of timid appeal which hardened to one of defiance.

"Nay," answered he coldly and lightly, "I never doubted it would — while there was oil to feed it."

On the morrow, then, I took up my station by the porch of the Cathedral, with a highly artistic wound in my left leg, a shade over my right eye, and beside me a crutch and a ragged cap. The first day brought me coppers only: but late on the second afternoon a stout citizen, pausing on the steps and catching his breath asthmatically before entering the Cathedral, dropped a paper pellet in with his penny. On the third day it began to rain pellets, and I drank that night to the assured success of our campaign.

I saw nothing of Fuentes. It had been agreed between us that I should play my part in my own fashion, and I played it so thoroughly as to take lodgings in the beggars' quarter, in a thieves' den — it was little better — off the Street of the Rosary. It was enough for me that, however Fuentes went about the sowing, the harvest kept pouring in. As for the Street of the Virgins, I had been brought to it and had quitted it in the dark, and it is a question if by daylight I could have found it again. At any rate, I did not try.

But on the fourth day, at about five in the afternoon, as the day's heat began to grow tolerable, I caught sight of Luisa herself picking her way towards the Cathedral porch along the pavement under the facade of the University. Before entering the great doors she paused on the step beside me, bent to drop a coin into my cap, and whispered —

"When I come out, follow me."

She passed on into the Cathedral and did not reappear for a quarter of an hour, perhaps. In this time I had made up my mind that, whatever the risk of my obeying her, she had probably weighed it against some risk more urgent, and perhaps brought the message direct from Fuentes. So when she came forth, and after pausing a moment to readjust her mantilla, tripped down the steps and away to the left down the street leading to the Porta del Rio, I picked up my crutch, yawned, shook the coppers in my wallet, and hobbled after her at a decent distance.

All the way I kept my eyes open and my ears too. In the streets around the Porta del Rio the city's traffic was beginning to flow again after the day's siesta: but I made pretty sure that we were not being tracked. Through half-a-dozen streets she led me, and so to one which I supposed to be the Street of the Virgins, and to a door which I recognised for that to which Fuentes had brought me four nights ago.

She had already knocked and been admitted: but the door opened again as I came abreast of it, and I stepped past the porter into the passage. Luisa stood halfway up the first flight of stairs under a sunny window and beckoned, and aloft I climbed after her to her attic. With her hand on the latch of her own door, she turned.

"You will find your clothes within," she said, and opened the door for me to pass. "Dress — dress with speed — and find Don Eugenio. Your work is done, and you must both be beyond the bridge before sunset."

"Is there treachery, Senorita?" I asked.

"There is treachery of a kind, but not of the kind you guess. It is important that Don Eugenio should be beyond the bridge tonight. Your beasts at the Four Crowns are ready saddled. Find your friend, and help him to go with all speed."

"But where shall I find him, Senorita? I have not set eyes on him for three or four days."

"Yet he has done his work surely, has he not?"

"Far better than I could have hoped."

"You ask where he is to be found? But where else than by the Archbishop's College, near by where the French have pulled down his own College of San Lorenzo, and are destroying more? You men!" She broke out into sudden passionate contempt. "The past is all you have eyes for — the poor, wild, blundering past. You have no eyes for the present, and with the past you poison its living joy. We women cannot be always seventeen: yet because we are not, you kill us—you kill us, I say!" Then, while I stared at her in downright amaze, "Go, dress!" she cried, thrusting me into the room. "In your coat you will find two letters. That without address you will give to Don Eugenio when you find him: that which is marked with a cross you will hand to him when you shall have passed the bridge—on no account before. And now be quick, I beseech you: for this one room is all my house."

Almost she thrust me within, and closed the door gently upon me. When I emerged, in my right and proper clothes, it was to find her yet waiting there upon the landing.

"I thank you for your speed, Senor Don Manuel; for I, too, am in haste to change my dress: and my dress will require care tonight, since I go to a masquerade." She gave me her hand. "Farewell, friend!" she said.

I found Don Eugenio behind the College of the Archbishop, seated on a mound and watching the French sappers at their work. I gave him Luisa's letter.

"The wench," said he calmly, having read it, "is a born conspirator. She cannot be happy unless she has a card hidden even from her fellow-plotters. Still, it is usually safe to follow her advice. Our work is pretty thoroughly done, I fancy?"

I nodded.

"We will see to our beasts then."

"She tells me they are ready saddled."

"Saints! She is in a hurry, that girl! Ah, well, then let us go and ask no questions."

We found our mare and mule, paid our reckoning, and rode forth from Salamanca. At the bridge-end we showed the passports, and were bidden to go in peace. As we climbed the hill beyond, I handed Fuentes Luisa's second letter.

"She bade me deliver it here," I explained.

He read it, turned in his saddle, and looked back towards the twilit sky. "A likely tale," said he, crushing the letter into his pocket.

★★★★

Scarcely a year later — to be precise, on the 17th of June, 1812 — the Allied forces crossed the fords above and below Salamanca, and invested the fortifications which still commanded the bridge. In the suburbs and outlying quarters the inhabitants lit up their houses and, cheering and weeping, thronged the streets to press the hands of the deliverers.

On the 27th the forts fell, and these scenes were renewed. I was passing through the Plaza Mayor that night, about eight o'clock, when a man plucked me by the sleeve, and, turning in the light of a bonfire, I confronted Fuentes. I had not seen him since our return to Lisbon: and his face, in the bonfire's glare, seemed to me to have aged woefully.

"The shells may have spared her house," said he. "Do you care to go with me and see what remains of it?"

He linked his arm in mine. We dived into the dark streets together.

The Street of the Virgins had suffered from the Allies' artillery, and we picked our way over fallen chimney-stacks and heaps of rubble to the remembered door. It stood open, no porter guarding it: but a lamp smoked in the stairway, and by the light of it we mounted together.

On the topmost landing all was dark, but here within the half-open door a light shone. Fuentes tapped on the door and pressed it open. From a deep armchair beside the empty fireplace a woman rose to greet us. It was the duenna, Dona Isabel. Behind her in the open window a lamp shone within a red shade, swaying a little in the draught.

"I give you welcome, Sirs," quavered the old lady in a voice that seemed to flicker, too, in the draught. "By the shouting I understood that the forts have fallen, and for some while I have been expecting you. It is dull up here, and a poor welcome for young gentlemen since my darling died. But on such a night as this------"

She gazed around her, resting both hands on the arms of her chair.

"Luisa! Where is Luisa?" cried Fuentes sharply.

"They come very seldom now," pursued the old woman, not hearing or not comprehending. "It is dull, you understand. You, Sir, are Don Eugenio, are you not?" She nodded palsywise toward the white bed, where a broken guitar lay between two baskets of withered flowers.

"I was to tell you------" She broke off and lifted a hand halfway to her brow, but let it drop. "I was to tell you, if you came, that her letter was true, and always the lamp had been lit for you only. It burns still, you see. She loved you, my little one did; and she was good — always, though she laughed, she was good."

Fuentes stepped to the bed and took the guitar in his hands. Some blow had broken in the sounding-board, and one of the strings had snapped.

"There is no blood upon it," went on the old woman in the same tone that seemed pitilessly striving not to hurt. "The little one scarcely bled at all. But Don Diego struck hard, and somehow the guitar was broken, yet it may have been with her elbow as she fell. It was not treachery, you understand. At first she believed that in his jealousy he meant to betray you, but he meant only to murder. And she, discovering this, dressed herself in your clothes and took your place in the line that night: I heard her playing down the stairs: they were all playing 'My love, she lives in Salamanca' — that was the tune — your own tune, Don Eugenio — and she, with her mask on, singing bravely, the third in the line. She was short, you remember — oh, perhaps a head and shoulders shorter than you! — but Don Diego, outside the door in the darkness, could not see well, or maybe he was misled by your guitar. And, afterwards, Don Sebastian ran him through. They brought her upstairs to me and laid her on the bed. She was breathing yet, but for a very little while: and I was to tell you — I was to tell you-----" She broke off again, seeking to remember.

"Was it something about the lamp, Dona Isabel?"

"Yes, that was it — but I have told you already, eh? Only for you she had ever lit it: for years, yet always and only for you . . . ."

He crept past me, the guitar beneath his arm, and I followed. He went like a blind man, groping between the stair-rail and the wall.

The Cellars of Rueda

1: I Enter the Cellars

It happened on a broiling afternoon in July 1812, and midway in a fortnight of exquisite weather, during which Wellington and Marmont faced each other across the Douro before opening the beautiful series of evolutions -- or, rather, of circumvolutions -- which ended suddenly on the 22nd, and locked the two armies in the prettiest pitched battle I have lived to see.

For the moment neither General desired a battle.

Marmont, thrust back from Salamanca, had found a strong position where he could safely wait for reinforcements, and had indeed already collected near upon forty thousand of all arms, when, on the 8th, Bonnet marched into camp from Asturias with another six thousand infantry.

He had sent, too, to borrow some divisions from Caffarelli's Army of the North.

But these he expected in vain: for Bonnet's withdrawal from Asturias had laid bare the whole line of French communication, and so frightened Caffarelli for the safety of his own districts that he at once recalled the twelve thousand men he was moving down to the Douro, and in the end sent but a handful of cavalry, and that grudgingly.

All this I had the honour to predict to Lord Wellington just twelve hours before Bonnet's arrival on the scene.

I staked my reputation that Caffarelli (on whom I had been watching and waiting for a month past) would not move.

And Lord Wellington on the spot granted me the few days'

The Cellars of Rueda

rest I deserved -- not so much in joy of the news (which, nevertheless, was gratifying) as because for the moment he had no work for me.

The knot was tied.

He could not attack except at great disadvantage, for the fords were deep, and Marmont held the one bridge at Tordesillas.

His business was to hold on, covering Salamanca and the road back to Portugal, and await Marmont's first move.

The French front stretched as a chord across an arc of the river, which here takes a long sweep to the south; and the British faced it around this arc, with their left, centre, and right, upon three tributary streams -- the Guarena, Trabancos, and Zapardiel -- over which last, and just before it joins the Douro, towers the rock of Rueda, crowned with a ruinated castle.

Upon this rock -- for my quarters lay in face of it, on the opposite bank of the stream -- I had been gazing for the best part of an idle afternoon. I was comfortable; my cigarritos lay within reach; my tent gave shade enough; and through the flapway I found myself watching a mighty pretty comedy, with the rock of Rueda for its back-scene. A more satisfactory one I could not have wished, and I have something of a connoisseur's eye.

To be sure, the triangular flapway narrowed the picture, and although the upstanding rock and castle fell admirably within the frame, it cut off an animated scene on the left, where their distant shouts and laughter told me that French and British were bathing together in the river below and rallying each other on the battles yet to be fought.

For during these weeks, and indeed through the operations which followed up to the moment of fighting, the armies behaved less like foes than like two teams before a cricket-match, or two wrestlers who shake hands and afterwards grin amicably as they move in circles seeking for a hitch.

As I lay, however, the bathing-place could only be brought

The Cellars of Rueda

into view by craning my neck beyond the tent-door: and my posture was too well chosen to be shifted.

Moreover, I had a more singular example of these amenities in face of me, on the rock of Rueda itself.

The cliff, standing out against the sun's glare like ivory beneath the blue, and quivering with heat, was flecked here and there with small lilac shadows; and these shadows marked the entrances of the caves with which Rueda was honeycombed.

I had once or twice resolved to visit these caves; for I had heard much of their renown, and even (although this I disbelieved) that they contained wine enough to intoxicate all the troops in the Peninsula.

Wine in abundance they certainly contained, and all the afternoon men singly and in clusters had been swarming in and out of these entrances like flies about a honeypot. For whatever might be happening on the Trabancos under Lord Wellington's eye, here at Rueda, on the extreme right, discipline for the while had disappeared: and presumably the like was true of Marmont's extreme left holding the bridge of Tordesillas.

For from the bridge a short roadway leads to Rueda; and among the figures moving about the rock, diminished by distance though they were, I counted quite a respectable proportion of Frenchmen.

No one who loves his calling ever quite forgets it: and though no one could well have appeared (or indeed felt) lazier, I was really giving my eye practice in discriminating, on this ant-hill, the drunk from the sober, and even the moderately drunk from the incapable.

There could be no doubt, at any rate, concerning one little Frenchman whom two tall British grenadiers were guiding down the cliff towards the road.

And against my will I had to drop my cigarette and laugh aloud: for the two guides were themselves unsteady, yet as desperately intent upon the job as though they handled a chest of treasure.

Now they would prop him up and run him over a few yards of easy ground: anon, at a sharp descent, one would clamber down ahead and catch the burden his comrade lowered by the collar, with a subsidiary grip upon belt or pantaloons.

But to the Frenchman all smooth and rugged came alike: his legs sprawled impartially: and once, having floundered on top of the leading Samaritan with a shock which rolled the pair to the very verge of a precipice, he recovered himself, and sat up in an attitude which, at half a mile's distance, was eloquent of tipsy reproach.

In short, when the procession had filed past the edge of my tent-flap, I crawled out to watch: and then it occurred to me as worth a lazy man's while to cross the Zapardiel by the pontoon bridge below and head these comedians off upon the highroad.

They promised to repay a closer view.

So I did; gained the road, and, seating myself beside it, hailed them as they came.

"My friend," said I to the leading grenadier, "you are taking a deal of trouble with your prisoner."

The grenadier stared at his comrade, and his comrade at him.

As if by signal they mopped their brows with their coat-sleeves.

The Frenchman sat down on the road without more ado.

"Prisoner?" mumbled the first grenadier.

"Ay," said I.

"Who is he? He doesn't look like a general of brigade."

"Devil take me if I know. Who will he be, Bill?"

Bill stared at the Frenchman blankly, and rooted him out of the dust with his toe.

"I wonder, now! Picked him up, somewheres -- Get up, you

little pig, and carry your liquor like a gentleman. It was Mike intoduced him."

"I did not," said Mike.

"Very well, then, ye did not. I must have come by him some other way."

"It was yourself tripped over him in the cellar, up yandhar."

He broke off and eyed me, meditating a sudden thought.

"It seems mighty queer, that -- speaking of a cellar as 'up yandhar.' Now a cellar, by rights, should be in the ground, under your fut."

"And so it is," argued Bill; "slap in the bowels of it."

"Ah, be quiet wid your bowels!

As I was saying, sor, Bill tripped over the little fellow: and the next I knew he was crying to be tuk home to camp, and Bill swearing to do it if it cost him his stripes. And that is where I come into this fatigue job: for the man's no friend of mine, and will not be looking it, I hope."

"Did I so?" Bill exclaimed, regarding himself suddenly from outside, as it were, and not without admiration.

"Did I promise that? Well, then" -- he fixed a sternly disapproving stare on the Frenchman -- "the Lord knows what possessed me; but to the bridgehead you go, if I fight the whole of Clausel's division single-handed. Take his feet, Mike; I'm a man of my word. Hep! -- ready is it? For'ard!"

For a minute or so, as they staggered down the road, I stared after them; and then upon an impulse mounted the track by which they had descended.

It was easy enough, or they had never come down alive; but the sun's rays smote hotly off the face of the rock, and at one point I narrowly missed being brained by a stone dislodged by some drunkard above me. Already, however, the stream of tipplers had begun to set back towards the camp, and my main difficulty was to steer against it, avoiding disputes as to the rule of the road.

I had no intention of climbing to the castle: my whim was -- and herein again I set my training a test -- to walk straight to the particular opening from which, across the Zapardiel, I had seen my comedians emerge.

I found it, not without difficulty -- a broad archway of rock, so low that a man of ordinary stature must stoop to pass beneath it; with, for threshold, a sill of dry fine earth which sloped up to a ridge immediately beneath the archway, and on the inner side dipped down into darkness so abruptly that as I mounted on the outer side I found myself staring, at a distance of two yards or less, into the face of an old man seated within the cave, out of which his head and shoulders arose into view as if by magic.

"Ah!" said he calmly.

"Good evening, senor. You will find good entertainment within."

He pointed past him into absolute night, or so it seemed to my dazzled eyes.

He spoke in Spanish, which is my native tongue -- although not my ancestral one. And as I crouched to pass the archway I found time to speculate on his business in this cavern. For clearly he had not come hither to drink, and as clearly he had nothing to do with either army. At first glance I took him for a priest; but his bands, if he wore them, were hidden beneath a dark poncho fitting tightly about his throat, and his bald head baffled any search for a tonsure.

Although a small book lay open on his lap, I had interrupted no reading; for when I came upon him his spectacles were perched high over his brows and gleamed upon me like a duplicate pair of eyes.

He was patently sober, too, which perhaps came as the greatest shock of all to me, after meeting so many on my path who were patently the reverse.

I answered his salutation.

The Cellars of Rueda

"But you will pardon me, excellent sir, for saying that you perhaps mistake the entertainment I seek. We gentlemen of Spain are temperate livers, and I will confess that curiosity alone has brought me -- or say, rather, the fame of your wonderful cellars of Rueda."

I put it thus, thinking he might perhaps be some official of the caves or of the castle above. But he let the shot pass.

His lean hands from the first had been fumbling with his poncho, to throw back the folds of it in courtesy to a stranger; but this seemed no easy matter, and at a sign from me he desisted.

"I can promise you," he answered, "nothing more amusing than the group with which you paused to converse just now by the road."

"Eh? You saw me?"

"I was watching from the path outside; for I too can enjoy a timely laugh."

No one, I am bound to say, would have guessed it.

With his long scrag neck and great moons of spectacles, which he had now drawn down, the better to study me, he suggested an absurd combination of the vulture and the owl.

"Dios! You have good eyes, then."

"For long distances. But they cannot see Salamanca."

His gaze wandered for a moment to the entrance beyond which, far below and away, a sunny landscape twinkled, and he sighed.

But before I could read any meaning in the words or the sigh, his spectacles were turned upon me again. "You are Spanish?" he asked abruptly.

"Of Castile, for that matter; though not, I may own to you, of pure descent. I come from Aranjuez, where a Scottish ancestor, whose name I bear, settled and married soon after the War of Succession."

"A Scot?"

He leaned forward, and his hands, which had been resting on his lap, clutched the book nervously.

"Of the Highlands?"

I nodded, wondering at his agitation.

"Even so, senor."

"They say that all Scotsmen in Spain know one another. Tell me, my son" -- he was a priest, then, after all -- "tell me, for the love of God, if you know where to find a certain Manuel McNeill, who, I hear, is a famous scout."

"That, reverend father, is not always easy, as the French would tell you; but for me, here, it happens to be very easy indeed, seeing that I am the unworthy sinner you condescend to compliment."

"You?"

He drew back, incredulous.

"You?" he repeated, thrusting the book into his pocket and groping on the rocky soil beside him. "The finger of God, then, is in this. What have I done with my candle? Ah, here it is. Oblige me by holding it -- so -- while I strike a light." I heard the rattle of a tinder-box.

"They sell these candles" -- here he caught a spark and blew -- "they sell these candles at the castle above. The quality is indifferent and the price excessive; but I wander at night and pick up those which the soldiers drop -- an astonishing number, I can assure you. See, it is lit!"

He stretched out a hand and took the candle from me.

"Be careful of your footsteps, for the floor is rough."

"But, pardon me; before I follow, I have a right to know upon what business."

He turned and peered at me, holding the candle high.

"You are suspicious," he said, almost querulously.

"It goes with my trade."

"I take you to one who will be joyful to see you. Will that suffice, my son?"

"Your description, reverend father, would include many persons -- from the Duke of Ragusa downwards -- whom, nevertheless, I have no desire to meet."

"Well, I will tell you, though I was planning it for a happy surprise. This person is a kinsman of yours -- a Captain Alan McNeill."

I stepped back a pace and eyed him.

"Then," said I, "your story will certainly not suffice; for I know it to be impossible. It was only last April that I took leave of Captain Alan McNeill on the road to Bayonne and close to the frontier. He was then a prisoner under escort, with a letter from Marmont ordering the Governor of Bayonne to clap him in irons and forward him to Paris, where (the Marshal hinted) no harm would be done by shooting him."

"Then he must have escaped."

"Pardon me, that again is impossible; for I should add that he was under some kind of parole."

"A prisoner under escort, in irons -- condemned, or at least intended, to be shot -- and all the while under parole! My friend, that must surely have been a strange kind of parole!"

"It was, and, saving your reverence, a cursed dirty kind. But it sufficed for my kinsman, as I know to my cost. For with the help of the partidas I rescued him, close to the frontier; and he -- like the fool, or like the noble gentleman he was -- declined his salvation, released the escort (which we had overpowered), shook hands with us, and rode forward to his death."

"A brave story."

"You would say so, did you know the whole of it. There is no man alive whose hand I could grasp as proudly as I grasped his at the last: and no other, alive or dead, of whom I could say, with the same conviction, that he made me at once think worse of myself and better of human nature."

"He seems, then, to have a mania for improving his fellow-men; for," said my guide, still pausing with the candle aloft and twinkling on his spectacles, "I assure you he has been trying to make a Lutheran of me!"

Wholly incredulous as I was, this took me fairly between wind and water. "Did he," I stammered, "did he happen to mention the Scarlet Woman?"

"Several times: though (in justice to his delicacy, I must say it) only in his delirium."

"His delirium?"

"He has been ill; almost desperately ill. A case of sunstroke, I believe. Do I understand that you believe sufficiently to follow me?"

"I cannot say that I believe. Yet if it be not Captain Alan McNeill, and if for some purpose which -- to be frank with you -- I cannot guess, I am being walked into a trap, you may take credit to yourself that it has been well, nay excellently, invented. I pay you that compliment beforehand, and for my kinsman's sake, or for the sake of his memory, I accept the risk."

"There is no risk," answered the reverend father, at once leading the way: "none, that is to say, with me to guide you."

"There is risk, then, in some degree?"

"We skirt a labyrinth," he answered quietly. "You will have observed, of course, that no one has passed us or disturbed our talk. To be sure, the archway under which you found me is one of the 'false entrances,' as they are called, of Rueda cellars. There are a dozen between this and the summit, and perhaps half a dozen below, which give easy access to the wine-vaults, and in any of which a crowd of goers and comers would have incommoded us. For the soldiers would seem -- and very wisely, I must allow -- to follow a chart and confine themselves to the easier outskirts of these caves. Wisely, because the few cellars they visit contain Val de Penas enough to keep two armies drunk until either Wellington enters Madrid or Marmont recaptures Salamanca. But they are not adventurous: and the few who dare, though no doubt they penetrate to better wine, are not in the end to be envied.... Now this passage of ours is popularly, but quite erroneously, supposed to lead nowhere, and is therefore by consent avoided."

"Excuse me," said I, "but it was precisely by this exit that I saw emerge three men as honestly drunk as any three I have met in my life."

For the moment he seemed to pay no heed, but stooped and held the candle low before his feet.

"The path, you perceive, here shelves downwards. By following it we should find ourselves, after ten minutes or so, at the end of a cul de sac. But see this narrow ledge to the right -- pay particular heed to your footsteps here, I pray you: it curves to the right, broadening ever so little before it disappears around the corner: yet here lies the true path, and you shall presently own it an excellent one."

He sprang forward like a goat, and turning, again held the candle low that I might plant my feet wisely.

Sure enough, just around the corner the ledge widened at once, and we passed into a new gallery.

"Ah, you were talking of those three drunkards? Well, they must have emerged by following this very path."

"Impossible."

"Excuse me, but for a scout whose fame is acknowledged, you seem fond of a word which Bonaparte (we are told) has banished from the dictionaries. Ask yourself, now. They were assuredly drunk, and your own eyes have assured you there is no wine between us and daylight. My son, I have inhabited Rueda long enough to acquire a faith in miracles, even had I brought none with me. Along this ledge our three drunkards strolled like children out of the very womb of earth. They will never know what they escaped: should the knowledge ever come to them it ought to turn their hair grey then and there."

The Cellars of Rueda

"Children and drunkards," said I.

"You know the byword?"

"And might believe it -- but for much evidence on the other side."

But I was following another thought, and for the moment did not hear him closely.

"I suppose, then, the owners guard the main entrances, but leave such as this, for instance, to be defended by their own difficulty?"

"Why should any be guarded?" he asked, pausing to untie a second candle from the bunch he had suspended from his belt. "Eh? Surely to leave all this wine exposed in a world of thieves -- "

The reverend father smiled as he lit the new candle from the stump of his old one.

"No doubt the wine-growers did not contemplate a visit from two armies, and such very thirsty ones. The peasants hereabouts are abstemious, and the few thieves count for no more than flies. For the rest -- "

He was stooping again, with his candle all but level with the ledge and a few inches wide of it. Held so, it cast a feeble ray into the black void below us: and down there -- thirty feet down perhaps -- as his talk broke in two like a snapped guitar-string, my eyes caught a blur of scarlet.

"For God's sake," I cried, "hold the light steady!"

"To what purpose?" he asked grimly. "That is one whom Providence did not lead out to light. See, he is broken to pieces -- you can tell from the way he lies; and dead, too. My son, the caves of Rueda protect themselves."

He shuffled to the end of the ledge, and there, at the entrance of a dark gallery, so low that our heads almost knocked against the rock-roof, he halted again and leaned his ear against the wall on the right.

"Sometimes where the wall is thin I have heard them crying and beating on it with their fists."

I shivered.

The reader knows me by this time for a man of fair courage: but the bravest man on earth may be caught off his own ground, and I do not mind confessing that here was a situation for which a stout parentage and a pretty severe training had somehow failed to provide. In short, as my guide pushed forward, I followed in knock-knee'd terror. I wanted to run.

I told myself that if this indeed were a trap, and he should turn and rush upon me, I was as a child at his mercy. And he might do worse: he might blow out the light and disappear. As the gallery narrowed and at the same time contracted in height, so that at length we were crawling on hands and knees, this insanity grew. Two or three times I felt for my knife, with an impulse to drive it through his back, seize the candles and escape: nor at this moment can I say what restrained me.

At length, and after crawling for at least two hundred yards, without any warning he stood erect: and this was the worst moment of all. For as he did so the light vanished -- or so nearly as to leave but the feeblest glimmer, the reason being (and I discovered it with a sob) that he stood in an ample vaulted chamber while I was yet beneath the roof of the tunnel.

The first thing I saw on emerging beside him was the belly of a great wine-tun curving out above my head, its recurve hidden, lost somewhere in upper darkness: and the first thing I heard was the whip of a bat's wing by the candle. My guide beat it off.

"Better take a candle and light it from mine. These creatures breed here in thousands -- hear them now above us!"

"But what is that other sound?" I asked, and together we moved towards it. Three enormous tuns stood in the chamber, and we halted by the base of the farthest, where, with a spilt pail beside him, lay a British sergeant of the 36th Regiment tranquilly snoring! That and no other was the sound, and a blesseder I never heard. I could have kicked the fellow awake for the mere pleasure of shaking hands with him.

My guide moved on.

"But we are not going to leave him here!"

"Oh, as for that, his sleep is good for hours to come. If you choose, we can pick him up on our return."

So we left him, and now I went forward with a heart strangely comforted, although on leaving the great cellar I knew myself hopelessly lost. Hitherto I might have turned, and, fortune aiding, have found daylight: but beyond the cellar the galleries ramified by the score, and we walked so rapidly and chose between them with such apparent lack of method that I lost count.

My one consolation was the memory of a burly figure in scarlet supine beneath a wine-tun.

I was thinking of him when, at the end of a passage to me indistinguishable from any of the dozen or so we had already followed, my guide put out a hand, and, drawing aside a goatskin curtain, revealed a small chamber with a lamp hanging from the roof, and under the lamp a bed of straw, and upon the bed an emaciated man, propped and holding a book.

His eyes were on the entrance; for he had heard our footsteps. And almost we broke into one cry of joy.

It was indeed my kinsman, Captain McNeill!

2: Captain McNeill's Adventures

"But how on earth came you here?" was the unspoken question in the eyes of both of us; and, each reading the reflection of his own, we both broke out together into a laugh -- though my kinsman's was all but inaudible -- and after it he lay back on his pillow (an old knapsack) and panted.

"My story must needs be the shorter," said I; "so let us have it over and get it out of the way. I come from watching Caffarelli in the north, and for the last four days have been taking a holiday and twiddling my fingers in camp here, just across the Zapardiel. Happening this afternoon to stroll to this amazing rock, I fell in with the reverend father here, and most incautiously told him my name: since which he has been leading me a dance which may or may not have turned my hair grey."

"The reverend father?" echoed Captain Alan.

"He has not," said I, turning upon my guide, who stood apart with a baffling smile, "as yet done me the honour to reciprocate my weak confidences."

Captain Alan too stared at him.

"Are you a priest, sir?" he demanded.

He was answered by a bow.

"You didn't know it?" cried I. "It's the one thing he has allowed me to discover."

"But I understood that you were a scholar, sir -- "

"The two callings are not incompatible, I hope?"

" -- of the University of Salamanca: a Doctor, too. My memory is yet weak, but surely I had it from your own lips that you were a Doctor?"

" -- of Moral Philosophy," the old man answered with another bow. "Of the College of the Conception -- now, alas! destroyed."

"The care with which you have tended me, sir, has helped my mistake: and now my gratitude for it must help my apologies. I fear I have, from time to time, allowed my tongue to take many liberties with your profession."

"You have, to be sure, been somewhat hard with us."

"My prejudice is an honest one, sir."

"Of that there can be no possible doubt."

"But it must frequently have pained you."

"Not the least in the world," the old Doctor assured him, almost with bonhomie. "Besides, you were suffering from sunstroke."

My kinsman eyed him; and I could have laughed to watch it -- that gaze betrayed a faint expiring hope that, after all, his diatribes against the Scarlet Woman had shaken the Doctor -- upon whom (I need scarcely say) they had produced about as much effect as upon the rock of Rueda itself. And I think that, though regretfully, he must at length have realised this, for he sank back on the pillow again with a gentle weariness in every line of his Don Quixote face.

"Ah, yes, from sunstroke!"

"My cousin" -- here he turned towards me -- "this gentleman -- or, as I must now learn to call him, this most reverend Doctor of Philosophy, Gil Gonsalvez de Covadonga -- found me some days ago stretched unconscious beside the highroad to Tordesillas, and in two ways has saved my life: first, by conveying me to this hiding-place, for the whole terrain was occupied by Marmont's troops, and I lay there in my scarlet tunic, a windfall for the first French patrol that might pass; and, secondly, by nursing me through delirium back to health of mind and strength of body."

"The latter has yet to come, Senor Capitano," the Doctor interposed.

And I: "My cousin, your distaste for disguise will yet be the death of you. But tell me, what were you doing in this neighbourhood?"

"Why, watching Marmont, to be sure, as my orders were."

"Your orders? You don't mean to tell me that Lord Wellington knows of your return!"

"I reported myself to him on the nineteenth of last month in the camp on San Christoval: he gave me my directions that same evening."

"But, Heavens!" I cried, "it is barely a week ago that I returned from the north and had an hour's interview with him; and he never mentioned your name, though aware (as he must be) that no news in the world could give me more joy."

"Is that so, cousin?"

He gazed at me earnestly and wistfully, as I thought.

"You know it is so," I answered, turning my face away that he might not see my emotion.

"As for Lord Wellington's silence," Captain Alan went on, after musing a while, "he has a great capacity for it, as you know; and perhaps he has persuaded himself that we work better apart. Our later performances in and around Sabugal might well excuse that belief."

"But now I suppose you have some message for him. Is it urgent? Or will you satisfy me first how you came here -- you, whom I left a prisoner on the road to Bayonne and, as I desperately thought, to execution?"

"There is no message, for I broke down before my work had well recommenced; and Wellington knows of my illness and my whereabouts, so there is no urgency."

He glanced at the Doctor and so did I.

"The reverend father's behaviour assuredly suggested urgency," I said.

"And was there none?" asked the old man quietly. "You sons of war chase the oldest of human illusions: to you nothing is of moment but the impact of brutal forces or the earthly cunning which arrays and moves them. To me all this is less hateful than contemptible, in moment not comparable with the joy of a single human soul. Believe me, my sons, although the French have destroyed my peerless University -- fortis Salamantina, arx sapientia -- I were less eager to hurry God's avenging hand on them than to bring together two souls which in the pure joy of meeting soar for a moment together, and, fraternising, forget this world. Nay, deny it not: for I saw it, standing by. Least of all be ashamed of it."

The Cellars of Rueda

"I am not sure that I understand you, holy father," I answered. "But you have done us a true service, and shall be rewarded by a confession -- from a stubborn heretic, too."

I glanced at Captain Alan mischievously.

My kinsman put up a hand in protest.

"Oh, I will prepare the way for you," said I: "and by and by you will be astonished to find how easy it comes."

I turned to the Doctor Gonsalvez.

"You must know, then, my father, that the Captain and I, though we follow the same business and with degrees of success we are too amiable to dispute about, yet employ very different methods. He, for instance, scorns disguises, while I pride myself upon mine. And, by the way, as a Professor of Moral Philosophy, you are doubtless used to deciding questions of casuistry?"

"For twenty years, more or less, I have presided at the public disputations in the Sala del Claustro of our University."

"Then perhaps you will resolve me the moral difference between hiding in a truss of hay and hiding under a wig? For, in faith, I can see none."

"That is matter for the private conscience," broke in Captain Alan.

"Pardon me," suggested the Doctor; "you promised me a narrative, I believe."

"We'll proceed, then. Our methods -- this, at least, is important -- were different: which made it the more distressing that the similarity of our names confused us in our enemies' minds, who grossly mistook us for one and the same person: which not only humiliated us as artists but ended in positive inconvenience. At Sabugal, in April last, after a bewildering comedy of errors, the Duke of Ragusa captured my kinsman here, and held him to account for some escapade of mine, of which, as a matter of fact, he had no knowledge whatever. You follow me?"

The Doctor nodded gravely.

"Well, Marmont showed no vindictiveness, but said in effect, 'You have done, sir, much damage to our arms, and without stretching a point I might have you hanged for a spy. I shall, however, treat you leniently, and send you to France into safe keeping, merely exacting your promise that you will not consent to be released by any of the partidas on the journey through Spain.' My cousin might have answered that he had never done an hour's scouting in his life save in the uniform of a British officer, and nothing whatever to deserve the death of a spy. Suspecting, however, that I might be mixed up in the business, he gave his parole and set out for the frontier under the guard of a young cavalry officer and one trooper.

"Meanwhile I had word of his capture: and knowing nothing of this parole, I posted to Lord Wellington, obtained a bond for twelve thousand francs payable for my kinsman's rescue, sought out the guerilla chief, Mina, borrowed two men on Wellington's bond -- the scoundrel would lend no more -- and actually brought off the rescue at Beasain, a few miles on this side of the frontier. One of our shots broke the young officer's sword-arm, the trooper was pitched from his horse and stunned, and behold! my kinsman in our hands, safe and sound.

"It was then, reverend father, that I first heard of his parole. He informed me of it, and while thanking me for my succour, refused to accept it. 'Very well done,' say you as a Doctor of Morality. But meanwhile I was searching the young officer, and finding a letter upon him from the Duke of Ragusa, broke the seal. 'Not so well done,' say you: but again wait a moment. This letter was addressed to the Governor of Bayonne, and gave orders that Captain McNeill, as a spy and a dangerous man, should be forwarded to Paris in irons. There was also a hint that a request for his execution might accompany him to Paris. And this was a prisoner who, on promise of clemency, had given his parole!

Now what, in your opinion, was a fair course for our friend here, on proof of this dirty treachery?"

"We will reserve this as Question Number Two," answered the Doctor gravely, "and proceed with the narrative, which (I opine) goes on to say that Captain McNeill preferred his oath to the excuse for considering it annulled, collected his escort, shook hands with you, and went forward to his fate."

"A man must save his soul," Captain McNeill explained modestly.

"You are to me, sir, a heretic (pardon my saying it); which prevents me from taking as cheerful a view as I could wish concerning your soul. But assuredly you saved your honour."

"Well, I hope so," the Captain answered, picking up the story: "but really, in the sequel, I had to take some decisions which, obvious as they seemed at the time, have since caused me grave searchings of heart, and upon which I shall be grateful for your opinion."

"Am I appealed to as a priest?"

"Most certainly not, but as a Professor -- a title for which, by the way, we have in Scotland an extraordinary reverence. I rode on, sir, with my escort, and that night we reached Tolosa, where the young Lieutenant -- his name was Gerard -- found a surgeon to set his bone. He suffered considerable pain, yet insisted next morning upon proceeding with me. I imagine his motives to have been mixed; but please myself with thinking that a latent desire to serve me made one of them. On the other hand, the seal of Marmont's letter had been broken in his keeping; a serious matter for a young officer, and one which he would naturally desire to defer explaining. At Tolosa he accounted for his wound by some tale of brigands and a chance shot at long range.

"On the morrow we rode to Irun and crossed the Bidassoa. We were now on French soil. Throughout the morning he had spoken little, and I too had preferred my own thoughts. But now, as we broke our fast and cracked a bottle together at the first tavern on the French shore, I opened fire by asking him if he yet carried the Marshal's letter with the broken seal. 'To be sure,' said he.

"'And what will you do with it?' I went on. 'Why, deliver it, I suppose, to the Governor of Bayonne, to whom it is addressed.'

"'And, when asked to account for the broken seal, you will tell him the exact truth about it and the rescue?'

"'I must,' he answered; 'and I hope my report will help you, sir. It will not be my fault if it does not.'

"'You are an excellent fellow,' said I; 'but it will help me little. You do not know the contents of that letter as I do -- not willingly, but because it was read aloud in my presence by the man who opened it.'

"And, before he could remonstrate, I had told him its purport. Now, sir, that was not quite fair to the young man, and I am not sure that it was strictly honourable?"

Captain McNeill paused with a question in his voice."

"Proceed, sir," said the Doctor: "I reserve this as Question Number Three, remarking only that the young man owed you something for having saved his life."

"Just so; and that is where the unfairness came in. He was inexpressibly shocked.

"'Why,' he cried, 'the Marshal had put you under parole!'

"'So far as the frontier,' said I.

"'The promise upon which I swore was that I would not consent to be released by the partidas on my journey through Spain. Once in France, I could not escape his vengeance. Now for this very reason I have a right to interpret my promise strictly, and I consider that during the past half-hour my parole has expired.'

"'I cannot deny it,' he allowed, and took a pace or two up and down the room, then halted in front of me. 'You would suggest, sir, that since this letter was taken from me by the partidas, and you and I alone know that it was restored, I owe you the favour of suppressing it.'

"'Good Heavens! my young friend,' I exclaimed, 'I suggest nothing of the sort. I may ask you to risk for my sake a professional ambition which is very dear to you, but certainly not to imperil your young soul by a falsehood. No, sir, if you will deliver me to the Governor of Bayonne as a prisoner on honourable parole -- which I will renew here and extend to the gates of that city only -- and will then request an interview for the purpose of delivering your letter and explaining how the seal came to be broken, with Joly' -- this was the trooper -- 'for witness, you will gain me all the time I hope to need.'

"'That will be little enough,' objected he.

"'I must make the most of it,' said I; 'and we must manage to time our arrival for the evening, when the Governor will either be supping or at the theatre, that the delay, if possible, may be of his creating.'

"'I owe you more than this,' said the ingenuous youth.

"'And I, sir, am even ashamed of myself for asking so much,' I answered.

"Well, so we contrived it; entered Bayonne at nightfall, presented ourselves at the Citadel, and were, to our inexpressible joy, received by the Deputy-Governor, who heard the Lieutenant's report and endorsed the false paper of parole which Marmont had given me, and which, in fact, had now expired.

"The fatal letter Lieutenant Gerard kept in his pocket, while demanding an interview with the Governor himself. This (he was told) could not be granted until the morning -- 'the Governor was entertaining that night' -- and with a well-feigned reluctance he saluted and withdrew.

"Outside the Deputy's door we parted without a word, and

at the Citadel gate, having shown my pass, which left me free to seek lodgings in the city, I halted, and, under the sentry's nose, dropped a note into the Governor's letter-box.

I had written it at Hendaye, and addressed it to the Duke of Ragusa; and it ran:

> "'MONSIEUR LE MARECHAL, -- I send this under cover of the Governor from the city of Bayonne, out of which I hope to escape to-night, having come so far in obedience to my word, which appears to be more sacred than that of a Marshal of France.
>
> My escort having been overpowered between Vittoria and Tolosa, I declined the rescue offered me, but not before your letter to the Governor had been broken open and its contents read, in my presence.
>
> This letter also I saw restored to its bearer, who during its perusal lay unconscious, of a severe and painful wound in his sword-arm.
>
> I beg to assure you that he has behaved in all respects as a gentleman of courage and honour: and, conceiving that you owe me some reparation, I shall rely on you that his prospects as a soldier are not in any way compromised by the miscarriage of your benevolent plans concerning me.'"

I laughed aloud, and even the Doctor relaxed his features. "Bravo, kinsman!" said I.

"If Marmont hates one thing more than another it's to see his majestic image diminished in the looking-glass. But -- faith! I'd have kept that letter in my pocket until I was many miles south of Bayonne."

"South? You don't suppose I had any intention of escaping towards the Pyrenees? Why, my dear fellow, that's the very direction in which they were bound to search."

The Cellars of Rueda

"Oh, very well," said I -- a trifle nettled, I will confess -- "perhaps you preferred Paris!"

"Precisely," was the cool answer. "I preferred Paris: and having but an hour or two to spare before the hotels closed, I at once inquired at the chief hotels if any French officer were starting that night for the capital. The first-named, if I remember, the Hotel du Sud -- I drew blank. At the second, the Trois Couronnes, I was informed that a chaise and four had been ordered by no less a man than General Souham, who would start that night as soon as he returned from supping with the Governor. I waited: the General arrived a few minutes before ten o'clock: I introduced myself -- "

"General Souham," I groaned. "Reverend father, I have not yet tasted the wine of Rueda: it appears to me that the fumes are strong enough. He tells me he introduced himself to General Souham!"

" -- and, I assure you, found him excellent company. We travelled three in the chaise -- the General, his aide-de-camp, and your fortunate kinsman. A second chaise followed with the General's baggage. He and the aide-de-camp at times beguiled the road with a game of picquet: for myself, I disapprove of cards."

"Doubtless you told them so at an early stage?" I suggested, with a last effort at irony.

"I was obliged to, seeing that the General challenged me to a partie; but I did not, I hope, adopt a tone inconsistent with good fellowship. We travelled through to Paris, with a few hours' break at Orleans -- an opportunity which I seized to purchase a suit of clothes more congruous than my uniform with the part I had to play in Paris. I had ventured to ask General Souham's advice, and he assured me that a British officer, though a prisoner on parole, might incur some risk from the Parisian mob by wearing his uniform in public."

"Cousin," said I, "henceforth pursue your tale without interruption. There was a time when, in my folly, I presumed to criticise your methods. I apologise."

"On leaving the tailor's shop I was accosted by a wretched creature who had seen me alight from the chaise in His Majesty's uniform, and had followed, but did not venture to introduce himself until I emerged in a less compromising garb.

"He was, it appeared, a British agent -- and a traitor to his own country -- and I gathered that a part of his dirty trade lay in assisting British prisoners to break their parole. He assumed that I travelled on parole, and insinuated that I might have occasion to break it: and, with all the will in the world to crack his head, I let the mistake and suspicion pass.

"For a napoleon I received the address of a Parisian agent in the Rue Carcassonne, whose name I will confide in you, in case you should ever require his services. For truly, although I had some difficulty in persuading him that I broke no faith in seeking to escape from France (a point in which self-respect obliged me to insist, though he himself treated it with irritating nonchalance), this agent proved a zealous fellow, and served me well.

"He fell in, too, with my proposals, complimented me on their boldness, and advanced me money to further them. I took a lodging au troisieme in the Faubourg St. Honore, and for a fortnight walked Paris without an attempt at concealment, frequenting the cafes, and spending my evenings atced the theatre.

"Once or twice I encountered Souham himself, with whom I had parted on the friendliest terms: but he did not choose to recognise me -- perhaps he had his good-natured suspicions. I lived unchallenged, though walking all the while on a razor's edge. I had reckoned on two fair chances in my favour.

"There was a chance that the Governor of Bayonne, on finding himself tricked, would for his own security suppress Marmont's letter, trusting that the affair would pass without inquiry: and there was the further chance that Marmont himself, on receipt of my note, would remember the magnanimity which (to do him justice) he usually has at call, and give orders whistling off the pursuit. At any rate, I spent a fortnight in Paris; and no man questioned or troubled me.

"On the same morning that I paid my second weekly bill the agent called on me with a capital plan of escape, which (being a facetious fellow) he announced as follows:

"'I wish you good morning, Mr. Buck,' he began.

"'Sir,' I answered, 'I have no claim to such a designation. My pleasures in Paris have been entirely respectable, and I dislike familiarity.'

"'Mr. Jonathan Buck, I should have said.'

"'Sir,' I corrected him, 'if your clients are so numerous that you confuse their names, I must remind you that mine is McNeill.'

"'Pardon me,' he replied, 'you have this morning inherited that of an American citizen who died suddenly last evening in an obscure lodging near the Barriere de Pantin; and, in addition, a passport now waiting for him at the Foreign Office, if you have the courage to claim it. You resemble the deceased sufficiently to answer a passport's description: and if you secure it, I advise a speedy departure, with Nantes for your objective.' Accordingly, that same evening I left Paris for the Loire."

"You had the coolness to apply for that passport?"

"And the good fortune to obtain it. If anything, my dear fellow, deserves the degree of astonishment your face expresses, it should rather be my consenting to use disguise, and so breaking through a self-denying ordinance on which you have sometimes rallied me. Suspense -- the danger from Bayonne hourly anticipated -- had perhaps shaken my nerves.

"To be brief, I travelled to Nantes as Mr. Jonathan Buck, and in that name took passage in a vessel bound for Philadelphia and on the point (as I understood) of lifting anchor.

"I slept that night on board the Minnie Dwight -- this was the vessel's name -- in full hope that my troubles were at an end. But next morning her captain came to me with a long face and a report that some hitch had occurred between him and the port authorities over his clearing-papers.

"And how long will this detain us?' I asked, cutting short an explanation too technical for my understanding.

"He answered that he had been to his Consul to protest, but could promise nothing short of a week's delay.

"Well, I saw nothing for it but to shut the cabin-door, make a clean breast of my fears, and desire him to help me in devising some new plan. He was a good fellow, and ingenious too; for after he had dashed up my hopes with the news that a similar embargo lay on all foreign ships in the port, his face cleared, and, said he,

"'There's no help for it, but you must play the sea-lawyer and I the brutal tyrant. It's hard, too, upon a man who treats his crew like his own children, and victuals his ship like an eating-house: but a seaman's rig and forty dollars is all you need, and with this you'll fare off to the American Consul's and swear that I've made life a burden to you.'

"'Why forty dollars?' I asked. He winked.

"'That's earnest money that when you reach the United States you'll have the law of me for ill-usage.'

"'And what shall I get in exchange?'

"'You will get a certificate enabling you to pass from port as a discharged sailor seeking a ship.'

"I thanked him warmly, and agreed; climbed down the ship's side in my new rig, waved an affecting farewell to my benevolent tyrant, and sought the American Consul who (it seemed) was used to discontented seamen. At all events, he accepted without suspicion his share in the dishonouring comedy, took my forty dollars, and made out my certificate."

Here the Captain glanced at Doctor Gonsalvez, who blinked.

Said I: "Even a Protestant must sometimes understand the relief of confession."

"Armed with this," he went on, "I made my way to the mouth of the Loire, to St. Nazaire, between which and Le Croisic lies a small island where, in the present weakness of the French marine, English ships of war are suffered to water unmolested. For ten napoleons I bribed an old fisherman to row me out at night to this island, which we reached at daybreak, and to our dismay found the anchorage empty.

"We cast our nets, however, for a blind, and taking a few fish on our way, worked slowly down to the south-west, where my comrade (and a faithful one he proved) had heard reports of an English frigate nosing about the coast. Sure enough, between breakfast and noon we caught sight of her topmasts: but to reach her we must pass in full view and almost within point-blank range of a coast battery.

"We were scarcely abreast of it when a round-shot plumped into the sea ahead of us and brought us to, and almost at once a boatful of soldiers put off to board us. Their object, it turned out, was merely to warn us not to pass the battery, or the chances were five to one that the Englishman would capture us.

"In no way discomposed, my friend maintained that we (he passed me off as his son) must either fish or starve; that we had come a long distance, knew every inch of the coast, and ran no danger. He backed this up by bribing the soldiers with our whole morning's catch, and in the end they contented themselves by insisting that we should wait under the battery until nightfall and so depart. And this we did: but in the meanwhile, pretending our anxiety to avoid her, we cross-questioned the soldiers so precisely on the Englishman's bearings that, when darkness fell and we slipped our anchor, we ran straight down on her without the slightest difficulty.

"She was the Agile sloop of twenty-four guns, and from her deck I waved good-bye to the fisherman, scarcely more delighted by my safety than he by his napoleons, which in my gratitude I had raised to fifteen. The Agile landed me in Plymouth without mishap: and so end my adventures.

"I ought to add, however, that, though my own conscience held no reproach for my trick upon Marmont, I sought and obtained permission from the War Office to select a prisoner of my own rank and exchange him with France; and with him I sent a precise account, which will afford some amusement to the Duke of Ragusa's enemies if he happen to have any at headquarters. You, my cousin, will doubtless consider this mere supererogation, but I should be glad of the reverend Doctor's opinion."

"We will reserve this," said the Doctor, "as Question Number Five."

"And you promptly reshipped for Lisbon, followed the army to Salamanca, and resumed your work?" said I.

"Even so: but I suspect that these adventures have rattled me. I am not the man I was: else I had not succumbed so easily to a mere coup-de-soleil. Will the reverend Doctor complete the narrative by describing how he found me?"

"In a ditch," said the reverend Doctor placidly. "My college was destroyed: my beloved Salamanca in ruins. 'To a philosopher,' said I, 'all the world is a home; but especially such wine-vaults as are found in Rueda.' I saddled, therefore, my mule; loaded her with a very few books and still fewer sticks of furniture; more frugal even than Juvenal's friend Umbricius, cui tota domus redo, componitur una. On my road, and almost under the shadow of this rock, my mule shied in the most ladylike fashion at sight of a redcoat prostrate in the dust. The rest you can guess: but assuredly I did not guess at the time that I had happened on one whose story will -- if ever God restores me to my University -- so illustrate my lectures as to make them appear that which they will not be -- an entirely new set of compositions."

"Well," said I, "the hour is late: and however cheerfully you men of conscience and of casuistry may look forward to spending the night in these caves, I have seen enough, and have enough imagination at the back of it, to desire nothing so little."

"I will escort you," said the Doctor.

"That was implied," I answered: and after shaking hands with my kinsman and promising to visit him on the morrow, I suffered myself to be guided back along the horrible passages.

On the way the Doctor Gonsalvez paused more than once to chuckle, and at each remove I found this indulgence more uncanny.

In the great cellar we came upon the sergeant of the 36th, still slumbering. I stirred him with my foot, and, sitting up, he amicably invited us to join him in a drink. I did so, the Doctor drawing it from the spigot into a pail.

"Might be worse!" hiccupped the sergeant, watching me. I agreed that it might be a great deal worse.

Between us we steered him out, through the tunnel, along the ledge, and so to the archway under which Venus sparkled in the purple heaven. Here the Doctor bade us good-night, and left me to pilot my drunkard down the cliff.

At the foot he shook hands with me in a fervour of tipsy gratitude: and I returned the grasp with an empressement, a passion almost, the exact grounds of which unless he should happen to read these lines and remember the circumstances -- contingencies equally remote -- he will spend his life without surmising.

Rain of Dollars

At nine o'clock or thereabouts in the morning of January 5, 1809, five regiments of British infantry and a troop of horse artillery with six guns were winding their way down the eastern slope of a ravine beyond Nogales, in the fastnesses of Galicia. They formed the reserve of Sir John Moore's army, retreating upon Corunna; and as they slid or skidded down the frozen road in the teeth of a snowstorm, the men of the 28th and 95th Rifles, who made up the rearguard — for the cavalry had been sent forward as being useless for protection in this difficult country — were forced to turn from time to time and silence the fire of the French, close upon their heels and galling them.

A dirty brown trail, trodden and churned by the main army and again frozen hard, gave them the course of the road as it zig-zagged into the ravine; but, even had the snow obliterated the track, the regiments could have found their way by the dead bodies strewing it — bodies of men, of horses, even of women and children — some heaped by the wind's eddies with thick coverlets of white, so that their forms could only be guessed; others half sunk, with a glazing of thin ice over upturned faces and wide-open eyes; others again flung in stiff contortions across the very road — here a man with his fists clenched to his ribs, there a horse on its back with all four legs in air, crooked, and rigid as poles.

The most of these horses had belonged to the dragoons, who, after leading them to the last, had been forced to slaughter them: for the poor brutes cast their shoes on the rough track, and the forage-carts with the cavalry contained neither spare shoes nor nails. The women and children, with sick stragglers and plunder-ers, had made up that horrible, shameful tail-pipe which every retreating army drags in its wake — a crowd to which the reserve had for weeks acted as whippers-in, herding them through Bembibre, Calcabellos, Villa Franca, Nogales; driving them out of wine-shops; shaking, pricking, clubbing them from drunken stupor into panic; pushing them forward through the snow until they collapsed in it to stagger up no more. Strewn between the corpses along the wayside lay broken carts and cartwheels, bundles, knapsacks, muskets, shakos, split boots, kettles, empty wine-flasks — whatever the weaker had dropped and the stronger had found not worth the gleaning.

The regiments lurched by sullenly, savagely. They were red-eyed with want of sleep and weary from an overnight march of thirty-five miles; and they had feasted their fill of these sights. On this side of Herrerias, for example, they had passed a group of three men, a woman, and a child, lying dead in a circle around a broken cask and a frozen pool of rum. And at Nogales they had drained a wine-vat, to discover its drowned owner at the bottom.

They themselves were sick and shaking with abstinence after drunkenness; heavy with shame, too. For though incomparably better behaved than the main body, the reserve had disgraced themselves once or twice, and incurred a stern lesson from Paget, their General. On a low hill before Calcabellos he had halted them, formed them in a hollow square with faces inwards, set up his triangles, and flogged the drunkards collected during the night by the patrols.

Then, turning to two culprits taken in the act of robbing a peaceful Spaniard, he had them brought forward with ropes around their necks and hoisted, under a tree, upon the shoulders of the provost-marshal's men. While the ropes were being knotted to the branches overhead, an officer rode up at a gallop to report that the French were driving in our picquets on the other side of the hill.

"I am sorry for it, Sir," answered Paget; "but though that angle of the square should be attacked, I shall hang these villains in this one." After a minute's silence he asked his men, "If I spare these two, will you promise me to reform?" There was no answer. "If I spare these men, shall I have your word of honour as soldiers that you will reform?" Still the men kept silence, until a few officers whispered them to say "Yes," and at once a shout of "Yes!" broke from every corner of the square. This had been their lesson, and from Calcabellos onward the division had striven to keep its word. But a sullen flame burned in their sick bodies; and when they fought they fought viciously, as men with a score to wipe off and a memory to drown.

A few hours ago they had resembled scarecrows rather than British soldiers; now, having ransacked at Nogales a train of carts full of Spanish boots and clothing — which had been sent thither by mistake and lay abandoned, without mules, muleteers, or guards — they showed a medley of costumes. Some wore grey breeches, others blue; some black boots, others white, others again black and white together; while not a few carried several pairs slung round their necks. Some had wrapped themselves in ponchos, others had replaced the regulation greatcoat with a simple blanket. But, wild crew as they seemed, they swung down the road in good order, kept steady by discipline and the fighting spirit and a present sense of the enemy close at hand.

Ahead of them, on the far side of the ravine, loomed a mountain white from base to summit save where a scarp of sheer cliff had allowed but a powder of snow to cling or, settling in the fissures, to cross-hatch the wrinkles of its forbidding face. A stream, hidden far out of sight by the near wall of the ravine, chattered aloud as it swept around the mountain's base on a sharp curve, rattling the boulders in its bed. During the first part of the descent mists and snow-wreaths concealed even the lip of the chasm through which this noisy water poured; but as the leading regiment neared it, the snowstorm lifted, the clouds parted, and a shaft of wintry sunshine pierced the valley, revealing a bridge of many arches. For the moment it seemed a fairy bridge spanning gulfs of nothingness; next — for it stood aslant to the road — its narrow archways appeared as so many portals, tall and cavernous, admitting to the bowels of the mountain. But beyond it the road resumed its zig-zags, plainly traceable on the snow. The soldiers, as they neared the bridge, grunted their disapproval of these zig-zags beyond it. A few lifted their muskets and took imaginary aim, as much as to say, "That's how the French from here will pick us off as we mount yonder."

The General had been the first to perceive this, and ran his forces briskly across the bridge — his guns first, then his infantry at the double. He found a party of engineers at work on the farther arches, preparing to destroy them as soon as the British were over; but ordered them to desist and make their way out of danger with all speed. For the stream — as a glance told him — was fordable both above and below the bridge, and they were wasting their labour. Moreover, arches of so narrow a span could be easily repaired.

Engineers, therefore, and artillery and infantry together pressed briskly up the exposed gradients, and were halted just beyond musket-shot from the bank opposite, having suffered little on the way from the few French voltigeurs who had arrived in time to fire with effect. Though beyond their range, the British position admirably commanded the bridge and the bridge-head; and Paget, warming to his work and willing to give tit-for-tat after hours of harassment, devised an open insult for his pursuers.

He ordered the guns to be unlimbered and their horses to be led out of sight. Then, regiment by regiment, he sent his division onward — 20th, 52nd, 91st, and Rifles — pausing only at his trusted 28th, whom he proceeded to post with careful inconspicuousness; the light company behind a low fence in flank of the guns and commanding the bridge, the grenadiers about a hundred yards behind them, and the battalion companies yet a little further to the rear. While the 28th thus disposed themselves, the rest of the division moved off, leaving the guns to all appearance abandoned. The General spread his greatcoat, and seating himself on the slope behind the light company, cheerfully helped himself to snuff from the pocket of his buff-leather waistcoat. Meanwhile the sky had been clearing steadily, and the sunshine, at first so feeble, fell on the slope with almost summer warmth. The 28th, under the lee of the mountain-cliffs, looked up and saw white clouds chasing each other across deep gulfs of blue, looked down and saw the noon rays glinting on their enemy's accoutrements beyond the bridge-head. The French were gathering fast, but could not yet make up their minds to assault.

"Our friends," said the General, pouring himself a drink from his pocket-flask, "don't seem in a hurry to add to their artillery."

The men of the light company, standing near him, laughed as they munched their rations. For three days they had plodded through snow and sleet with hot hearts, nursing their Commander-in-Chief's reproof at Calcabellos: "You, 28th, are not the men you used to be. You are no longer the regiment who to a man fought by my side in Egypt!" So Moore had spoken, and ridden off contemptuously, leaving the words to sting. They not only stung, but rankled; for to the war-cry of "Remember Egypt!" the 28th always went into action: and they had been rebuked in the presence of Paget, now their General of Division, but once their Colonel, and the very man under whom they had won their proudest title, "the Backplates." It was Paget who, when once in Egypt the regiment had to meet two simultaneous attacks, in front and rear, had faced his rear rank about and gloriously repulsed both charges.

Rain of Dollars

At the moment of Moore's reproof Paget had said nothing, and he made no allusion to it now. But the 28th understood. They knew why he had posted them alone here, and why he remained to watch. He was giving them a splendid chance, if a forlorn one. In the recovered sunshine their hearts warmed to him.

Unhappily, the French did not seem disposed to walk into the trap. Their fire slackened — from the first it had not been serious — and they loitered by the bridge-end awaiting reinforcements. Yet from time to time they pushed small parties across the fords above and below the bridge; and at length Paget sent a young subaltern up to the crest of the ridge on his flank, to see how many had collected thus on the near side of the stream. The subaltern reported — "Two or three hundred."

By this time the 28th had been posted for an hour or more; time enough to give the main body of the reserve a start of four miles. General Paget consulted his watch, returned it to his fob, and ordered the guns to be horsed again. As the artillerymen led their horses forward, he turned to the infantry, eyed their chap-fallen faces, and composedly took snuff.

"Twenty-eighth, if you don't get fighting enough it's not my fault."

This was all he said, but it went to the men's hearts. "You'll give us another chance, Sir?" answered one or two. He had given them back already some of their old self-esteem, and if they were disappointed of a scrimmage, so was he.

But it would never do, since the French shirked a direct attack, to linger and be turned in flank by the numbers crossing the fords. So, having horsed his guns and sent them forward to overtake the reserve, Paget ordered the 28th to quit their position and resume the march.

No sooner were they in motion than the enemy's leading column began to pour across the bridge; its light companies, falling in with the scattered troops from the fords, pressed down upon the British rear; and the 28th took up once more the Parthian game in which they were growing expert. For three miles along the climbing road they marched, faced about for a skirmish, drove back their pursuers, and marched forward again, always in good order; the enemy being encumbered by its cavalry, which, useless from the first in this rough and wavering track, at length became an impediment and a serious peril. It was by fairly stampeding a troop back upon the foot-soldiers following that the British in the end checked the immediate danger, and, hurrying forward unmolested for a couple of miles, gained a new position in which they could not easily be assailed. The road here wound between a line of cliffs and a precipice giving a sheer drop into the ravine; and here, without need of flankers or, indeed, possibility of using them, the rearmost (light) company, halted for a while and faced about.

This brought their right shoulders round to the precipice, at the foot of which, and close upon three hundred feet below, a narrow plateau (or so it seemed) curved around the rock-face. The French, held at check, and once more declining a frontal attack, detached a body of cavalry and voltigeurs to follow this path in the hope of turning one flank. But a week's snow had smoothed over the true contour of the valley, and this apparent plateau proved to be but a gorge piled to its brim with drifts, in which men and horses plunged and sank until, repenting, they had much ado to extricate themselves.

On the ledge over their heads a young subaltern of the 28th — the same that Paget had sent to count the numbers crossing the fords — was looking down and laughing, when a pompous voice at his elbow inquired —

"Pray, Sir, where is General Paget?"

The subaltern, glancing up quickly, saw, planted on horseback before him, with legs astraddle, a podgy, red-faced man in a blue uniform buttoned to the chin. The General himself

Rain of Dollars

happened to be standing less than five yards away, resting his elbows on the wall of the road while he scanned the valley and the struggling Frenchmen through his glass: and the subaltern, knowing that he must have heard the question, for the moment made no reply.

"Be so good as to answer at once, Sir? Where is General Paget?"

The General closed his glass leisurably and came forward.

"I am General Paget, Sir — at your commands."

"Oh — ah — er, I beg pardon," said the little blue-coated man, slewing about in his saddle. "I am Paymaster-General, and — er — the fact is-------"

"Paymaster-General?" echoed Paget in a soft and musing tone, as if deliberately searching his memory.

"Assistant," the little man corrected.

"Get down from your horse, Sir."

"I beg pardon------"

"Get down from your horse."

The Assistant-Paymaster clambered off. His vanity was wounded and he showed it; the mottles on his face deepened to crimson. "Beg pardon — ceremony — hardly an occasion — treasure of the army in danger."

Paget eyed him calmly, but with a darkening at the corner of the eye; a sign which the watching subaltern knew to be ominous.

"Be a little more explicit, if you please."

"The treasure, Sir, for which I am responsible -----"

"Yes? How much?"

"I am not sure that I ought------"

"How much?"

"If you press the question, Sir, it might be twenty-five thousand pounds. I should not have mentioned it in the hearing of your men-----" he hesitated.

The General concluded his sentence for him. "—Had not your foresight placed it in safety and out of their reach: that's understood. Well, Sir, — what then?"

" But, on the contrary, General, it is in imminent peril! The carts conveying it have stuck fast, not a mile ahead: the bullocks are foundered and cannot proceed; and I have ridden back to request that you supply me with fresh animals."

"Look at me, Sir, and then pray look about you."

"I beg your pardon-------"

"You ought to. Am I a bullock-driver, Sir, or a muleteer? And in this country"— with a sharp wave of his hand—"can I breed full-grown mules or bullocks at a moment's notice to repair your d------d incompetence? Or, knowing me, have you the assurance to tell me coolly that you have lost — yes, lost — the treasure committed to you? — to confess that you, who ought to be a day's march ahead of the main body, are hanging back upon the rearmost company of the rearguard? — and come to me whining when that company is actually engaged with the enemy? Look, Sir" — and it seemed to some of the 28th that their General mischievously prolonged his address to give the Assistant-Paymaster a taste of rearguard work, for Soult's heavy columns were by this time pressing near to the entrance of the defile — "Observe the kind of strife in which we have been engaged since dawn; reflect that our tempers must needs be short; and congratulate yourself that, if this mountain be bare of fresh bullocks, it also fails to supply a handy tree."

The little man waited no longer on the road, along which French bullets were beginning to whistle, but clambered on his horse, and galloped off with hunched shoulders to rejoin his carts.

The rearguard, galled now by musketry and finding that, for all their floundering, the enemy were creeping past the rocky barrier below, retired in good order but briskly, and so, in about twenty minutes, overtook the two treasure-carts and their lines of exhausted cattle. Plainly this procession had come to the end of its powers and could not budge: and as plainly the officers in charge of it were at loggerheads. Paget surveyed the scene, his brow darkening thunderously: for, of the guns he had sent forward to overtake the reserve, two stood planted to protect the carts, and the artillery-captain in charge of them was being harangued by the fuming Assistant-Paymaster, while the actual guard of the treasure — a subaltern's party of the 4th (King's Own) — stood watching the altercation in surly contempt. Now the 28th and the King's Own were old friends, having been brigaded together through the early days of the campaign. As Paget rode forward they exchanged hilarious grins.

"Pray, Sir," he addressed the artilleryman, "why are you loitering here when ordered to overtake the main body with all speed? And what are you discussing with this person?"

"The Colonel, Sir, detached me at this officer's request."

"Hey?" Paget swung round on the Assistant-Paymaster. "You dared to interfere with an order of mine? And, having done so, you forbore to tell me, just now, the extent of your impudence!"

"But — but the bullocks can go no farther!" stammered the poor man.

"And if so, who is responsible? Are you, Sir?" Paget demanded suddenly of the subaltern.

"No, General," the young man answered, saluting. "I beg to say that as far back as Nogales I pointed out the condition of these beasts, and also where in that place fresh animals were to be found: but I was bidden to hold my tongue."

"Do you admit this?" Paget swung round again upon the Assistant-Paymaster.

"Upon my word, Sir," the poor man tried to bluster, "I am

not to be cross-examined in this fashion. I do not belong to the reserve, and I take my orders-----"

"Then what the devil are you doing here? And how is it I catch you ordering my reserve about? By the look of it, a moment ago you were even attempting to teach my horse-artillery its business."

"He was urging me, Sir," said the artillery-captain grimly, "to abandon my guns and hitch my teams on to his carts."

The General's expression changed, and he bent upon the little man in blue a smile that was almost caressing. "I beg your pardon, Sir: it appears that I have quite failed to appreciate you."

"Do not mention it, Sir. You see, with a sum of twenty-five thousand pounds at stake-----"

"And your reputation."

"To be sure, and my reputation; though that, I assure you, was less in my thoughts. With all this at stake-----"

"Say rather 'lost.' I am going to pitch it down the mountain."

"But it is money!" almost screamed the little man.

"So are shot and shells. Twenty-eighth, forward, and help the guard to overturn the carts!"

Even the soldiers were staggered for a moment by this order. Impossible as they saw it to be to save the treasure, they were men; and the instinct of man revolts from pouring twenty-five thousand pounds over a precipice. They approached, unstrapped the tarpaulin covers, and feasted their eyes on stacks of silver Spanish dollars.

"You cannot mean it, Sir! I hold you responsible -----" Speech choked the Assistant-Paymaster, and he waved wild arms in dumbshow.

But the General did mean it. At a word from him the artillerymen stood to their guns, and at another word the fatigue party of the 28th climbed off the carts, put their shoulders to the wheels and axle-trees, and with a heave sent the treasure over in a jingling avalanche. A few ran and craned their necks to mark where it fell: but the cliffs just here were sharply undercut, and everywhere below spread deep drifts to receive and cover it noiselessly. After the first rush and slide no sound came up from the depths into which it had disappeared. The men strained their ears to listen. They were listening still when, with a roar, the two guns behind them spoke out, hurling their salutation into Soult's advance guard as it swung into view around the corner of the road.

2

In a mud-walled hut perched over the brink of the ravine and sheltered there by a shelving rock, an old Gallegan peasant sat huddled over a fire and face to face with starvation. The fire, banked in the centre of the earthen floor, filled all the cabin with smoke, which escaped only by a gap in the thatch and a window-hole overlooking the ravine. An iron crock, on a chain furred with soot, hung from the rafters, where sooty cobwebs, a foot and more in length, waved noiselessly in the draught. It was empty, but he had no strength to lift it off its hook; and at the risk of cracking it he had piled up the logs on the hearth, for the cold searched his old bones. The windowhole showed a patch of fading day, wintry and sullen: but no beam of it penetrated within, where the firelight flickered murkily on three beds of dirty straw, a table like a butcher's block, and, at the back of the hut, an alcove occupied by three sooty dolls beneath a crucifix — the Virgin, St. Joseph, and St. James.

The alcove was just a recess scooped out of the adobe wall: and the old man himself could not have told why his house had been built of unbaked mud when so much loose stone lay strewn about the mountain-side ready to hand. Possibly even his ancestors, who had built it, could not have told. They had come from the plain-land near Zamora, and built in the only fashion they knew — a fashion which their ancestors had learnt from the Moors: but time and the mountain's bad habit of dropping stones had taught them to add a stout roof. For generations they had clung to this perch, and held body and soul together by the swine-herding. They pastured their pigs three miles below, where the ravine opened upon a valley moderately fertile and wooded with oak and chestnut; and in midwinter drove them back to the hill and styed them in a large pen beside the hut, in which, if the pen were crowded, they made room for the residue.

The family now consisted of the old man, Gil Chaleco (a widower and past work); his son Gil the Younger, with a wife, Juana; their only daughter, Mercedes, her young husband, Sebastian May, and their two-year-old boy. The two women worked with the men in herding the swine and were given sole charge of them annually, when Gil the Younger and Sebastian tramped it down to the plains and hired themselves out for the harvest.

But this year Sebastian, instead of harvesting, had departed for Corunna to join the insurrectionary bands and carry a gun in defence of his country. To Gil the Elder this was a piece of youthful folly. How could it matter, in this valley of theirs, what King reigned in far-away Madrid? And would a Spaniard any more than a Corsican make good the lost harvest-money?

The rest of the family had joined him in raising objections; for in this den of poverty the three elders thought of money morning, noon, and night, and of nothing but money; and Mercedes was young and in love with her husband, and sorely unwilling to lend him to the wars. Sebastian, however, had smiled and kissed her and gone his way; and at the end of his soldiery had found himself, poor lad, in hospital in Leon, one of the many hundreds abandoned by the Marquis of Romana to the French.

News of this had not reached the valley, where indeed his wife's family had other trouble to concern them: for a forage party from the retreating British main guard had descended upon the cabin four days ago and carried off all the swine, leaving in exchange some scraps of paper, which (they said) would be honoured next day by the Assistant-Paymaster: he could not be more than a day's march behind. But a day had passed, and another, and now the household had gone off to Nogales to meet him on the road, leaving only the old man, and taking even little Sebastianillo. The pigs would be paid for handsomely by the rich English; Juana had some purchases to make in the town; and Mercedes needed to buy a shawl for the child, and thought it would be a treat for him to see the tall foreign redcoats marching past.

So they had started, leaving the old man with a day's provision (for the foragers had cleared the racks and the larder as well as the sty), and promising to be home before nightfall. But two days and a night had passed without news of them.

With his failing strength he had made shift to keep the fire alight; but food was not to be found. He had eaten his last hard crust of millet-bread seven or eight hours before, and this had been his only breakfast. His terror for the fate of the family was not acute. Old age had dulled his faculties, and he dozed by the fire with sudden starts of wakefulness, blinking his smoke-sored eyes and gazing with a vague sense of evil on the straw beds and the image in the alcove. His thoughts ran on the swine and the price to be paid for them by the Englishman: they faded into dreams wherein the family saints stepped down from their shrine and chaffered with the foreign paymaster; dreams in which he found himself grasping silver dollars with both hands. And all the while he was hungry to the point of dying; yet the visionary dollars brought no food — suggested only the impulse to bury them out of sight of thieves.

So vivid was the dream that, waking with a start and a shiver, he hobbled towards the window-hole and stopped to pick up the wooden shutter that should close it. Standing so, still half asleep, with his hand on the shutter-bar, he heard a rushing sound behind him, as though the mountain-side were breaking away overhead and rushing down upon the roof and back of the cabin.

He had spent all his life on these slopes and knew the sounds of avalanche and land-slips — small land-slips in this Gallegan valley were common enough. This noise resembled both, yet resembled neither, and withal was so terrifying that he swung round to face it, aquake in his shoes — to see the rear wall bowing inwards and crumbling, and the roof quietly subsiding upon it, as if to bury him alive.

For a moment he saw it as the mirror of his dream, cracking and splitting; then, as the image of the Virgin tilted itself forward from its shrine and fell with a crash, he dropped the shutter, and running to the door, tugged at its heavy wooden bolt. The hut was collapsing, and he must escape into the open air.

He neither screamed nor shouted, for his terror throttled him; and after the first rushing noise the wall bowed inwards silently, with but a trickle of dry and loosened mud. His gaze, cast back across his shoulder, was on it while he tugged at the bolt. Slowly — very slowly, the roof sank, and stayed itself, held up on either hand by its two corner-props. Then, while it came to a standstill, sagging between them, the wall beneath it burst asunder, St. Joseph and St. James were flung head-over-heels after the Virgin, and through the rent poured a broad river of silver.

He faced around gradually, holding his breath. His back was to the door now, and he leaned against it with outspread palms while his eyes devoured the miracle.

Dollars! Silver dollars!

He could not lift his gaze from them. If he did, they would

surely vanish, and he awake from his dream. Yet in the very shock of awe, and starving though he was, the master-habit of his life, the secretive peasant cunning, had already begun to work. Never once relaxing his fixed stare, fearful even of blinking with his smoke-sored eyes, he shuffled sideways toward the window-hole, his hands groping the wall behind him. The wooden shutter and its fastening bar — a short oak pole — lay where he had dropped them, on the floor beneath the window. He crouched, feeling backwards for them; found, lifted them on to the inner ledge, and, with a half-turn of his body, thrust one arm deep into the recess and jammed the shutter into its place. To fix the bolt was less easy; it fitted across the back of the shutter, its ends resting in two sockets pierced in the wall of the recess. He could use but one hand; yet in less than a minute he found the first socket, slid an end of the bolt into it as far as it would go, lifted the other end and scraped with it along the opposite side of the recess until it dropped into the second socket. He was safe now — safe from prying eyes. In all this while — these two, perhaps three, minutes — his uppermost terror had been lest strange eyes were peering in through the window-hole: it had cost him anguish not to remove his own for an instant from the miracle to assure himself. But he had shut out this terror now: and the miracle had not vanished.

A few coins trickled yet. He crawled forward across the floor, crouching like a beast for a spring. But as he drew close his old legs began to shake under him. He dropped on his knees and fell forward, plunging both hands into the bright pile.

Dollars! Real silver dollars!

He lay on the flood of wealth, stretched like a swimmer, his fingers feebly moving among the coins which slid and poured over the back of his hands. He did not ask how the miracle had befallen. He was starving? dying in fact, though he did not know it; and lo! he had found a heaven beyond all imagination, and lay in it and panted, at rest. The firelight played on the heave and fall of his gaunt shoulder-blades, and on the glass eyes of the Virgin, whose head had rolled half-way across the floor and lay staring up foolishly at the rafters.

★ ★ ★ ★ ★ ★

"Mother, open! Ah, open quickly, mother, for the love of God!"

Whose voice was that? Yes, yes — Mercedes', to be sure, his granddaughter's. She had gone to Nogales . . . long ago . . . Yet that was her voice. Had he come, then, to Paradise that her voice was pleading for him — pleading for the door to open?

"Mother —Father! It is I, Mercedes! Open quickly — It is Mercedes, do you hear? I want my child — Sebastianillo — my child — quick!"

The voice broke into short agonised cries, into sobs. The door rattled.

At the sound of this last the old man raised himself on his knees. His eyes fell again on the shining dollars all around him. His throat worked.

Suddenly terror broke out in beads on his forehead. Someone was shaking the door! Thieves were there trying the door: they were come to rob him!

He drew himself up slowly. As he did so the door ceased to rattle, and presently, somewhere near the windy edge of the ravine, a faint cry sounded.

But long after the door had ceased to rattle, old Gil Chaleco stared at it, fascinated. And long after the cry had died away it beat from side to side within the walls of his head, while he listened and life trickled from him, drop by drop.

"Thou shalt not be afraid for the terror by night." But he was listening for it: it would come again. . . .

And it came — with a rough summons on the door, and, a moment later, with a thunderous blow. The old man stood up, knee-deep in dollars, lifting both arms to cover his head. As the door fell he seemed to bow himself toward it, toppled, and slid forward — still with his arms crooked — amid a rush of silver.

3

Although crushed in the rear and broken inwards there, the hut showed its ordinary face to the path as Mercedes reached it in the failing daylight. She ran like a madwoman, and with short, distraught cries, as she neared her home. Her eyes were wild as a hunted creature's, her coarse black hair streamed over her shoulders, her bare feet bled where the rocks and ice had cut them. But one thing she did not doubt — would not allow herself to doubt — that at home she would find her child. For two days she had been parted from him, and in those two days . . . God had been good to her, very good: but she could not thank God yet — not until she clutched Sebastianillo in her arms, held his small, wriggling body, felt his feet kick against her breast. . . .

The great sty beside the cabin was empty, of course: and the cabin itself looked strange to her and desolate and unfriendly. For some hours the snow had ceased falling, and, save in a snowstorm or a gale, it was not the family custom to close door or window before dark: indeed, the window-hole usually stood open night and day the year round. Now both were closed. But warm firelight showed under the chink of the door; and on the door she bowed her head, to take breath, and beat with her hands while she called urgently —

"Mother! Quickly, mother —open to me for the love of God!"

No answer came from within.

"Mother! Father! Open to me — it is I, Mercedes!"

Then, after listening a moment, she began to beat again, frantically, for at length she was afraid.

"Quick! Quick! Ah, do not be playing a trick on me: I want my child — Sebastianillo!"

Again and again she called and beat. No answer came from the hut or from the sombre twilight around her. She drew back, to fling her full weight against the door. And at this moment she heard, some way down the path, a man's footstep crunching the snow.

She never doubted that this must be her father returning up the mountain-side, perhaps after a search for her. What other man — now that her husband had gone soldiering — ever trod this path? She ran down to meet him.

The path, about forty yards below, rounded an angle of the sheer cliff, and at this angle she came to a terrified halt. The man, too, had halted a short gunshot away. He did not see her, but was staring upward at the cliff overhead; and he was not her father. For an instant there flashed across her brain an incredible surmise — that he was her husband, Sebastian: for he wore a soldier's overcoat and shako, and carried a musket and knapsack. But no: this man was taller than Sebastian by many inches; taller and thinner.

He was a soldier, then: and to Mercedes all soldiers were by this time incarnate devils — or all but one, and that one a plucky little British officer who had snatched her from his men just as she fell swooning into their clutches, and had dragged and thrust her through the convent doorway at Nogales and slammed the door upon her; and (though this she did not know) held the doorstep, sword in hand, while the Fathers within shot the heavy bolts.

The British had gone, and after them — close after — came the French: and these broke down the convent door and ransacked the place. But the Fathers had hidden her and a score or so more of trembling women, nor would allow her to creep out and search for Sebastianillo in the streets through which swept, hour after hour, a flood of drunken yelling devils. So now Mercedes, who had left home two days ago to watch an army pass, turned from this one soldier with a scream and ran back towards the cabin.

In her terror lest he should overtake and catch her by the closed door, she darted aside, clambered across the wall of the empty sty, and crouched behind it in the filth, clutching at her bodice: for within her bodice was a knife, which she had borrowed of the Fathers at Nogales.

The footsteps came up the path and went slowly past her hiding-place. Then they came to a halt before the hut. Still Mercedes crouched, not daring to lift her head.

Rat, rat-a-tat!

Well, let him knock. Her father was a strong man, and always kept a loaded gun on the shelf. If this soldier meant mischief, he would find his match: and she, too, could help.

She heard him call to the folks within once or twice in bad Spanish. Then his voice changed and seemed to threaten in a language she did not know.

Her hand was thrust within her bodice now, and gripped the handle of her knife; nevertheless, what followed took her by surprise, though ready for action. A terrific bang sounded on the timbers of the door. Involuntarily she raised her head above the wall's coping. The man had stepped back a pace into the path, and was swinging his musket up for another blow with the butt.

She stood up, white, with her jaw set. Her father could not be inside the hut, or he would have answered that blow on his door as a man should. But Sebastianillo might be within —-nay, must be! She put her hands to the wall's coping and swung herself over and on to the path, again unseen, for the dusk hid her, and a dark background of cliff behind the sty: nor could the man hear, for he was raining blow after blow upon the door. At length, having shaken it loose from its hasp, he stepped back and made a run at it, using the butt of his musket for a ram, and finishing up the charge with the full weight of one shoulder. The door crashed open before him, and he reeled over it into the hut. A second later, Mercedes had sprung after him.

"Sebastianillo! You shall not harm him! You shall not-----"

The door, falling a little short of the fire, had scattered some of the buring brands about the floor and fanned the rest into a blaze. In the light of it he faced round with a snarl, his teeth showing beneath his moustache. The light also showed — though Mercedes neither noted it nor could have read its signification — a corporal's chevron on his sleeve.

"Who the devil are you?" The snarl ended in a snap.

Mercedes stood swaying on the threshold, knife in hand.

"You shall not harm him!"

She spoke in her own tongue and he understood it, after a fashion; for he answered in broken Spanish, catching up her word —

"Harm? Who means any harm? When a man is perishing with hunger and folks will not open to him-----"

He paused, wondering at her gaze. Travelling past him, it had fastened itself on the back wall of the hut, across the fire. "Hullo! What's the matter?" He swung round. "Good Lord!" said he, with a gulp.

He sprang past the fire and stooped over the old man's body, which lay face downward on the shelving heap of silver. It did not stir. By-and-by he took it by one of the rigid arms and turned it over, not roughly.

"Warm," said he: "warm, but dead as a herring! Come and see for yourself."

Mercedes did not move. Her eyes sought the dark corners of the cabin, fixed themselves for a moment on the shattered image of the Virgin, and met his across the firelight in desperate inquiry.

"What is this? What have you done?"

"Done? I tell you I never touched the man; never saw him before in my life. Who is he? Your father? No: grandfather, more like. Eh? Am I right?"

She bent her head, staring at the money.

"This? This is dollars, my girl: dollars enough to set a man up for life, with a coach and lads in livery, and dress you in diamonds from head to heel. Don't stand playing with that knife. I tell you I never touched the old man. What's more, I'm willing to be friendly and go shares." He stared at her with quick suspicion. "You're alone here, hey?"

She did not answer.

"But answer me," he insisted, "do you live alone with him?" And he pointed to the body at his feet.

"There was my mother," said Mercedes slowly, in her turn pointing to the third bed of straw by the fire. "We journeyed over to Nogales, she and I. Your soldiers came and took away our pigs, giving us pieces of paper for them. They said that if we took these to Nogales someone would pay us: so we started, leaving him. And at Nogales your men were rough and parted us, and I have not seen her since."

The Corporal eyed her with the beginnings of a leer. She faced him with steady eyes. "Well, well," said he, after a pause, "I mean no harm to you, anyway. Lord! but you're in luck. Here you reach home and find a fortune at your door — a sort of fortune a man can dig into with a spade; while a poor devil like me——" He paused again and stood considering.

"You knew about this?" She nodded towards the dollars. "You knew how it came here, and you came after it?"

"I did and I didn't. I knew 'twas somewhere hereabouts; but strike me, if a man could dream of finding it like this!"

"Yet you came to this door and beat it open!"

"You've wits, my girl," said the Corporal admiringly; "but

they are on the wrong tack. I mean no harm; and the best proof is that here I'm standing with a loaded musket and not offering to hurt you. As it happens, I came to the door asking a bite of bread. I'm cruel hungry."

Mercedes pulled a crust of millet-bread from her pocket. The Fathers at the convent had given it to her at parting, but she had forgotten to eat. She stepped forward; the Corporal stretched out a hand.

"No," said she, and, avoiding him, laid the crust on the block-table. He caught it up and gnawed it ravenously. "I think there is no other food in the house."

"You don't get rid of me like that." He ran a hand along the shelves, searching them. "Hullo! a gun?" He took it down and examined it beside the fire, while Mercedes' heart sank. She had hoped to possess herself of it, snatching it from the shelf when he should be off his guard. "Loaded, too!" He laid it gently on the block and eyed her, munching his crust.

"You'd best put down that knife and talk friendly," said he at length. "What's the use? — you a woman, and me with two guns, both loaded? It's silliness; you must see for yourself it is. Now look here: I've a notion — a splendid notion. Come sit down alongside of me, and talk it over. I promise you there's no harm meant."

But she had backed to her former position in the doorway and would not budge.

"It's treating me suspicious, you are," he grumbled: "hard and suspicious."

"Cannot you take the money and go?" she begged, breathing hard, speaking scarcely above a whisper.

"No, I can't: it stands to reason I can't. What can I do in a country like this with dollars it took two carts to drag here — two carts with six yoke of bullocks apiece? And that's where my cruel luck comes in. All I can take, as things are, is just so much as this knapsack will carry: and even for this I've run some risks."

The man — it was the effect of hunger, perhaps, and exposure and drunkenness on past marches — had an ugly, wolfish face; but his eyes, though cunning, were not altogether evil, not quite formidably evil. She divined that, though lust for the money was driving him, some weakness lay behind it.

"You are a deserter," she said.

"We'll pass that." He seated himself, flinging a leg over the block and laying the two guns side by side on his knees. "I can win back, maybe. As things go, between stragglers and deserters it's hard to choose in these times, and I'll get the benefit of the doubt. I've taken some risks," he repeated, glancing from the guns on his knees to the pile of silver and back: "pretty bad risks, and only to fill my knapsack. But, now it strikes me----- Can't you come closer?"

But she held her ground and waited.

"It strikes me, why couldn't we collar the whole of this, we two? We're alone: no one knows; I've but to lift one of these" — he tapped the guns — "and where would you be? But I don't do it. I don't want to do it. You hear me?"

"You don't do it," said Mercedes slowly, "because without me you can't get away with more than a handful of this money. And you want the whole of it."

"You're a clever girl. Yes, I want the whole of it. Who wouldn't? And you can help. Can't you see how?"

"No."

He sat swinging his legs. "Well, that's where my notion comes in. I wish you'd drop that knife and be friendly: it's a fortune I'm offering you. Now my notion is that we two ought to marry." He stood up.

Mercedes lifted the knife with its point turned inward against her breast. "If you take another step!"

"Oh, but look here: look at it every way. I like you. You're a fine build of a woman, with plenty of spirit — the very woman to help a man. We should get along famously. One country's as good as another to me: I'm tired of soldiering, and there's no woman at home, s' help me!" He was speaking rapidly now, not waiting to cast about for words in Spanish, but falling back on English whenever he found himself at a loss. "I dare say you can fit me out with a suit of clothes." His glance ran round the hut and rested on the body of the old man.

Mercedes had understood scarce half of his words: but she divined the meaning of that look and shuddered.

"No, no; you cannot do that!"

"Hark!" said he raising his head and listening. "What's that noise?"

"The wolves. We hear them every night in winter."

"A nice sort of place for a woman to live alone in! See here, my dear; it's sense I'm talking. Better fix it up with me and say 'yes.'"

She appeared to be considering this. "One thing you must promise."

"Well?"

"You won't touch him" — she nodded towards her grandfather's corpse. "You won't touch him to — to------"

"Is it strip him you mean? Very well, then, I won't."

"You will help me to bury him? He cannot lie here. I can give you no answer while he lies here."

"Right you are, again. Only, no tricks, mind!"

He stowed the guns under his left arm and gripped the collar of the old man. Mercedes took the feet; and together they bore him out — a light burden enough. Outside the hut a pale radiance lay over all the snow, forerunner of the moon now rising over the crags across the ravine.

"Where?" grunted the Corporal.

Mercedes guided him. A little way down the path, beyond

Rain of Dollars

the wall of the sty, they came to a recess in the base of the cliff where the wind's eddies had piled a smooth mound of snow. Here, under a jutting rock, they laid the body.

"Cover him as best you can," the Corporal ordered. "My hands are full."

He stood, clasping his guns, and watched Mercedes while she knelt and shovelled the snow with both hands. Yet always her eyes were alert and she kept her knife ready. From their mound they looked down upon the ravine in front and over the wall of the sty towards the cabin. Behind them rose the black cliff.

"Hark to the wolves!" said the Corporal, listening: and at that moment something thudded down from the cliff, striking the snow a few yards from him; rolled heavily down the slope and came to a standstill against the wall of the sty, where it lay bedded.

The round moon had risen over the ravine, and was flooding the mound with light. The Corporal stared at Mercedes: for the moment he could think of nothing but that a large, loose stone had dropped from the cliff. He ran to the thing and turned it over.

It was a knapsack.

He did not at once understand, but stepped back a few paces and gazed up at the crags mounting tier by tier into the vague moonlight. And while he gazed a lighter object struck the wall over head, glanced from it, went spinning by him, and disappeared over the edge of the ravine. As it passed he recognized it — a soldier's shako.

Then he understood. Someone had found the spot on the road above where the treasure had been upset, and these things were being dropped to guide his search. The Corporal ran to Mercedes and would have clutched her by the wrist. The knife flashed in her hand as she evaded him.

Rain of Dollars

"Quick, my girl — back with you, quick! They're after the money, I tell you!"

He caught up the knapsack. They ran back together and flung themselves into the cabin. The Corporal bolted the door.

"King's Own," he announced, having dragged the knapsack to the firelight. "If there's only one, we'll do for him."

He stepped to the window-hole, pulled open the shutter, laid the two guns on the ledge, and waited, straining his ears.

"Got such a thing as a shovel or a mattock?" he asked after a while. "I reckon you could make shift to cover up the dollars: there's a deal of loose earth come down with them."

It took her some time to guess what he wanted, for he spoke in a hoarse whisper. He listened again for a while, then pointed to the treasure.

"Cover it up. If there's more than one, we'll have trouble."

She produced a mattock from a corner of the cabin and began, through the broken wall, to rake down mud and earth and cover the coins. For an hour and more she worked, the Corporal still keeping watch. Once or twice he growled at her to make less noise.

He did not stand the suspense well, but after the first hour grew visibly uneasy.

"I've a mind to give this over," he grumbled, and fell to unstrapping his knapsack. "Here!" — he tossed it to her — "pack it, full as you can. Half a loaf may turn out better than no bread."

She laid the knapsack open on the floor and set to work, cramming it with dollars.

"Talking of bread," he went on by-and-by, "that's going to be a question. My stomach's feeling at this moment like as if it had two rows of teeth inside."

"Hist!" Mercedes rose, finger to lip. He turned again to the window-hole and peered out, gun in hand, his shoulder blocking the recess.

A man's footsteps were coming up the path — coming cautiously. Their crunch upon the snow was just audible, and no more. Mercedes stole towards the window and crept close behind the Corporal's back; stood there, holding her breath.

The man on the path halted for a moment, and came on again, still cautiously.... There was a jet of flame, a roar; and the Corporal, after the kick of his musket, strained himself forward on the window-ledge to see if his shot had told.

"Settled him!" he announced, drawing back and turning to face her with a triumphant grin.

But Mercedes confronted him with her father's fowling-piece in hand. She had slipped it off the window-ledge from under his elbow as he leaned forward.

"Unbar the door!" she commanded.

"Look here, no nonsense!"

"Unbar the door!" She believed him to be a coward, and he was.

"You just wait a bit, my lady!" he threatened, but drew the bolt, nevertheless; when he turned, the muzzle of the fowling-piece still covered him.

She nodded toward the knapsack. "Pick up that, if you will - now turn your back - your back to me, if you please - and go."

He hesitated, rebellious: but there was no help for it.

"Go!" she repeated. And he went.

Above the cabin the path ended almost at once in a cul de sac — a wall of frowning cliff. There was no way for him, whether he wished to descend or climb the mountain, but that which led him past the body of the man he had just murdered. He went past it tottering, fumbling with the straps of his knapsack: and Mercedes stood in the moonlit doorway and watched him out of sight.

By-and-by she seated herself before the threshold, and, laying the gun across her knees, prepared herself to wait for the dawn. The dead man lay huddled on his side, a few paces from her. Overhead, along the waste mountain heights, the wolves howled.

Hours passed. Still the wolves howled, and once from the upper darkness Mercedes heard, or fancied that she heard, a scream.

At noon, next day, two men — a priest and a young peasant — were climbing the mountain-path leading to the hut. The young man carried on his shoulder a two-year-old child; and, because the sun shone and the crisp air put a spirit of life into all things untroubled by thought, the child crowed and tugged gleefully at his father's berret. But his father paid no heed, and strode forward at a pace which forced the priest (who was stout) now and again into a run.

"She will not be there," he kept repeating, steeling himself against the worst. "She cannot be there. When she missed her child------"

"She is waiting on her grandfather, belike," urged the priest. "They left him with one day's food: so she told the Brothers. And they, like fools, let her go with just sufficient for her own needs. Yet I ought not to blame them for losing their heads in so small a matter. They saved many women."

He told again how he — the parish priest of Nogales — had found Gil the Younger and his wife dead and drunken, with their heads in a gutter and the child wailing in the mud beside them. "Your wife had given her mother the child to guard but a minute before she fell in with the soldiers. A young officer saved her, the Brothers said."

"Mercedes will have sought her child first," persisted Sebastian; and rounding the corner of the cliff, they came in sight of the hut and of her whom they sought.

She sat in the path before it, still with the fowling-piece across her knees. But to reach her they had to pass the body of a soldier lying with clenched hands in a crimson patch of snow. The child, who had passed by many horrors on the road, and all with gay unconcern, stretched out his arms across this one, recognising his mother at once, and kicking in his father's clasp.

She raised her eyes dully. She was too weak even to move. "I knew you would come," she said in a whisper; and with that her eyes shifted and settled on the body in the path.

"Take him away! I — I did not kill him."

Her husband set down the child. "Run indoors, little one: you shall kiss mamma presently."

He bent over her, and, unstringing a small wine-skin from his belt, held the mouth of it to her lips. The priest stooped over the dead man, on whose collar the figures "28" twinkled in the sunlight. The child, for a moment rebellious, toddled towards the doorway of the hut.

Mercedes' eyelids had closed: but some of the wine found its way down her throat, and as it revived her, they flickered again.

"Sebastian," she whispered.

"Be at rest, dear wife. It is I, Sebastian."

"I did not kill him."

"I hear. You did not kill him."

"The child?"

"He is safe — safe and sound," he assured her, and called, "Sebastianillo!"

For a moment there was no answer: but as he lifted Mercedes and carried her into the hut, on its threshold the boy met them, his both hands dropping silver dollars.

The Laird's Luck

[In a General Order issued from the Horse-Guards on New Year's Day, 1836, His Majesty, King William IV., was pleased to direct, through the Commander-in-Chief, Lord Hill, that "with the view of doing the fullest justice to Regiments, as well as to Individuals who had distinguished themselves in action against the enemy," an account of the services of every Regiment in the British Army should be published, under the supervision of the Adjutant General.

With fair promptitude this scheme was put in hand, under the editorship of Mr. Richard Cannon, Principal Clerk of the Adjutant General's Office. The duty of examining, sifting, and preparing the records of that distinguished Regiment which I shall here call the Moray Highlanders (concealing its real name for reasons which the narrative will make apparent) fell to a certain Major Reginald Sparkes; who in the course of his researches came upon a number of pages in manuscript sealed under one cover and docketed "Memoranda concerning Ensign D.M.J. Mackenzie. J.R., Jan. 3rd, 1816" -- the initials being those of Lieut.-Colonel Sir James Ross, who had commanded the 2nd Battalion of the Morays through the campaign of Waterloo. The cover also bore, in the same handwriting, the word "Private," twice underlined.

Of the occurrences related in the enclosed papers -- of the private ones, that is -- it so happened that of the four eye-witnesses none survived at the date of Major Sparkes' discovery. They had, moreover, so carefully taken their secret with them that the Regiment preserved not a rumour of it. Major Sparkes' own commission was considerably more recent than the Waterloo year, and he at least had heard no whisper of the story. It lay outside the purpose of his inquiry, and he judiciously omitted it from his report. But the time is past when its publication might conceivably have been injurious; and with some alterations in the names -- to carry out the disguise of the Regiment -- it is here given. The reader will understand that I use the *ipsissima verba* of Colonel Ross. Q.]

1

I had the honour of commanding my Regiment, the Moray Highlanders, on the 16th of June, 1815, when the late Ensign David Marie Joseph Mackenzie met his end in the bloody struggle of Quatre Bras (his first engagement). He fell beside the colours, and I gladly bear witness that he had not only borne himself with extreme gallantry, but maintained, under circumstances of severest trial, a coolness which might well have rewarded me for my help in procuring the lad's commission. And yet at the moment I could scarcely regret his death, for he went into action under a suspicion so dishonouring that, had it been proved, no amount of gallantry could have restored him to the respect of his fellows. So at least I believed, with three of his brother officers who shared the secret. These were Major William Ross (my half-brother), Captain Malcolm Murray, and Mr. Ronald Braintree Urquhart, then our senior ensign. Of these, Mr. Urquhart fell two days later, at Waterloo, while steadying his men to face that heroic shock in which Pack's skeleton regiments were enveloped yet not overwhelmed by four brigades of the French infantry. From the others I received at the time a promise that the accusation against young Mackenzie should be wiped off the slate by his death, and the affair kept secret between us. Since then, however, there has come to me an explanation which -- though hard indeed to credit -- may, if true, exculpate the lad. I laid it before the others, and they agreed that if, in spite of precautions, the affair should ever come to light, the explanation ought also in justice to be forthcoming; and hence I am writing this memorandum.

It was in the late September of 1814 that I first made acquaintance with David Mackenzie. A wound received in the battle of Salamanca -- a shattered ankle -- had sent me home invalided, and on my partial recovery I was appointed to command the 2nd Battalion of my Regiment, then being formed at Inverness. To this duty I was equal; but my ankle still gave trouble (the splinters from time to time working through the flesh), and in the late summer of 1814 I obtained leave of absence with my step-brother, and spent some pleasant weeks in cruising and fishing about the Moray Firth. Finding that my leg bettered by this idleness, we hired a smaller boat and embarked on a longer excursion, which took us almost to the south-west end of Loch Ness.

Here, on September 18th, and pretty late in the afternoon, we were overtaken by a sudden squall, which carried away our mast (we found afterwards that it had rotted in the step), and put us for some minutes in no little danger; for my brother and I, being inexpert seamen, did not cut the tangle away, as we should have done, but made a bungling attempt to get the mast on board, with the rigging and drenched sail; and thereby managed to knock a hole in the side of the boat, which at once began to take in water. This compelled us to desist and fall to baling with might and main, leaving the raffle and jagged end of the mast to bump against us at the will of the waves. In short, we were in a highly unpleasant predicament, when a coble or row-boat, carrying one small lug-sail, hove out of the dusk to our assistance. It was manned by a crew of three, of whom the master (though we had scarce light enough to distinguish features) hailed us in a voice which was patently a gentleman's. He rounded up, lowered sail, and ran his boat alongside; and while his two hands were cutting us free of our tangle, inquired very civilly if we were strangers. We answered that we were, and desired him to tell us of the nearest place alongshore where we might land and find a lodging for the night, as well as a carpenter to repair our damage.

"In any ordinary case," said he, "I should ask you to come aboard and home with me. But my house lies five miles up the lake; your boat is sinking, and the first thing is to beach her. It happens that you are but half a mile from Ardlaugh and a decent carpenter who can answer all requirements. I think, if I stand by you, the thing can be done; and afterwards we will talk of supper."

By diligent baling we were able, under his direction, to bring our boat to a shingly beach, over which a light shone warm in a cottage window. Our hail was quickly answered by a second light. A lantern issued from the building, and we heard the sound of footsteps.

"Is that you, Donald?" cried our rescuer (as I may be permitted to call him).

Before an answer could be returned, we saw that two men were approaching; of whom the one bearing the lantern was a grizzled old carlin with bent knees and a stoop of the shoulders. His companion carried himself with a lighter step. It was he who advanced to salute us, the old man holding the light obediently; and the rays revealed to us a slight, up-standing youth, poorly dressed, but handsome, and with a touch of pride in his bearing.

"Good evening, gentlemen." He lifted his bonnet politely, and turned to our rescuer. "Good evening, Mr. Gillespie," he said -- I thought more coldly. "Can I be of any service to your friends?"

Mr. Gillespie's manner had changed suddenly at sight of the young man, whose salutation he acknowledged more coldly and even more curtly than it had been given. "I can scarcely claim them as my friends," he answered. "They are two gentlemen, strangers in these parts, who have met with an accident to their boat: one so serious that I brought them to the nearest landing, which happened to be Donald's." He shortly explained our mishap, while the young man took the lantern in hand and inspected the damage with Donald.

"There is nothing," he announced, "which cannot be set right in a couple of hours; but we must wait till morning. Meanwhile if, as I gather, you have no claim on these gentlemen, I shall beg them to be my guests for the night."

We glanced at Mr. Gillespie, whose manners seemed to have deserted him. He shrugged his shoulders. "Your house is the nearer," said he, "and the sooner they reach a warm fire the better for them after their drenching." And with that he lifted his cap to us, turned abruptly, and pushed off his own boat, scarcely regarding our thanks.

A somewhat awkward pause followed as we stood on the beach, listening to the creak of the thole-pins in the departing boat. After a minute our new acquaintance turned to us with a slightly constrained laugh.

"Mr. Gillespie omitted some of the formalities," said he. "My name is Mackenzie -- David Mackenzie; and I live at Ardlaugh Castle, scarcely half a mile up the glen behind us. I warn you that its hospitality is rude, but to what it affords you are heartily welcome."

He spoke with a high, precise courtliness which contrasted oddly with his boyish face (I guessed his age at nineteen or twenty), and still more oddly with his clothes, which were threadbare and patched in many places, yet with a deftness which told of a woman's care. We introduced ourselves by name, and thanked him, with some expressions of regret at inconveniencing (as I put it, at hazard) the family at the Castle.

"Oh!" he interrupted, "I am sole master there. I have no parents living, no family, and," he added, with a slight sullenness which I afterwards recognised as habitual, "I may almost say, no friends: though to be sure, you are lucky enough to have one

The Laird's Luck

fellow-guest to-night -- the minister of the parish, a Mr. Saul, and a very worthy man."

He broke off to give Donald some instructions about the boat, watched us while we found our plaids and soaked valises, and then took the lantern from the old man's hand. "I ought to have explained," said he, "that we have neither cart here nor carriage: indeed, there is no carriage-road. But Donald has a pony."

He led the way a few steps up the beach, and then halted, perceiving my lameness for the first time. "Donald, fetch out the pony. Can you ride bareback?" he asked: "I fear there's no saddle but an old piece of sacking." In spite of my protestations the pony was led forth; a starved little beast, on whose over-sharp ridge I must have cut a sufficiently ludicrous figure when hoisted into place with the valises slung behind me.

The procession set out, and I soon began to feel thankful for my seat, though I took no ease in it. For the road climbed steeply from the cottage, and at once began to twist up the bottom of a ravine so narrow that we lost all help of the young moon. The path, indeed, resembled the bed of a torrent, shrunk now to a trickle of water, the voice of which ran in my ears while our host led the way, springing from boulder to boulder, avoiding pools, and pausing now and then to hold his lantern over some slippery place. The pony followed with admirable caution, and my brother trudged in the rear and took his cue from us. After five minutes of this the ground grew easier and at the same time steeper, and I guessed that we were slanting up the hillside and away from the torrent at an acute angle. The many twists and angles, and the utter darkness (for we were now moving between trees) had completely baffled my reckoning when -- at the end of twenty minutes, perhaps -- Mr. Mackenzie halted and allowed me to come up with him.

I was about to ask the reason of this halt when a ray of his lantern fell on a wall of masonry; and with a start almost laugh-

The Laird's Luck

able I knew we had arrived. To come to an entirely strange house at night is an experience which holds some taste of mystery even for the oldest campaigner; but I have never in my life received such a shock as this building gave me -- naked, unlit, presented to me out of a darkness in which I had imagined a steep mountain scaur dotted with dwarfed trees -- a sudden abomination of desolation standing, like the prophet's, where it ought not. No light showed on the side where we stood -- the side over the ravine; only one pointed turret stood out against the faint moonlight glow in the upper sky: but feeling our way around the gaunt side of the building, we came to a back courtyard and two windows lit. Our host whistled, and helped me to dismount.

In an angle of the court a creaking door opened. A woman's voice cried, "That will be be you, Ardlaugh, and none too early! The minister -- "

She broke off, catching sight of us. Our host stepped hastily to the door and began a whispered conversation. We could hear that she was protesting, and began to feel awkward enough. But whatever her objections were, her master cut them short.

"Come in, sirs," he invited us: "I warned you that the fare would be hard, but I repeat that you are welcome."

To our surprise and, I must own, our amusement, the woman caught up his words with new protestations, uttered this time at the top of her voice.

"The fare hard? Well, it might not please folks accustomed to city feasts; but Ardlaugh was not yet without a joint of venison in the larder and a bottle of wine, maybe two, maybe three, for any guest its master chose to make welcome. It was 'an ill bird that 'filed his own nest'" -- with more to this effect, which our host tried in vain to interrupt.

"Then I will lead you to your rooms," he said, turning to us as soon as she paused to draw breath.

"Indeed, Ardlaugh, you will do nothing of the kind." She ran into the kitchen, and returned holding high a lighted torch -- a grey-haired woman with traces of past comeliness, overlaid now by an air of worry, almost of fear. But her manner showed only a defiant pride as she led us up the uncarpeted stairs, past old portraits sagging and rotting in their frames, through bleak corridors, where the windows were patched and the plastered walls discoloured by fungus. Once only she halted. "It will be a long way to your appartments. A grand house!" She had faced round on us, and her eyes seemed to ask a question of ours. "I have known it filled," she added -- "filled with guests, and the drink and fiddles never stopping for a week. You will see it better to-morrow. A grand house!"

I will confess that, as I limped after this barbaric woman and her torch, I felt some reasonable apprehensions of the bedchamber towards which they were escorting me. But here came another surprise. The room was of moderate size, poorly furnished, indeed, but comfortable and something more. It bore traces of many petty attentions, even -- in its white dimity curtains and valances -- of an attempt at daintiness. The sight of it brought quite a pleasant shock after the dirt and disarray of the corridor. Nor was the room assigned to my brother one whit less habitable. But if surprised by all this, I was fairly astounded to find in each room a pair of candles lit -- and quite recently lit -- beside the looking-glass, and an ewer of hot water standing, with a clean towel upon it, in each wash-hand basin. No sooner had the woman departed than I visited my brother and begged him (while he unstrapped his valise) to explain this apparent miracle. He could only guess with me that the woman had been warned of our arrival by the noise of footsteps in the court-yard, and had dispatched a servant by some back stairs to make ready for us.

Our valises were, fortunately, waterproof. We quickly exchanged our damp clothes for dry ones, and groped our way together along the corridors, helped by the moon, which shone through their uncurtained windows, to the main staircase. Here we came on a scent of roasting meat -- appetising to us after our day in the open air -- and at the foot found our host waiting for us. He had donned his Highland dress of ceremony -- velvet jacket, phillabeg and kilt, with the tartan of his clan -- and looked (I must own) extremely well in it, though the garments had long since lost their original gloss. An apology for our rough touring suits led to some few questions and replies about the regimental tartan of the Morays, in the history of which he was passably well informed.

Thus chatting, we entered the great hall of Ardlaugh Castle -- a tall, but narrow and ill-proportioned apartment, having an open timber roof, a stone-paved floor, and walls sparsely decorated with antlers and round targes -- where a very small man stood warming his back at an immense fireplace. This was the Reverend Samuel Saul, whose acquaintance we had scarce time to make before a cracked gong summoned us to dinner in the adjoining room.

The young Laird of Ardlaugh took his seat in a roughly carved chair of state at the head of the table; but before doing so treated me to another surprise by muttering a Latin grace and crossing himself. Up to now I had taken it for granted he was a member of the Scottish Kirk. I glanced at the minister in some mystification; but he, good man, appeared to have fallen into a brown study, with his eyes fastened upon a dish of apples which adorned the centre of our promiscuously furnished board.

Of the furniture of our meal I can only say that poverty and decent appearance kept up a brave fight throughout. The table-cloth was ragged, but spotlessly clean; the silver-ware scanty and worn with high polishing. The plates and glasses displayed a noble range of patterns, but were for the most part chipped or cracked. Each knife had been worn to a point, and a few of them joggled in their handles. In a lull of the talk I caught myself idly counting the darns in my table-napkin. They were -- if I remember -- fourteen, and all exquisitely stitched. The dinner, on the other hand, would have tempted men far less hungry than we -- grilled steaks of salmon, a roast haunch of venison, grouse, a milk-pudding, and, for dessert, the dish of apples already mentioned; the meats washed down with one wine only, but that wine was claret, and beautifully sound. I should mention that we were served by a grey-haired retainer, almost stone deaf, and as hopelessly cracked as the gong with which he had beaten us to dinner. In the long waits between the courses we heard him quarrelling outside with the woman who had admitted us; and gradually -- I know not how -- the conviction grew on me that they were man and wife, and the only servants of our host's establishment. To cover the noise of one of their altercations I began to congratulate the Laird on the quality of his venison, and put some idle question about his care for his deer.

"I have no deer-forest," he answered. "Elspeth is my only housekeeper."

I had some reply on my lips, when my attention was distracted by a sudden movement by the Rev. Samuel Saul. This honest man had, as we shook hands in the great hall, broken into a flood of small talk. On our way to the dining-room he took me, so to speak, by the button-hole, and within the minute so drenched me with gossip about Ardlaugh, its climate, its scenery, its crops, and the dimensions of the parish, that I feared a whole evening of boredom lay before us. But from the moment we seated ourselves at table he dropped to an absolute silence. There are men, living much alone, who by habit talk little during their meals; and the minister might be reserving himself. But I had almost forgotten his presence when I heard a sharp exclamation, and, looking across, saw him take from his lips his

The Laird's Luck

wine-glass of claret and set it down with a shaking hand. The Laird, too, had heard, and bent a darkly questioning glance on him. At once the little man -- whose face had turned to a sickly white -- began to stammer and excuse himself.

"It was nothing -- a spasm. He would be better of it in a moment. No, he would take no wine: a glass of water would set him right -- he was more used to drinking water," he explained, with a small, nervous laugh.

Perceiving that our solicitude embarrassed him, we resumed our talk, which now turned upon the last peninsular campaign and certain engagements in which the Morays had borne part; upon the stability of the French Monarchy, and the career (as we believed, at an end) of Napoleon. On all these topics the Laird showed himself well informed, and while preferring the part of listener (as became his youth) from time to time put in a question which convinced me of his intelligence, especially in military affairs.

The minister, though silent as before, had regained his colour; and we were somewhat astonished when, the cloth being drawn and the company left to its wine and one dish of dessert, he rose and announced that he must be going. He was decidedly better, but (so he excused himself) would feel easier at home in his own manse; and so, declining our host's offer of a bed, he shook hands and bade us good-night. The Laird accompanied him to the door, and in his absence I fell to peeling an apple, while my brother drummed with his fingers on the table and eyed the faded hangings. I suppose that ten minutes elapsed before we heard the young man's footsteps returning through the flagged hall and a woman's voice uplifted.

"But had the minister any complaint, whatever -- to ride off without a word? She could answer for the collops -- "

"Whist, woman! Have done with your clashin', ye doited old fool!" He slammed the door upon her, stepped to the table, and with a sullen frown poured himself a glass of wine. His brow cleared as he drank it. "I beg your pardon, gentlemen; but this indisposition of Mr. Saul has annoyed me. He lives at the far end of the parish -- a good seven miles away -- and I had invited him expressly to talk of parish affairs."

"I believe," said I, "you and he are not of the same religion?"

"Eh?" He seemed to be wondering how I had guessed. "No, I was bred a Catholic. In our branch we have always held to the Old Religion. But that doesn't prevent my wishing to stand well with my neighbours and do my duty towards them. What disheartens me is, they won't see it." He pushed the wine aside, and for a while, leaning his elbows on the table and resting his chin on his knuckles, stared gloomily before him. Then, with sudden boyish indignation, he burst out: "It's an infernal shame; that's it -- an infernal shame! I haven't been home here a twelvemonth, and the people avoid me like a plague. What have I done? My father wasn't popular -- in fact, they hated him. But so did I. And he hated me, God knows: misused my mother, and wouldn't endure me in his presence. All my miserable youth I've been mewed up in a school in England -- a private seminary. Ugh? what a den it was, too! My mother died calling for me -- I was not allowed to come: I hadn't seen her for three years. And now, when the old tyrant is dead, and I come home meaning -- so help me! -- to straighten things out and make friends -- come home, to the poverty you pretend not to notice, though it stares you in the face from every wall -- come home, only asking to make the best of of it, live on good terms with my fellows, and be happy for the first time in my life -- damn them, they won't fling me a kind look! What have I done? -- that's what I want to know. The queer thing is, they behaved more decently at first. There's that Gillespie, who brought you ashore: he came over the first week, offered me shooting, was altogether as pleasant as could be. I quite took to the fellow. Now, when we meet, he looks the other way! If he has anything against me, he might at least explain: it's all I ask. What have I done?"

Throughout this outburst I sat slicing my apple and taking now and then a glance at the speaker. It was all so hotly and honestly boyish! He only wanted justice. I know something of youngsters, and recognised the cry. Justice! It's the one thing every boy claims confidently as his right, and probably the last thing on earth he will ever get. And this boy looked so handsome, too, sitting in his father's chair, petulant, restive under a weight too heavy (as anyone could see) for his age. I couldn't help liking him.

My brother told me afterwards that I pounced like any recruiting-sergeant. This I do not believe. But what, after a long pause, I said was this: "If you are innocent or unconscious of offending, you can only wait for your neighbours to explain themselves. Meanwhile, why not leave them? Why not travel, for instance?"

"Travel!" he echoed, as much as to say, "You ought to know, without my telling, that I cannot afford it."

"Travel," I repeated; "see the world, rub against men of your age. You might by the way do some fighting."

He opened his eyes wide. I saw the sudden idea take hold of him, and again I liked what I saw.

"If I thought -- " He broke off. "You don't mean -- " he began, and broke off again.

"I mean the Morays," I said. "There may be difficulties; but at this moment I cannot see any real ones."

By this time he was gripping the arms of his chair. "If I thought -- " he harked back, and for the third time broke off. "What a fool I am! It's the last thing they ever put in a boy's head at that infernal school. If you will believe it, they wanted to make a priest of me!"

He sprang up, pushing back his chair. We carried our wine

into the great hall, and sat there talking the question over before the fire. Before we parted for the night I had engaged to use all my interest to get him a commission in the Morays; and I left him pacing the hall, his mind in a whirl, but his heart (as was plain to see) exulting in his new prospects.

And certainly, when I came to inspect the castle by the next morning's light, I could understand his longing to leave it. A gloomier, more pretentious, or worse-devised structure I never set eyes on. The Mackenzie who erected it may well have been (as the saying is) his own architect, and had either come to the end of his purse or left his heirs to decide against planting gardens, laying out approaches or even maintaining the pile in decent repair. In place of a drive a grassy cart-track, scored deep with old ruts, led through a gateless entrance into a courtyard where the slates had dropped from the roof and lay strewn like autumn leaves. On this road I encountered the young Laird returning from an early tramp with his gun; and he stood still and pointed to the castle with a grimace.

"A white elephant," said I.

"Call it rather the corpse of one," he answered. "Cannot you imagine some genie of the Oriental Tales dragging the beast across Europe and dumping it down here in a sudden fit of disgust? As a matter of fact my grandfather built it, and cursed us with poverty thereby. It soured my father's life. I believe the only soul honestly proud of it is Elspeth."

"And I suppose," said I, "you will leave her in charge of it when you join the Morays?"

"Ah!" he broke in, with a voice which betrayed his relief: "you are in earnest about that? Yes Elspeth will look after the castle, as she does already. I am just a child in her hand. When a man has one only servant it's well to have her devoted." Seeing my look of surprise, he added, "I don't count old Duncan, her husband; for he's half-witted, and only serves to break the plates.

Does it surprise you to learn that, barring him, Elspeth is my only retainer?"

"H'm," said I, considerably puzzled -- I must explain why.

I am by training an extraordinarily light sleeper; yet nothing had disturbed me during the night until at dawn my brother knocked at the door and entered, ready dressed.

"Hullo!" he exclaimed, "are you responsible for this?" and he pointed to a chair at the foot of the bed where lay, folded in a neat pile, not only the clothes I had tossed down carelessly overnight, but the suit in which I had arrived. He picked up this latter, felt it, and handed it to me. It was dry, and had been carefully brushed.

"Our friend keeps a good valet," said I; "but the queer thing is that, in a strange room, I didn't wake. I see he has brought hot water too."

"Look here," my brother asked: "did you lock your door?"

"Why, of course not -- the more by token that it hasn't a key."

"Well," said he, "mine has, and I'll swear I used it; but the same thing has happened to me!"

This, I tried to persuade him, was impossible; and for the while he seemed convinced. "It must be," he owned; "but if I didn't lock that door I'll never swear to a thing again in all my life."

The young Laird's remark set me thinking of this, and I answered after a pause, "In one of the pair, then, you possess a remarkably clever valet."

It so happened that, while I said it, my eyes rested, without the least intention, on the sleeve of his shooting-coat; and the words were scarcely out before he flushed hotly and made a motion as if to hide a neatly mended rent in its cuff. In another moment he would have retorted, and was indeed drawing himself up in anger, when I prevented him by adding --

"I mean that I am indebted to him or to her this morning for a neatly brushed suit; and I suppose to your freeness in plying me with wine last night that it arrived in my room without waking me. But for that I could almost set it down to the supernatural."

I said this in all simplicity, and was quite unprepared for its effect upon him, or for his extraordinary reply. He turned as white in the face as, a moment before, he had been red. "Good God!" he said eagerly, "you haven't missed anything, have you?"

"Certainly not," I assured him. "My dear sir -- "

"I know, I know. But you see," he stammered, "I am new to these servants. I know them to be faithful, and that's all. Forgive me; I feared from your tone one of them -- Duncan perhaps ..."

He did not finish his sentence, but broke into a hurried walk and led me towards the house. A minute later, as we approached it, he began to discourse half-humorously on its more glaring features, and had apparently forgotten his perturbation.

I too attached small importance to it, and recall it now merely through unwillingness to omit any circumstance which may throw light on a story sufficiently dark to me. After breakfast our host walked down with us to the loch-side, where we found old Donald putting the last touches on his job. With thanks for our entertainment we shook hands and pushed off: and my last word at parting was a promise to remember his ambition and write any news of my success.

2

I anticipated no difficulty, and encountered none. The Gazette of January, 1815, announced that David Marie Joseph Mackenzie, gentleman, had been appointed to an ensigncy in the -- th Regiment of Infantry (Moray Highlanders); and I timed my letter of congratulation to reach him with the news. Within a week he had joined us at Inverness, and was made welcome.

I may say at once that during his brief period of service I could find no possible fault with his bearing as a soldier. From the first he took seriously to the calling of arms, and not only showed himself punctual on parade and in all the small duties of barracks, but displayed, in his reserved way, a zealous resolve to master whatever by book or conversation could be learned of the higher business of war. My junior officers -- though when the test came, as it soon did, they acquitted themselves most creditably -- showed, as a whole, just then no great promise. For the most part they were young lairds, like Mr. Mackenzie, or cadets of good Highland families; but, unlike him, they had been allowed to run wild, and chafed under harness. One or two of them had the true Highland addiction to card-playing; and though I set a pretty stern face against this curse -- as I dare to call it -- its effects were to be traced in late hours, more than one case of shirking "rounds," and a general slovenliness at morning parade.

In such company Mr. Mackenzie showed to advantage, and I soon began to value him as a likely officer. Nor, in my dissatisfaction with them, did it give me any uneasiness -- as it gave me no surprise -- to find that his brother-officers took less kindly to him. He kept a certain reticence of manner, which either came of a natural shyness or had been ingrained in him at the Roman Catholic seminary. He was poor, too; but poverty did not prevent his joining in all the regimental amusements, figuring modestly but sufficiently on the subscription lists, and even taking a hand at cards for moderate stakes. Yet he made no headway, and his popularity diminished instead of growing. All this I noted, but without discovering any definite reason. Of his professional promise, on the other hand, there could be no question; and the men liked and respected him.

Our senior ensign at this date was a Mr. Urquhart, the eldest son of a West Highland laird, and heir to a considerable estate.

He had been in barracks when Mr. Mackenzie joined; but a week later his father's sudden illness called for his presence at home, and I granted him a leave of absence, which was afterwards extended. I regretted this, not only for the sad occasion, but because it deprived the battalion for a time of one of its steadiest officers, and Mr. Mackenzie in particular of the chance to form a very useful friendship. For the two young men had (I thought) several qualities which might well attract them each to the other, and a common gravity of mind in contrast with their companions' prevalent and somewhat tiresome frivolity. Of the two I judged Mr. Urquhart (the elder by a year) to have the more stable character. He was a good-looking, dark-complexioned young Highlander, with a serious expression which, without being gloomy, did not escape a touch of melancholy. I should judge this melancholy of Mr. Urquhart's constitutional, and the boyish sullenness which lingered on Mr. Mackenzie's equally handsome face to have been imposed rather by circumstances.

Mr. Urquhart rejoined us on the 24th of February. Two days later, as all the world knows, Napoleon made his escape from Elba; and the next week or two made it certain not only that the allies must fight, but that the British contingent must be drawn largely, if not in the main, from the second battalions then drilling up and down the country. The 29th of March brought us our marching orders; and I will own that, while feeling no uneasiness about the great issue, I distrusted the share my raw youngsters were to take in it.

On the 12th of April we were landed at Ostend, and at once marched up to Brussels, where we remained until the middle of June, having been assigned to the 5th (Picton's) Division of the Reserve. For some reason the Highland regiments had been massed into the Reserve, and were billeted about the capital, our own quarters lying between the 92nd

(Gordons) and General Kruse's Nassauers, whose lodgings stretched out along the Louvain road; and although I could have wished some harder and more responsible service to get the Morays into training, I felt what advantage they derived from rubbing shoulders with the fine fellows of the 42nd, 79th, and 92nd, all First Battalions toughened by Peninsular work. The gaieties of life in Brussels during these two months have been described often enough; but among the military they were chiefly confined to those officers whose means allowed them to keep the pace set by rich civilians, and the Morays played the part of amused spectators. Yet the work and the few gaieties which fell to our share, while adding to our experiences, broke up to some degree the old domestic habits of the battalion. Excepting on duty I saw less of Mr. Mackenzie and thought less about him; he might be left now to be shaped by active service. But I was glad to find him often in company with Mr. Urquhart.

I come now to the memorable night of June 15th, concerning which and the end it brought upon the festivities of Brussels so much has been written. All the world has heard of the Duchess of Richmond's ball, and seems to conspire in decking it out with pretty romantic fables. To contradict the most of these were waste of time; but I may point out (1) that the ball was over and, I believe, all the company dispersed, before the actual alarm awoke the capital; and (2) that all responsible officers gathered there shared the knowledge that such an alarm was impending, might arrive at any moment, and would almost certainly arrive within a few hours. News of the French advance across the frontier and attack on General Zieten's outposts had reached Wellington at three o'clock that afternoon. It should have been brought five hours earlier; but he gave his orders at once, and quietly, and already our troops were massing for defence upon Nivelles. We of the Reserve had secret orders to hold ourselves prepared. Obedient to a hint from their Commander-in-chief, the generals of division and brigade who attended the Duchess' ball withdrew themselves early on various pleas. Her Grace had honoured me with an invitation, probably because I represented a Highland regiment; and Highlanders (especially the Gordons, her brother's regiment) were much to the fore that night with reels, flings, and strathspeys. The many withdrawals warned me that something was in the wind, and after remaining just so long as seemed respectful, I took leave of my hostess and walked homewards across the city as the clocks were striking eleven.

We of the Morays had our headquarters in a fairly large building -- the Hôtel de Liège -- in time of peace a resort of commis-voyageurs of the better class. It boasted a roomy hall, out of which opened two coffee-rooms, converted by us into guard- and mess-room. A large drawing-room on the first floor overlooking the street served me for sleeping as well as working quarters, and to reach it I must pass the entresol, where a small apartment had been set aside for occasional uses. We made it, for instance, our ante-room, and assembled there before mess; a few would retire there for smoking or card-playing; during the day it served as a waiting-room for messengers or any one whose business could not be for the moment attended to.

I had paused at the entrance to put some small question to the sentry, when I heard the crash of a chair in this room, and two voices broke out in fierce altercation. An instant after, the mess-room door opened, and Captain Murray, without observing me, ran past me and up the stairs. As he reached the entresol, a voice -- my brother's -- called down from an upper landing, and demanded, "What's wrong there?"

"I don't know, Major," Captain Murray answered, and at the same moment flung the door open. I was quick on his heels, and he wheeled round in some surprise at my voice, and to see me interposed between him and my brother, who had come running downstairs, and now stood behind my shoulder in the entrance.

"Shut the door," I commanded quickly. "Shut the door, and send away any one you may hear outside. Now, gentlemen, explain yourselves, please."

Mr. Urquhart and Mr. Mackenzie faced each other across a small table, from which the cloth had been dragged and lay on the floor with a scattered pack of cards. The elder lad held a couple of cards in his hand; he was white in the face.

"He cheated!" He swung round upon me in a kind of indignant fury, and tapped the cards with his forefinger.

I looked from him to the accused. Mackenzie's face was dark, almost purple, rather with rage (as it struck me) than with shame.

"It's a lie." He let out the words slowly, as if holding rein on his passion. "Twice he's said so, and twice I've called him a liar." He drew back for an instant, and then lost control of himself. "If that's not enough -- ." He leapt forward, and almost before Captain Murray could interpose had hurled himself upon Urquhart. The table between them went down with a crash, and Urquhart went staggering back from a blow which just missed his face and took him on the collar-bone before Murray threw both arms around the assailant.

"Mr. Mackenzie," said I, "you will consider yourself under arrest. Mr. Urquhart, you will hold yourself ready to give me a full explanation. Whichever of you may be in the right, this is a disgraceful business, and dishonouring to your regiment and the cloth you wear: so disgraceful, that I hesitate to call up the guard and expose it to more eyes than ours. If Mr. Mackenzie" -- I turned to him again -- "can behave himself like a gentleman, and accept the fact of his arrest without further trouble, the scandal can at least be postponed until I discover how much it is necessary to face. For the moment,

The Laird's Luck

sir, you are in charge of Captain Murray. Do you understand?"

He bent his head sullenly. "He shall fight me, whatever happens," he muttered.

I found it wise to pay no heed to this. "It will be best," I said to Murray, "to remain here with Mr. Mackenzie until I am ready for him. Mr. Urquhart may retire to his quarters, if he will -- I advise it, indeed -- but I shall require his attendance in a few minutes. You understand," I added significantly, "that for the present this affair remains strictly between ourselves." I knew well enough that, for all the King's regulations, a meeting would inevitably follow sooner or later, and will own I looked upon it as the proper outcome, between gentlemen, of such a quarrel. But it was not for me, their Colonel, to betray this knowledge or my feelings, and by imposing secrecy I put off for the time all the business of a formal challenge with seconds. So I left them, and requesting my brother to follow me, mounted to my own room. The door was no sooner shut than I turned on him.

"Surely," I said, "this is a bad mistake of Urquhart's? It's an incredible charge. From all I've seen of him, the lad would never be guilty ..." I paused, expecting his assent. To my surprise he did not give it, but stood fingering his chin and looking serious.

"I don't know," he answered unwillingly. "There are stories against him."

"What stories?"

"Nothing definite." My brother hesitated. "It doesn't seem fair to him to repeat mere whispers. But the others don't like him."

"Hence the whispers, perhaps. They have not reached me."

"They would not. He is known to be a favourite of yours. But they don't care to play with him." My brother stopped, met my look, and answered it with a shrug of the shoulders, adding, "He wins pretty constantly."

"Any definite charge before to-night's?"

"No: at least, I think not. But Urquhart may have been put up to watch."

"Fetch him up, please," said I promptly; and seating myself at the writing-table I lit candles (for the lamp was dim), made ready the writing materials and prepared to take notes of the evidence.

Mr. Urquhart presently entered, and I wheeled round in my chair to confront him. He was still exceedingly pale -- paler, I thought, than I had left him. He seemed decidedly ill at ease, though not on his own account. His answer to my first question made me fairly leap in my chair.

"I wish," he said, "to qualify my accusation of Mr. Mackenzie. That he cheated I have the evidence of my own eyes; but I am not sure how far he knew he was cheating."

"Good heavens, sir!" I cried. "Do you know you have accused that young man of a villainy which must damn him for life? And now you tell me -- " I broke off in sheer indignation.

"I know," he answered quietly. "The noise fetched you in upon us on the instant, and the mischief was done."

"Indeed, sir," I could not avoid sneering, "to most of us it would seem that the mischief was done when you accused a brother-officer of fraud to his face."

He seemed to reflect. "Yes, sir," he assented slowly; "it is done. I saw him cheat: that I must persist in; but I cannot say how far he was conscious of it. And since I cannot, I must take the consequences."

"Will you kindly inform us how it is possible for a player to cheat and not know that he is cheating?"

He bent his eyes on the carpet as if seeking an answer. It was long in coming. "No," he said at last, in a slow, dragging tone, "I cannot."

"Then you will at least tell us exactly what Mr. Mackenzie did."

Again there was a long pause. He looked at me straight, but with hopelessness in his eyes. "I fear you would not believe me. It would not be worth while. If you can grant it, sir, I would ask time to decide."

"Mr. Urquhart," said I sternly, "are you aware you have brought against Mr. Mackenzie a charge under which no man of honour can live easily for a moment? You ask me without a word of evidence in substantiation to keep him in torture while I give you time. It is monstrous, and I beg to remind you that, unless your charge is proved, you can -- and will -- be broken for making it."

"I know it, sir," he answered firmly enough; "and because I knew it, I asked -- perhaps selfishly -- for time. If you refuse, I will at least ask permission to see a priest before telling a story which I can scarcely expect you to believe." Mr. Urquhart too was a Roman Catholic.

But my temper for the moment was gone. "I see little chance," said I, "of keeping this scandal secret, and regret it the less if the consequences are to fall on a rash accuser. But just now I will have no meddling priest share the secret. For the present, one word more. Had you heard before this evening of any hints against Mr. Mackenzie's play?"

He answered reluctantly, "Yes."

"And you set yourself to lay a trap for him?"

"No, sir; I did not. Unconsciously I may have been set on the watch: no, that is wrong -- I did watch. But I swear it was in every hope and expectation of clearing him. He was my friend. Even when I saw, I had at first no intention to expose him until -- "

"That is enough, sir," I broke in, and turned to my brother. "I have no option but to put Mr. Urquhart too under arrest. Kindly convey him back to his room, and send Captain Murray to me. He may leave Mr. Mackenzie in the entresol."

My brother led Urquhart out, and in a minute Captain Mur-

The Laird's Luck

ray tapped at my door. He was an honest Scot, not too sharp-witted, but straight as a die. I am to show him this description, and he will cheerfully agree with it.

"This is a hideous business, Murray," said I as he entered. "There's something wrong with Urquhart's story. Indeed, between ourselves it has the fatal weakness that he won't tell it."

Murray took a minute to digest this, then he answered, "I don't know anything about Urquhart's story, sir. But there's something wrong about Urquhart." Here he hesitated.

"Speak out, man," said I: "in confidence. That's understood."

"Well, sir," said he, "Urquhart won't fight."

"Ah! so that question came up, did it?" I asked, looking at him sharply.

He was not abashed, but answered, with a twinkle in his eye, "I believe, sir, you gave me no orders to stop their talking, and in a case like this -- between youngsters -- some question of a meeting would naturally come up. You see, I know both the lads. Urquhart I really like; but he didn't show up well, I must own -- to be fair to the other, who is in the worse fix."

"I am not so sure of that," I commented; "but go on."

He seemed surprised. "Indeed, Colonel? Well," he resumed, "I being the sort of fellow they could talk before, a meeting was discussed. The question was how to arrange it without seconds -- that is, without breaking your orders and dragging in outsiders. For Mackenzie wanted blood at once, and for awhile Urquhart seemed just as eager. All of a sudden, when...." here he broke off suddenly, not wishing to commit himself.

"Tell me only what you think necessary," said I.

He thanked me. "That is what I wanted," he said. "Well, all of a sudden, when we had found out a way and Urquhart was discussing it, he pulled himself up in the middle of a sentence, and with his eyes fixed on the other -- a most curious look it was -- he waited while you could count ten, and, 'No,' says he, 'I'll not fight you at once' -- for we had been arranging something of the sort -- 'not to-night, anyway, nor to-morrow,' he says. 'I'll fight you; but I won't have your blood on my head in that way.' Those were his words. I have no notion what he meant; but he kept repeating them, and would not explain, though Mackenzie tried him hard and was for shooting across the table. He was repeating them when the Major interrupted us and called him up."

"He has behaved ill from the first," said I. "To me the whole affair begins to look like an abominable plot against Mackenzie. Certainly I cannot entertain a suspicion of his guilt upon a bare assertion which Urquhart declines to back with a tittle of evidence."

"The devil he does!" mused Captain Murray. "That looks bad for him. And yet, sir, I'd sooner trust Urquhart than Mackenzie, and if the case lies against Urquhart -- "

"It will assuredly break him," I put in, "unless he can prove the charge, or that he was honestly mistaken."

"Then, sir," said the Captain, "I'll have to show you this. It's ugly, but it's only justice."

He pulled a sovereign from his pocket and pushed it on the writing-table under my nose.

"What does this mean?"

"It is a marked one," said he.

"So I perceive." I had picked up the coin and was examining it.

"I found it just now," he continued, "in the room below. The upsetting of the table had scattered Mackenzie's stakes about the floor."

"You seem to have a pretty notion of evidence," I observed sharply. "I don't know what accusation this coin may carry; but why need it be Mackenzie's? He might have won it from Urquhart."

"I thought of that," was the answer. "But no money had

changed hands. I enquired. The quarrel arose over the second deal, and as a matter of fact Urquhart had laid no money on the table, but made a pencil-note of a few shillings he lost by the first hand. You may remember, sir, how the table stood when you entered."

I reflected. "Yes, my recollection bears you out. Do I gather that you have confronted Mackenzie with this?"

"No. I found it and slipped it quietly into my pocket. I thought we had trouble enough on hand for the moment."

"Who marked this coin?"

"Young Fraser, sir, in my presence. He has been losing small sums, he declares, by pilfering. We suspected one of the orderlies."

"In this connection you had no suspicion of Mr. Mackenzie?"

"None, sr." He considered for a moment, and added: "There was a curious thing happened three weeks ago over my watch. It found its way one night to Mr. Mackenzie's quarters. He brought it to me in the morning; said it was lying, when he awoke, on the table beside his bed. He seemed utterly puzzled. He had been to one or two already to discover the owner. We joked him about it, the more by token that his own watch had broken down the day before and was away at the mender's. The whole thing was queer, and has not been explained. Of course in that instance he was innocent: everything proves it. It just occurred to me as worth mentioning, because in both instances the lad may have been the victim of a trick."

"I am glad you did so," I said; "though just now it does not throw any light that I can see." I rose and paced the room. "Mr. Mackenzie had better be confronted with this, too, and hear your evidence. It's best he should know the worst against him; and if he be guilty it may move him to confession."

"Certainly, sir," Captain Murray assented. "Shall I fetch him?"

"No, remain where you are," I said; "I will go for him myself."

I understood that Mr. Urquhart had retired to his own quarters or to my brother's, and that Mr. Mackenzie had been left in the entresol alone. But as I descended the stairs quietly I heard within that room a voice which at first persuaded me he had company, and next that, left to himself, he had broken down and given way to the most childish wailing. The voice was so unlike his, or any grown man's, that it arrested me on the lowermost stair against my will. It resembled rather the sobbing of an infant mingled with short strangled cries of contrition and despair.

"What shall I do? What shall I do? I didn't mean it -- I meant to do good! What shall I do?"

So much I heard (as I say) against my will, before my astonishment gave room to a sense of shame at playing, even for a moment, the eavesdropper upon the lad I was to judge. I stepped quickly to the door, and with a warning rattle (to give him time to recover himself) turned the handle and entered.

He was alone, lying back in an easy chair -- not writhing there in anguish of mind, as I had fully expected, but sunk rather in a state of dull and hopeless apathy. To reconcile his attitude with the sounds I had just heard was merely impossible; and it bewildered me worse than any in the long chain of bewildering incidents. For five seconds or so he appeared not to see me; but when he grew aware his look changed suddenly to one of utter terror, and his eyes, shifting from me, shot a glance about the room as if he expected some new accusation to dart at him from the corners. His indignation and passionate defiance were gone: his eyes seemed to ask me, "How much do you know?" before he dropped them and stood before me, sullenly submissive.

"I want you upstairs," said I: "not to hear your defence on this charge, for Mr. Urquhart has not yet specified it. But there is another matter."

The Laird's Luck

"Another?" he echoed dully, and, I observed, without surprise.

I led the way back to the room where Captain Murray waited. "Can you tell me anything about this?" I asked, pointing to the sovereign on the writing-table.

He shook his head, clearly puzzled, but anticipating mischief.

"The coin is marked, you see. I have reason to know that it was marked by its owner in order to detect a thief. Captain Murray found it just now among your stakes."

Somehow -- for I liked the lad -- I had not the heart to watch his face as I delivered this. I kept my eyes upon the coin, and waited, expecting an explosion -- a furious denial, or at least a cry that he was the victim of a conspiracy. None came. I heard him breathing hard. After a long and very dreadful pause some words broke from him, so lowly uttered that my ears only just caught them.

"This too? O my God!"

I seated myself, the lad before me, and Captain Murray erect and rigid at the end of the table. "Listen, my lad," said I. "This wears an ugly look, but that a stolen coin has been found in your possession does not prove that you've stolen it."

"I did not. Sir, I swear to you on my honour, and before Heaven, that I did not."

"Very well," said I: "Captain Murray asserts that he found this among the moneys you had been staking at cards. Do you question that assertion?"

He answered almost without pondering. "No, sir. Captain Murray is a gentleman, and incapable of falsehood. If he says so, it was so."

"Very well again. Now, can you explain how this coin came into your possession?"

At this he seemed to hesitate; but answered at length, "No, I cannot explain."

"Have you any idea? Or can you form any guess?"

Again there was a long pause before the answer came in low and strained tones: "I can guess."

"What is your guess?"

He lifted a hand and dropped it hopelessly. "You would not believe," he said.

I will own a suspicion flashed across my mind on hearing these words -- the very excuse given a while ago by Mr. Urquhart -- that the whole affair was a hoax and the two young men were in conspiracy to fool me. I dismissed it at once: the sight of Mr. Mackenzie's face, was convincing. But my temper was gone.

"Believe you?" I exclaimed. "You seem to think the one thing I can swallow as creditable, even probable, is that an officer in the Morays has been pilfering and cheating at cards. Oddly enough, it's the last thing I'm going to believe without proof, and the last charge I shall pass without clearing it up to my satisfaction. Captain Murray, will you go and bring me Mr. Urquhart and the Major?"

As Captain Murray closed the door I rose, and with my hands behind me took a turn across the room to the fireplace, then back to the writing-table.

"Mr. Mackenzie," I said, "before we go any further I wish you to believe that I am your friend as well as your Colonel. I did something to start you upon your career, and I take a warm interest in it. To believe you guilty of these charges will give me the keenest grief. However unlikely your defence may sound -- and you seem to fear it -- I will give it the best consideration I can. If you are innocent, you shall not find me prejudiced because many are against you and you are alone. Now, this coin -- " I turned to the table.

The coin was gone.

I stared at the place where it had lain; then at the young man. He had not moved. My back had been turned for less than two seconds, and I could have sworn he had not budged from the square of carpet on which he had first taken his stand, and on which his feet were still planted. On the other hand, I was equally positive the incriminating coin had lain on the table at the moment I turned my back.

"It is gone!" cried I.

"Gone?" he echoed, staring at the spot to which my finger pointed. In the silence our glances were still crossing when my brother tapped at the door and brought in Mr. Urquhart, Captain Murray following.

Dismissing for a moment this latest mystery, I addressed Mr. Urquhart. "I have sent for you, sir, to request in the first place that here in Mr. Mackenzie's presence and in colder blood you will either withdraw or repeat and at least attempt to substantiate the charge you brought against him."

"I adhere to it, sir, that there was cheating. To withdraw would be to utter a lie. Does he deny it?"

I glanced at Mr. Mackenzie. "I deny that I cheated," said he sullenly.

"Further," pursued Mr. Urquhart, "I repeat what I told you, sir. He may, while profiting by it have been unaware of the cheat. At the moment I thought it impossible; but I am willing to believe -- "

"You are willing!" I broke in. "And pray, sir, what about me, his Colonel, and the rest of his brother officers? Have you the coolness to suggest -- "

But the full question was never put, and in this world it will never be answered. A bugle call, distant but clear, cut my sentence in half. It came from the direction of the Place d'Armes. A second bugle echoed, it from the height of the Montagne du

The Laird's Luck

Parc, and within a minute its note was taken up and answered across the darkness from quarter after quarter.

We looked at one another in silence. "Business," said my brother at length, curtly and quietly.

Already the rooms above us were astir. I heard windows thrown open, voices calling questions, feet running.

"Yes," said I, "it is business at length, and for the while this inquiry must end. Captain Murray, look to your company. You, Major, see that the lads tumble out quick to the alarm-post. One moment!" -- and Captain Murray halted with his hand on the door -- "It is understood that for the present no word of to-night's affair passes our lips." I turned to Mr. Mackenzie and answered the question I read in the lad's eyes. "Yes, sir; for the present I take off your arrest. Get your sword. It shall be your good fortune to answer the enemy before answering me."

To my amazement Mr. Urquhart interposed. He was, if possible, paler and more deeply agitated than before. "Sir, I entreat you not to allow Mr. Mackenzie to go. I have reasons -- I was mistaken just now -- "

"Mistaken, sir?"

"Not in what I saw. I refused to fight him -- under a mistake. I thought -- "

But I cut his stammering short. "As for you," I said, "the most charitable construction I can put on your behaviour is to believe you mad. For the present you, too, are free to go and do your duty. Now leave me. Business presses, and I am sick and angry at the sight of you."

It was just two in the morning when I reached the alarm-post. Brussels by this time was full of the rolling of drums and screaming of pipes; and the regiment formed up in darkness rendered tenfold more confusing by a mob of citizens, some wildly excited, others paralysed by terror, and all intractable. We had, moreover, no small trouble to disengage from our ranks the wives and families who had most unwisely followed many officers abroad, and now clung to their dear ones bidding them farewell. To end this most distressing scene I had in some instances to use a roughness which it still afflicts me to remember. Yet in actual time it was soon overhand dawn scarcely breaking when the Morays with the other regiments of Pack's brigade filed out of the park and fell into stride on the road which leads southward to Charleroi.

In this record it would be immaterial to describe either our march or the since-famous engagement which terminated it. Very early we began to hear the sound of heavy guns far ahead and to make guesses at their distance; but it was close upon two in the afternoon before we reached the high ground above Quatre Bras, and saw the battle spread below us like a picture. The Prince of Orange had been fighting his ground stubbornly since seven in the morning. Ney's superior artillery and far superior cavalry had forced him back, it is true; but he still covered the cross-roads which were the key of his defence, and his position remained sound, though it was fast becoming critical. Just as we arrived, the French, who had already mastered the farm of Piermont, on the left of the Charleroi road, began to push their skirmishers into a thicket below it and commanding the road running east to Namur. Indeed, for a short space they had this road at their mercy, and the chance within grasp of doubling up our left by means of it.

This happened, I say, just as we arrived; and Wellington, who had reached Quatre Bras a short while ahead of us (having fetched a circuit from Brussels through Ligny, where he paused to inspect Field-Marshal Blücher's dispositions for battle), at once saw the danger, and detached one of our regiments, the 95th Rifles, to drive back the tirailleurs from the thicket; which, albeit scarcely breathed after their march, they did with a will, and so regained the Allies' hold upon the Namur road. The rest

The Laird's Luck

of us meanwhile defiled down this same road, formed line in front of it, and under a brisk cannonade from the French heights waited for the next move.

It was not long in coming. Ney, finding that our artillery made poor play against his, prepared to launch a column against us. Warned by a cloud of skirmishers, our light companies leapt forward, chose their shelter, and began a very pretty exchange of musketry. But this was preliminary work only, and soon the head of a large French column appeared on the slope to our right, driving the Brunswickers slowly before it. It descended a little way, and suddenly broke into three or four columns of attack. The mischief no sooner threatened than Picton came galloping along our line and roaring that our division would advance and engage with all speed. For a raw regiment like the Morays this was no light test; but, supported by a veteran regiment on either hand, they bore it admirably. Dropping the Gordons to protect the road in case of mishap, the two brigades swung forward in the prettiest style, their skirmishers running in and forming on either flank as they advanced. Then for a while the work was hot; but, as will always happen when column is boldly met by line, the French quickly had enough of our enveloping fire, and wavered. A short charge with the bayonet finished it, and drove them in confusion up the slope: nor had I an easy task to resume a hold on my youngsters and restrain them from pursuing too far. The brush had been sharp, but I had the satisfaction of knowing that the Morays had behaved well. They also knew it, and fell to jesting in high good-humour as General Pack withdrew the brigade from the ground of its exploit and posted us in line with the 42nd and 44th regiments on the left of the main road to Charleroi.

To the right of the Charleroi road, and some way in advance of our position, the Brunswickers were holding ground as best they could under a hot and accurate artillery fire. Except for this, the battle had come to a lull, when a second mass of the enemy began to move down the slopes: a battalion in line heading two columns of infantry direct upon the Brunswickers, while squadron after squadron of lancers crowded down along the road into which by weight of numbers they must be driven. The Duke of Brunswick, perceiving his peril, headed a charge of his lancers upon the advancing infantry, but without the least effect. His horsemen broke. He rode back and called on his infantry to retire in good order. They also broke, and in the attempt to rally them he fell mortally wounded.

The line taken by these flying Brunswickers would have brought them diagonally across the Charleroi road into our arms, had not the French lancers seized this moment to charge straight down it in a body. They encountered, and the indiscriminate mass was hurled on to us, choking and overflowing the causeway. In a minute we were swamped -- the two Highland regiments and the 44th bending against a sheer weight of Trench horsemen. So suddenly came the shock that the 42nd had no time to form square, until two companies were cut off and well-nigh destroyed; then that noble regiment formed around the horsemen who could boast of having broken it, and left not one to bear back the tale. The 44th behaved more cleverly, but not more intrepidly: it did not attempt to form square, but faced its rear rank round and gave the Frenchmen a volley; before they could checks their impetus the front rank poured in a second; and the light company, which had held its fire, delivered a third, breaking the crowd in two, and driving the hinderpart back in disorder and up the Charleroi road. But already the fore-part had fallen upon the Morays, fortunately the last of the three regiments to receive the shock. Though most fortunate, they had least experience, and were consequently slow in answering my shout. A wedge of lancers broke through us as we formed around the two standards, and I saw Mr. Urquhart with the King's colours hurled back in the rush. The pole fell with

The Laird's Luck

him, after swaying within a yard of a French lancer, who thrust out an arm to grasp it. And with that I saw Mackenzie divide the rush and stand -- it may have been for five seconds -- erect, with his foot upon the standard. Then three lancers pierced him, and he fell. But the lateral pressure of their own troopers broke the wedge which the French had pushed into us. Their leading squadrons were pressed down the road and afterwards accounted for by the Gordons. Of the seven-and-twenty assailants around whom the Morays now closed, not one survived.

Towards nightfall, as Ney weakened and the Allies were reinforced, our troops pushed forward and recaptured every important position taken by the French that morning. The Morays, with the rest of Picton's division, bivouacked for the night in and around the farmstead of Gemiancourt.

So obstinately had the field been contested that darkness fell before the wounded could be collected with any thoroughness; and the comfort of the men around many a camp-fire was disturbed by groans (often quite near at hand) of some poor comrade or enemy lying helpless and undiscovered, or exerting his shattered limbs to crawl towards the blaze. And these interruptions at length became so distressing to the Morays, that two or three officers sought me and demanded leave to form a fatigue party of volunteers and explore the hedges and thickets with lanterns. Among them was Mr. Urquhart: and having readily given leave and accompanied them some little way on their search, I was bidding them good-night and good-speed when I found him standing at my elbow.

"May I have a word with you, Colonel?" he asked.

His voice was low and serious. Of course I knew what subject filled his thoughts. "Is it worth while, sir?" I answered. "I have lost to-day a brave lad for whom I had a great affection. For him the account is closed; but not for those who liked him and are still concerned in his good name. If you have anything further against him, or if you have any confession to make, I warn you that this is a bad moment to choose."

"I have only to ask," said he, "that you will grant me the first convenient hour for explaining; and to remind you that when I besought you not to send him into action to-day, I had no time to give you reasons."

"This is extraordinary talk, sir. I am not used to command the Morays under advice from my subalterns. And in this instance I had reasons for not even listening to you." He was silent. "Moreover," I continued, "you may as well know, though I am under no obligation to tell you, that I do most certainly not regret having given that permission to one who justified it by a signal service to his king and country."

"But would you have sent him knowing that he must die? Colonel," he went on rapidly, before I could interrupt, "I beseech you to listen. I knew he had only a few hours to live. I saw his wraith last night. It stood behind his shoulder in the room when in Captain Murray's presence he challenged me to fight him. You are a Highlander, sir: you may be sceptical about the second sight; but at least you must have heard many claim it. I swear positively that I saw Mr. Mackenzie's wraith last night, and for that reason, and no other, tried to defer the meeting. To fight him, knowing he must die, seemed to me as bad as murder. Afterwards, when the alarm sounded and you took off his arrest, I knew that his fate must overtake him -- that my refusal had done no good. I tried to interfere again, and you would not hear. Naturally you would not hear; and very likely, if you had, his fate would have found him in some other way. That is what I try to believe. I hope it is not selfish, sir; but the doubt tortures me."

"Mr. Urquhart," I asked, "is this the only occasion on which you have possessed the second sight, or had reason to think so?"

"No, sir."

"Was it the first or only time last night you believed you were granted it?"

"It was the second time last night," he said steadily.

We had been walking back to my bivouac fire, and in the light of it I turned and said: "I will hear your story at the first opportunity. I will not promise to believe, but I will hear and weigh it. Go now and join the others in their search."

He saluted, and strode away into the darkness. The opportunity I promised him never came. At eleven o'clock next morning we began our withdrawal, and within twenty-four hours the battle of Waterloo had begun. In one of the most heroic feats of that day -- the famous resistance of Pack's brigade -- Mr. Urquhart was among the first to fall.

3

Thus it happened that an affair which so nearly touched the honour of the Morays, and which had been agitating me at the very moment when the bugle sounded in the Place d'Armes, became a secret shared by three only. The regiment joined in the occupation of Paris, and did not return to Scotland until the middle of December.

I had ceased to mourn for Mr. Mackenzie, but neither to regret him nor to speculate on the mystery which closed his career, and which, now that death had sealed Mr. Urquhart's lips, I could no longer hope to penetrate, when, on the day of my return to Inverness, I was reminded of him by finding, among the letters and papers awaiting me, a visiting-card neatly indited with the name of the Reverend Samuel Saul. On inquiry I learnt that the minister had paid at least three visits to Inverness during the past fortnight, and had, on each occasion, shown much anxiety to learn when the battalion might be expected. He had also left word that he wished to see me on a matter of much importance.

Sure enough, at ten o'clock next morning the little man presented himself. He was clearly bursting to disclose his business, and our salutations were scarce over when he ran to the door and called to some one in the passage outside.

"Elspeth! Step inside, woman. The housekeeper, sir, to the late Mr. Mackenzie of Ardlaugh," he explained, as he held the door to admit her.

She was dressed in ragged mourning, and wore a grotesque and fearful bonnet. As she saluted me respectfully I saw that her eyes indeed were dry and even hard, but her features set in an expression of quiet and hopeless misery. She did not speak, but left explanation to the minister.

"You will guess, sir," began Mr. Saul, "that we have called to learn more of the poor lad." And he paused.

"He died most gallantly," said I: "died in the act of saving the colours. No soldier could have wished for a better end."

"To be sure, to be sure. So it was reported to us. He died, as one might say, without a stain on his character?" said Mr. Saul, with a sort of question in his tone.

"He died," I answered, "in a way which could only do credit to his name."

A somewhat constrained silence followed. The woman broke it. "You are not telling us all," she said, in a slow, harsh voice.

It took me aback. "I am telling all that needs to be known," I assured her.

"No doubt, sir, no doubt," Mr. Saul interjected. "Hold your tongue, woman. I am going to tell Colonel Ross a tale which may or may not bear upon anything he knows. If not, he will interrupt me before I go far; but if he says nothing I shall take it I have his leave to continue. Now, sir, on the 16th day of June last, and at six in the morning -- that would be the day of Quatre Bras -- "

He paused for me to nod assent, and continued. "At six in the morning or a little earlier, this woman, Elspeth Mackenzie, came to me at the Manse in great perturbation. She had walked all the way from Ardlaugh. It had come to her (she said) that the young Laird abroad was in great trouble since the previous evening. I asked, 'What trouble? Was it danger of life, for instance?' -- asking it not seriously, but rather to compose her; for at first I set down her fears to an old woman's whimsies. Not that I would call Elspeth old precisely -- "

Here he broke off and glanced at her; but, perceiving she paid little attention, went on again at a gallop. "She answered that it was worse -- that the young Laird stood very near disgrace, and (the worst of all was) at a distance she could not help him. Now, sir, for reasons I shall hereafter tell you, Mr. Mackenzie's being in disgrace would have little surprised me; but that she should know of it, he being in Belgium, was incredible. So I pressed her, and she being distraught and (I verily believe) in something like anguish, came out with a most extraordinary story: to wit, that the Laird of Ardlaugh had in his service, unbeknown to him (but, as she protested, well known to her), a familiar spirit -- or, as we should say commonly, a 'brownie' -- which in general served him most faithfully but at times erratically, having no conscience nor any Christian principle to direct him. I cautioned her, but she persisted, in a kind of wild terror, and added that at times the spirit would, in all good faith, do things which no Christian allowed to be permissible, and further, that she had profited by such actions. I asked her, 'Was thieving one of them?' She answered that it was, and indeed the chief.

"Now, this was an admission which gave me some eagerness to hear more. For to my knowledge there were charges lying against young Mr. Mackenzie -- though not pronounced -- which pointed to a thief in his employment and presumably in his confidence. You will remember, sir, that when I had the honour of meeting you at Mr. Mackenzie's table, I took my leave with much abruptness. You remarked upon it, no doubt. But you will no longer think it strange when I tell you that there -- under my nose -- were a dozen apples of a sort which grows nowhere within twenty miles of Ardlaugh but in my own Manse garden. The tree was a new one, obtained from Herefordshire, and planted three seasons before as an experiment. I had watched it, therefore, particularly; and on that very morning had counted the fruit, and been dismayed to find twelve apples missing. Further, I am a pretty good judge of wine (though I taste it rarely), and could there and then have taken my oath that the claret our host set before us was the very wine I had tasted at the table of his neighbour Mr. Gillespie. As for the venison -- I had already heard whispers that deer and all game were not safe within a mile or two of Ardlaugh. These were injurious tales, sir, which I had no mind to believe; for, bating his religion, I saw everything in Mr. Mackenzie which disposed me to like him. But I knew (as neighbours must) of the shortness of his purse; and the multiplied evidence (particularly my own Goodrich pippins staring me in the face) overwhelmed me for a moment.

"So then, I listened to this woman's tale with more patience -- or, let me say, more curiosity -- than you, sir, might have given it. She persisted, I say, that her master was in trouble; and that the trouble had something to do with a game of cards, but that Mr. Mackenzie had been innocent of deceit, and the real culprit was this spirit I tell of -- "

Here the woman herself broke in upon Mr. Saul. "He had nae conscience -- he had nae conscience. He was just a poor luck-child, born by mischance and put away without baptism. He had nae conscience. How should he?"

I looked from her to Mr. Saul in perplexity.

"Whist!" said he; "we'll talk of that anon."

"We will not," said she. "We will talk of it now. He was my own child, sir, by the young Laird's own father. That was before he was married upon the wife he took later -- "

Here Mr. Saul nudged me, and whispered: "The old Laird -- had her married to that daunderin' old half-wit Duncan, to cover things up. This part of the tale is true enough, to my knowledge."

"My bairn was overlaid, sir," the woman went on; "not by purpose, I will swear before you and God. They buried his poor body without baptism; but not his poor soul. Only when the young Laird came, and my own bairn clave to him as Mackenzie to Mackenzie, and wrought and hunted and mended for him -- it was not to be thought that the poor innocent, without knowledge of God's ways -- "

She ran on incoherently, while my thoughts harked back to the voice I had heard wailing behind the door of the entresol at Brussels; to the young Laird's face, his furious indignation, followed by hopeless apathy, as of one who in the interval had learnt what he could never explain; to the marked coin so mysteriously spirited from sight; to Mr. Urquhart's words before he left me on the night of Quatre Bras.

"But he was sorry," the woman ran on; "he was sorry -- sorry. He came wailing to me that night; yes, and sobbing. He meant no wrong; it was just that he loved his own father's son, and knew no better. There was no priest living within thirty miles; so I dressed, and ran to the minister here. He gave me no rest until I started."

I addressed Mr. Saul. "Is there reason to suppose that, besides this woman and (let us say) her accomplice, any one shared the secret of these pilferings?"

"Ardlaugh never knew," put in the woman quickly. "He may have guessed we were helping him; but the lad knew nothing, and may the saints in heaven love him as they ought! He trusted me with his purse, and slight it was to maintain him. But until too late, he never knew -- no, never, sir!"

I thought again of that voice behind the door of the entresol.

"Elspeth Mackenzie," I said, "I and two other living men alone know of what your master was accused. It cannot affect him; but these two shall hear your exculpation of him. And I will write the whole story down, so that the world, if it ever hears the charge, may also hear your testimony, which of the two (though both are strange) I believe to be not the less credible."